Her Last Secret

By

Renée Bess

eBook ISBN: 978-1-61929-569-8
Paperback ISBN: 978-1-61929-568-1
Hardback ISBN: 978-1-61929-570-4

Flashpoint Publications First Edition: October, 2024

Printed in the United States of America.

Cover design by TreeHouse Studio

www.flashpointpublications.com

A Note to Readers

The time frame when this story unfolds is the 1930's. It was commonplace during that era to use the words colored and Negro when identifying or describing a person of color. Those terms are not used today. They are considered politically incorrect and are held in a negative light.

Dedication

To my mother who took my sister and me to Europe for the first time in 1964. Each country we visited opened a new world for our curious eyes, ears, and minds to experience. It was our short stay in Paris however, that invited us to return.

To my sister, who has traveled with me to Paris three or four times after that first visit, and consequently shares many wonderful memories.

To my unselfish wife, who gave me space and time to write this book and all the others because she understood I needed to tell the stories.

To all the Black American soldiers, writers, and artists who called Paris their home when France and its people invited them to stay.

We learn from history that we don't learn from history!

~Desmond Tutu

Prelude

Summer, 1976

Our former neighbors said they didn't want to sound like they were complaining, but the family that bought our house two years ago was letting it go downhill. They sent us notes and photos so we could see the downward spiral for ourselves. Even though we were no longer responsible for the property, the images we saw in those pictures hurt our feelings.

One of the shutters outside a second-story window was dangling and left at the mercy of its only remaining bolt. The shrubs in front of the living room and dining room windows hadn't been pruned since God-knows-when, and the weed-invaded grass was four times higher than it ought to be. A drain spout that had always been attached to the left side of the house was pulled away. It stuck out from its lower section like a rebellious teenager's presence after an angry confrontation with her parents. This was *not* how we'd left our home and it wasn't how we'd maintained it all those years.

Several neighbors *said* they didn't blame us for the present state of our former property, but we could sense an aura of resentment floating just above their words, and we could hear the slightest tone of reproach vibrate in their voices when we spoke on the phone. Although they said they didn't blame us for selling the house and moving, we didn't believe them. We'd known most of them for many years, traded homemade desserts and gossip dozens of times. A few of those folks knew we had struggled with the decision to sell and move to a smaller place that didn't need so much upkeep, one that reminded us of a French country cottage. There was absolutely nothing we could do about our former property, other than regret the new owners lacked respect for it and the neighborhood.

Imagine our surprise the day we saw our old house's picture among others in the local newspaper's weekly real estate section. Imagine our disdain when we read it was described as a fixer-upper. Tilting toward self-centeredness, I hoped to heck that anyone who'd known the fixer-upper had once belonged to us would also have known we'd sold it.

It turned out the realtor who'd listed the property described it correctly. The house sold in a week and the transaction was posted in the newspaper a few months later. We both smiled when we read the buyers' names. Two women, no doubt young and ambitious, bought the undervalued house and began working to bring it back to its former state.

My old neighbors were happy when the house sold and happier when they saw contractors' trucks in the driveway and in front of the property. The emails and texts flowed between us. Pleased to witness the house's revival, they sprinkled their messages with, *Thank God*, and *Our block won't have a house on it that looks like it's abandoned*, and, *I think they're lesbians, but who cares*? Or, slightly more subtle, *They're just like you two, only younger*.

A couple of months after they bought the house, one of the women, Sharon, found my contact information and sent me an email. She wrote about one of their contractors who was working in the attic and found three boxes with my name affixed to them. She'd spoken to her next-door neighbor who figured I'd forgotten to take the boxes with me when we moved. In no time at all Sharon and her wife, Michelle, delivered the boxes to me.

I'm not a detective, but I could tell one of the boxes had been opened. Its contents were no longer as I'd arranged them years ago. They were not in chronological order. Documents such as these were best read according to the date when they were written.

I didn't set out to read every word of every entry I'd written in the diaries or every letter I'd received over a period of years. That task would take too much time and cost too high an emotional price. But I would read some parts, if only to better understand the things I'd experienced, the people whom I'd known, and where I'd been.

Chapter One

Autumn, 1936

According to the first page of my diary, six days after I left Philadelphia and found my way to the pier in the Port of New York City, I grabbed the handle of my small suitcase and joined the line of third-class passengers disembarking the *SS Leviathan*. I'd planned my departure from home for quite a long time. I wasn't afraid to travel by myself, not even to a foreign country. I'd borrowed a lot of books about France from my local branch of the public library and I'd read them all, especially the ones about Paris. And my aunt's letters described landmarks and places so well, I expected to be able to recognize certain streets, parks, and stores on first sight. I gave up all attempts to memorize that city's street map. Unlike my native Philadelphia whose streets were laid out in a grid-like pattern, Parisian thoroughfares looked more like a tangle of spider webs whose threads began and ended abruptly. I wondered why the city, divided as it was by the undulating Seine River, couldn't have been organized more logically, like Philadelphia was. After all, Philadelphia was also divided by a river.

Despite my consternation about the streets in Paris, I hadn't hesitated to make that city my destination. I'd held onto my four years of high school French plus two additional years during college, so I knew I'd be able to communicate, at least a little. The idea of going to France didn't intimidate me in the least. In fact, the notion of venturing to a distant place attracted me as if I were a magnet meeting a strip of metal.

I knew I might miss my parents and our home, but I didn't want to dwell on anything that suggested I might become homesick. I'd miss seeing Angela, also, even though we'd both pulled back from what could have been a relationship, albeit a secret hidden one. I was determined to visit my Aunt Vangie who had been living in Paris for the last five years.

Our household was usually quiet, even after my father went against my mother's wishes and bought a combination radio-record player. He always kept the volume turned down, especially when he played his jazz recordings. His consideration of my mother's attitude toward the music made little sense to me. If there were times when tapping your feet and humming alongside loud trumpets, trombones, bass guitars, and drums could lift him away from a bad mood, then he should have turned that volume button as far to the right as he wished. But that act of rebellion wasn't part of my father's repertoire.

My mother didn't mount much of a battle about the music, maybe because she was grateful my dad never lost his job during the hardest times of the Great Depression. Like many of his friends who also worked for the United States Postal Service, my dad remained employed. My mother cut a few items from our weekly grocery lists, and in the winter, she supervised our house's thermostat setting while reminding us to wear the sweaters she'd knitted over the years. Unlike a few of our neighbors who were forced to find odd jobs to eke out a subsistence income, we pretty much sailed through the last three years of the country's economic disaster without feeling the pain of it.

My parents didn't have an automobile, so paying off a car loan wasn't an issue. They did carry a loan for our house, but they never missed a mortgage payment. Consequently, the thought of having to leave our home and find cheaper shelter never crossed my mind.

Our house was where I'd learned to find solace, first by being anywhere my aunt was, and later by spending countless hours alone in the quiet stillness of my bedroom. My bedroom was where I read and daydreamed. It was also where I kept all the letters my aunt wrote to me after she left Philadelphia.

Aunt Vangie was twenty-six years older than I was, but she'd always talked with me as if we were the same age. It followed that the letters she wrote to me quite regularly were in that same voice. She filled each page with descriptions of her life in France and invitations to come visit and stay for as long as I wanted. I placed those letters in a box I labeled *Someday*. The night before my departure, I gathered some of the letters and put them in my suitcase. No doubt, I'd read them all over again during the long voyage to France.

The morning of my departure, I paused and looked carefully at everything in my parents' living room. I smiled at my father's chair placed next to the walnut side table ever burdened with the oversized ash tray that sheltered two of my father's pipes. The red tin can of tobacco had barely enough room to roost next to the ashtray on that small table. I breathed in the odor of burned tobacco that remained welded to the bowls of both pipes. Had they not been smoked by my father, I would have frowned at the slightly acrid odor that was now part and parcel of each pipe.

I approached the spinet piano and let my fingers travel the distance of an octave. The sounds from the untuned keys made me wince, and the memories of my hips becoming numb after what seemed like hours of practicing scales and one piece of sheet music after another deepened my pained expression.

I walked toward the fireplace. Its tiled hearth, rough-textured faux logs, and brass tools beckoned. When I looked at the four silver-framed photographs aligned atop the mantle, I whispered. "Mother, Dad, you have been the anchors tethering me to safety, to my beliefs, to this house."

The fifth picture frame, a dark stained wooden one, held my picture within its borders. The photo, taken the morning of my graduation from college, showed a young, brown girl with straightened hair styled in a pageboy cut, wearing a cap and gown. I stared at that photo and wondered why my smile was almost imperceptible. Over time, I'd wondered also why each frame surrounded a portrait of a single individual. I realized I didn't know if my parents had ever posed together as a couple. And for that matter, why couldn't *I* recall being photographed with both of my parents?

I took a half-step back from the mantle, and then I reached out and gently touched my parents' pictures.

"Well, I'm off," I said. "Wish me luck. I'll see you when I get back."

Chapter Two

I stepped across the last of the raised rungs nailed cross-ways on the ship's wooden walkway. When my feet touched solid land, I looked up at the leaden sky and silently said a prayer of gratitude for having crossed the Atlantic Ocean safely and in one piece. From the first whistle that signaled the ship's departure from New York City and every morning and evening afterward, my cabin-mate had assured me we would have good weather for the duration of the crossing. To prove it, the devout young woman said a prayer twice a day to the little statue of St. Medard she'd placed on the table next to her bed.

"Don't worry," she said. "We will travel safely. He will see to it."

"You mean that little statue is going to protect us?" I asked.

Maybe she was Catholic, even though she'd told me she was British. Weren't many people from Great Britain Anglican?

"Indeed, it will. We must stay safe because I'm returning home to be married."

I couldn't see the line of logic that tied her marriage plans to a statuette. Nor did I think a statuette could prevent storms at sea. But maybe there was no logic. Maybe it was simply her faith that let her believe we'd be okay. I'd been brought up Episcopalian. Although it was a close cousin of Catholicism, it wasn't its twin. The two sects differed sufficiently enough to keep me in a state of perpetual skepticism regarding religious miracles. By the voyage's end though, I had to concede my cabin-mate's prediction about our safety had been correct. From time to time, the ocean beneath us rolled, but it never roiled. Not once. The part of my soul that sought new experiences on the cusp of danger had to be satisfied with the ship's routine rhythm as it moved according to the sea's will.

I secured the metal clamps that closed my suitcase and

then looked over at my cabin-mate.

"Best wishes for your wedding, Mary. I hope you and your fiancé enjoy many happy years of marriage."

I truly meant that. When I booked passage on this ship, I knew I'd have to share the sleeping quarters with two or three other passengers. Then I received a letter offering me a different cabin, breathing-room-only, smaller, but shared with one other person, not three. Immediately, I ditched my worries about being outnumbered, three against one, and agreed to share one of the ship's three tiniest sleeping quarters.

"Oh, thanks awfully, Vera. You were so quiet each evening whilst I prattled on endlessly. I hope I wasn't a bother."

"No, you didn't bother me at all."

That was the truth. Any last-minute concerns I'd had about the possibility of feeling attracted to my cabin-mate vanished the second we met each other. After all, Mary was a white woman, and English to boot. The taboo against dating out of my race was as strong as the one against my having feelings for a woman. Early on, I'd received the message about both kinds of relationships. They were not permitted. End of story. Up to that point in my life, I'd known only one interracial married couple. That marriage represented a colored wife and her husband who was from India. Because neither one was white, I'd speculated their union wasn't *really* an interracial one. I'd never met a colored and white interracial couple. Such was the power of that particular taboo, even in Pennsylvania where such marriages were legal.

As Mary and I talked, I discovered how important religion was to her. Perhaps her religious beliefs played a role in the ease with which she'd met me. Or maybe she seemed comfortable being in close quarters with a Negro because she was English, not American. There were differences forged by the nationality of white people.

Too bad religious beliefs didn't steer more human interactions. If there were a saint who oversaw civility between white and colored people, I would have packed that saint's little statue in my suitcase and then wielded it every opportunity I had.

That last morning as I climbed the steps to the ship's disembarkation deck and joined the phalanx of suitcase-burdened passengers making their way from the ship to the Customs and Immigration Office, I recalled the one disturbing incident I'd experienced aboard the *S.S. Leviathan.* I felt proud of myself because I knew I'd handled the situation with the rudely obnoxious man and his wife satisfactorily.

The gray sky above the port of Le Havre began surrendering to rain, a soft, fine mist that I welcomed as the moisture kissed my face.

I watched the long line of passengers grow shorter as some people siphoned off to the left toward a sign that read, *Citoyens de L.R.F.*

I remained where I was, my ears surrounded by voices speaking all sorts of languages. The tide of different inflections washed over me, arriving at full speed, and leaving diminished as the sounds receded. I adjusted quickly to the timbre of male voices blending with female tones, along with the high-pitched staccato notes bursting from the mouths of children. There was something about the richness of this noise that wrapped itself around my shoulders and reminded me I was at the borderline of a new reality.

I, Vera Clay, had arrived in the port city of Le Havre, France. America was almost a week and definitely a sea away from me.

Refusing to be cowed by the newness of everything, I read aloud the words posted on another sign. *Passagers d'Outre-Mer.* Enough vocabulary remained embedded in my memory of high school French classes, that I easily figured out, *Passagers* meant passengers. *D'outre* looked like its English counterpart, other and *mer* meant the sea.

I watched many of the ship's passengers, including other Americans, veer toward that sign, so I did the same. In no time at all I'd arrived at the front of the line and stood close to a small wooden structure. When summoned forward by a man wearing a black jacket, pristine white shirt, black tie, and hat accented by a bill that was both broad and shiny, I stepped closer to the box-like shelter.

"*Bonjour, mademoiselle.* May I see your passport and

arrival papers?"

I handed him my documents.

The immigration officer opened my passport, turned to the page that bore my photo, and alternately looked at me and my likeness.

"You are a citizen of the United States?" he asked.

"Yes," I answered.

"And where do you live in the United States?" he asked.

"In Philadelphia."

The officer nodded, though clearly not finished with me and my passport.

"What is your address in Philadelphia?"

"125 North Fiftieth Street." An answer I'd recited from memory since I was four years old.

"And what is the purpose of your visit to France?"

I recalled my aunt's instructions about answering this question.

"I'm a student. I study journalism and I've come here to research how life is for Americans who remained in France instead of returning to the United States when World War I ended."

Barely waiting to hear my last syllable, the customs agent exhaled another question.

"How long do you plan to stay in France, *Mademoiselle*?"

I delivered my aunt's coached response. "For a month, or maybe two."

The immigration officer stamped my passport and documents and handed me the former.

"Welcome to France, *Mademoiselle* Clay." He tilted his head forward, politely dismissing me.

"Thank you." I turned to the right and started walking away. Suddenly I stopped. "Oh, could you tell me where I can get the train to Paris?" I asked.

"Certainly, *Mademoiselle*." The officer pointed toward large doors at the other end of the Customs and Arrivals Hall.

"Leave by that exit and look to the left. You will see a large building with an open roof. That is the train shed."

"*Merci, Monsieur*." I smiled coquettishly and began

walking the length of the cavernous hall.

Once outside, I saw the train building at the end of a long cobblestone path, now made slick by the rain. My shoes had flat heels, but common sense warned me to pay attention and step cautiously over the stones. The last thing I wanted to do was fall and twist an ankle or break a bone, any bone.

Before I could stop it, I felt my left foot slide forward too quickly for my right foot to follow. I gave into gravity and swung my suitcase behind me to soften the backward fall that mercifully didn't happen.

"Dammit!"

The near accident sealed my determination to concentrate on the cobblestones. I knew there had to be a trick to keeping my balance. What if all the streets in Paris were paved like this path?

The walk to the train shed was a short one. I entered the huge structure and looked up to see where the openness ended and the oval glass ceiling began. It was grayed with layers of soot left by the burned coal that pre-dated steam engines and made even darker by today's rain-filled clouds. I spotted a row of ticket-seller windows, their destinations clearly posted under their window number. Le Havre, Rouen, Les Andelys, were names I'd seen each time I'd examined my worn map of France. I scanned the destination names until I read Paris printed above a ticket window in the center of the span. A line of travelers, no doubt newly departed from the *SS Leviathan*, awaited their turn to purchase tickets. I tightened my fingers around my suitcase's handle and joined the line of Paris-bound passengers.

In front of me stood a well-dressed man, his overcoat draped neatly over one arm. The woman standing next to him was equally well-dressed.

The man turned slightly and noticed I was standing in his shadow.

Somewhat startled, he looked down at me.

"*C'est vous encore.* It is you, again," he said. His mustachioed upper lip spread into a snarl.

Taken aback for a second, I stood erect, hoping to equal the man's height. I glared at him and willed my eyes and the set of my mouth to wither his hostility.

"Yes. It's me again," I said.

The man's companion turned and looked at me. Startled, she reversed her movement until once again she faced the ticket booth.

The man scowled before he turned around and showed me the back of his carefully tailored suit.

As the line of ticket buyers slowly crept forward, I resurrected the still-fresh memory of my previous encounter with this couple.

****

Two evenings ago, in violation of the rules that segregated the *S.S. Leviathan's* passengers according to the price they'd paid for their tickets, I ventured from the ship's third-class area to one of the decks designated for first class passengers only. From the first day I'd boarded the ship and met my cabinmate Mary, I'd heard all sorts of tales about the monied passengers.

"Oh, they're upper crust, you know," Mary explained. "Some of them are travelling with their own maids, valets, and nannies. A few of the older, infirm first-class passengers brought along their private nurses."

"You mean they've paid their employees' fares in addition to their own?"

I thought this was incredible because I knew how long it had taken me and Aunt Vangie to save enough money to buy only one ticket, mine.

"Oh, yes indeed," Mary continued. "And their staterooms are enormous. They come with their own ensuites. The first-class passengers have their own dining room, men-only smoking lounges, and parlors. There are at least two different playrooms for the children. And there's a swimming pool!"

It wasn't that I didn't believe what Mary told me. I wasn't naive about the divisive power of class difference. It was my curiosity that spurred me on. I wanted to enter the prohibited territory to see it for myself. I knew I had to be careful to avoid being discovered. Although there had been plenty of times in my life when I knew I'd been invisible to

those who surrounded me, that evening I would have welcomed not being seen. I knew my brown skin would call
attention to itself immediately. So far, I'd spotted only one
other person on the ship who looked like me, and he'd been
busy carrying a huge sack filled with dirty laundry.

After eating dinner in the third-class passenger dining
room, I climbed what seemed like a million steps up a
never-ending stairwell located mid-ship. The stairs ended
near a door whose sign read, Promenade Deck. First-Class
Only. I nudged the door open and stepped onto a wide
expanse of deck that smelled of sea air mixed with wood
polish. A regiment of deck chairs stood at attention, their
alignment interrupted here and there by the protrusion of
closets, no doubt filled with blankets for those passengers
who were hardy or arrogant enough to ensconce themselves
in one of the chairs during a fall or winter crossing.

I stepped closer to the deck's railing and looked to my
left and right. I didn't see a soul. I figured the passengers
who'd chosen to dine during the first sitting were still seated
at their assigned tables, enjoying their evening meal. The
second-seating passengers were probably in their staterooms, getting dressed to the nines or maybe sipping pre-
dinner drinks in one of the ship's first-class lounges.

The further I walked along the deck, the more I questioned the whole idea of class differences and how they separated one group of people from another one. I covered one
half of the deck's perimeter before my exploration came to a
halt. I saw a door open and a man and woman stepped onto
the deck. My mind raced, but not as quickly as my heart.
Should I play it safe and disguise my fear by being servile
and apologetic, or should I feign ignorance about where I
was and assume the upper hand?

"Excuse me, *Mademoiselle*."

The tuxedo clad man spoke as he and his female companion approached me. "You do know this deck is for first-
class passengers only, don't you?"

"Yes, I do," I answered calmly and disguised the anger
I felt because of the man's feckless assumption that I wasn't
one of the first-class travelers.

"Well then, why are you here?"

"I'm here to enjoy the evening air," I said.

The man frowned, somewhat confused.

"You are enjoying the evening air?" he asked, his voice filled with incredulity.

"Yes."

The man's eyes narrowed to slits.

"How much can you enjoy anything while traveling in third class? Or is it steerage?" He leaned closer to me.

I wanted to say, "Steerage beats the crossings on slave ships that my ancestors had to endure."

I was adequately educated about the history of slavery, but I was also intelligent enough to recognize this was neither the time nor the place to say these things to a white man in formal dress who sneered at me as we stood toe-to-toe on the first-class passengers' promenade deck of the *S.S. Leviathan*.

I took a deep breath and answered him. "I've made a mistake coming up here."

"Yes," he huffed. "You have made a serious mistake."

"Oh, Hervé, she admits her error. You do not need to argue with her."

The man's female companion nudged his forearm.

"There is nothing to worry about, Bette."

He squared his shoulders and stepped so close to me that I saw the suggestion of the next morning's stubble breaking through the pores of his chin.

"I shall make sure the First Officer knows about your intrusion into this area," he said.

As I took a step backward, I saw the woman stare at me intently and then quickly look away.

I turned from the pair of first-class passengers and continued my circuit around the promenade deck. I hoped they weren't watching me too closely because I didn't want them to see I was barely breathing as I retreated. I held onto every molecule of oxygen until I found the staircase I'd used earlier and began my trek down the steps that ended in the third-class area.

I walked past the ship's laundry and inhaled the odor of lavender infused steam mixed with human sweat. I heard the sounds of women's voices folded within the sleeves of dress shirts, the precise creases in trousers, and the whitened bed linens on their way to the laundry's industrial iron presses.

All of this reminded me of Aunt Vangie's description of the laundry where she had worked when she first arrived in Paris.

"I hated it there," Aunt Vangie wrote in one of her letters. "Being a dishwasher in a bistro is a better job for me, Vera."

When I returned to my shared two-berth quarters, I went directly to the wash basin and splashed cold water on my face. Then, I pulled my suitcase from under my bed and extracted the pile of letters that were traveling with me. I'd arranged them in chronological order, starting with the oldest, written five springs ago and ending with the latest one, penned thirteen days prior to my departure for France.

I began to reread my aunt's first letter.

Vangie, the shortened version of her real name, Evangeline, was my mother's younger sister. My mother, Ethel, usually spoke about Aunt Vangie, with sighs of exasperation surrounding, "She's-a-disgrace-to-our-family." Vangie always seemed delighted whenever she sensed that she and I were a two-person coalition united in opposition to my mother.

When Vangie announced her intention to leave Philadelphia and live in France, I felt crushed under the boulder of losing an older but beloved ally. Who would defend me when I spoke about the importance of books and my desire to be a writer? Who would smile indulgently at me as she had every September since I was in elementary school, as I described the beauty and intelligence of my favorite instructor? Who would advise me to ignore my mother's annoyance when she heard once again, my favorite instructor was a woman? That was way before I'd had a chance to figure out the why's and wherefores of my own existence.

"You want to be a writer?" My mother asked before she opined. "That's no way to make a living."

"Now, Ethel. You don't know that for sure," Vangie would counter. "Your daughter writes beautifully. She has a way with words. I bet she could go far in life with her name printed on book covers."

"It's not practical, Vangie. She'd go farther in life if her name appeared next to a man's name on a marriage certificate. A man with a good job, of course."

At that point, Aunt Vangie would always go silent, glance at me, and squeeze out a smile she meant to be consoling, or at least understanding.

I always interpreted my aunt's smile as an all-knowing gesture, even though I wasn't sure what all Aunt Vangie knew. Something else I didn't know was exactly why my mother thought Vangie was such a disgrace.

Family mysteries aside, I felt proud I was the first college graduate in my family. I vowed to become a writer. It was my determination to write for a living that led me to accept Aunt Vangie's long-standing invitation to come to Paris where I might find opportunities that were non-existent in Philadelphia in 1936.

I smoothed the crease in the middle of my aunt's letter and proceeded to read it once again. The letter's words were far more important than those I'd exchanged with the pair of snobs on the first-class promenade deck.

25 March, 1933

My Dear Niece,
I am still here in Paris, happy, healthy, and employed. The last few years have passed by so quickly. While you've continued your studies, I've gone from being a laundress in a hotel, to a dishwasher in a small restaurant, and after that, to a server in an after-hours watering hole. The best description of my current job is a combination hostess and barman in a swanky jazz club not far from where I live. I used the word barman because in Paris it's rare to be served drinks or meals by a woman. Almost all the waiters are men.

Every night when I come to work, I feel like I'm sitting on top of the world. You should see all the club-goers! How they do dress. And the music swings from the time the club opens until it closes. (And sometimes, for an hour after that.)

The musicians are from Chicago, New York City, St. Louis, Cleveland. Many of them had been soldiers who brought jazz over here when they arrived. When the war ended, these veterans decided to stay in France instead of going back to the States. They learned to speak French and got jobs and places to live. Some of them found wives. Life in France is better for them than it is in the United States, Vera.

Life here is better for me also. Most Parisians don't look at me and the ex-GI's like we shouldn't be walking on the same side of the street with them or breathing the same air. And guess what? In the club where I work colored and white patrons dance together, and I'm the only one who notices it. Nobody seems to care one whit.

In your letters, you never mentioned how you were treated by the professors at the university. I hope they treated you with respect and gave you the grades you earned. Did you ever have any classes taught by Negro professors? *Were* there any Negro professors at your university?

Lately I've struck up conversations with some of the regulars at the club. They're Negro Americans just like me, except they're painters and musicians and writers. They tell me they feel freer here to paint and compose and write than they ever felt in the U.S. Isn't that something, Vera? They had to leave their birthplace and move to a foreign country in order to succeed. A few of them, mostly men, have told me about other kinds of freedom. But more about that at a later date.

Vera. If you still want to be a writer, maybe you should come to Paris. Think about it, honey, and start saving your money. I'll stash away some of my salary for you every week. That way I can help you pay for a steamship ticket when you're ready to travel.

That's about it for now. Don't forget to tell your mother that "You're-a-disgrace-to-our-family" says "Hi."

Love,
Aunt Vangie

Chapter Three

Train ticket in hand, I stopped in front of the large board where a uniformed man was posting the trains' numbers, destinations, departure times, and platform designations. I waited for him to add the information about my Paris-bound train and then I searched the train shed's perimeter until I spotted the sign for the correct platform.

As I approached, I saw passengers already boarding. Well ahead of me were the hostile man and woman from the ship's first-class promenade deck. The pair was headed toward the front of the train, no doubt to the *Première Classe* cars.

I knew my less expensive train ticket guaranteed I didn't need to worry about being seated anywhere near the uppity couple. I did wonder though if Aunt Vangie had it right about France being different from the United States, because so far, I'd been reminded in no uncertain terms that I belonged to the lower class. And I was certain the reminders were rooted in suppositions triggered by my color… suppositions, not facts.

I stepped off the platform and climbed three steps into a third-class car where I spotted a vacant, well-worn seat next to a window. Settling in, I reached into my handbag and pulled out another one of my aunt's letters.

Its first page was filled with Aunt Vangie's anger about all the rejection notes I'd received in response to job applications. Not one daily newspaper within five hundred miles of Philadelphia was interested in hiring me. It appeared the many articles I had written for the *Temple University News* meant nothing to the people charged with finding new staff writers.

The hiring committee of both the *Philadelphia Tribune* and the *Pittsburgh Courier* praised my abilities but declined my applications. They advised me to keep writing, but suggested their readers and advertisers might not be enthusiastic about reading a young woman's point of view. They said they didn't want to risk losing any of their readership or any of the advertisers who kept their newspapers on solid financial ground.

I shrugged away the memories of disappointment that were briefly reborn when I read Aunt Vangie's letter and began to reread its second page.

"The time has come for me to explain myself to you, Vera. I need to share two of my truths. Do you remember Charles Mercer, the guy I used to date shortly after the war ended? Charles was in the Army during the war and his unit was sent here to France. When the war ended, the Army shipped his unit back to the States. That's about the same time we met each other. Charles used to tell me all kinds of things about France, and I always got the impression he liked it here much better than in the U.S. One day he told me exactly why. He'd always preferred the company of other men more than women. That kind of thing was more tolerated in France than it was in America.

Charles said, in France, they wouldn't put you in jail if they found out you were homosexual, or gay, as they say here. He said he felt he could trust me with his secret because he suspected I might be gay also.

I denied it at first, Vera. I'd denied it ever since I'd had my first crush on a female schoolmate. Charles helped me understand there was nothing wrong with loving a person who's the same sex as you. He believes people like him and me are born with those tendencies. I've thought about it a lot, and I've come to believe it too.

I figure everyone has at least three truths that see the light of day when the time is right. My first truth is... I love women. My second truth is... loving women does not make me inverted or mentally sick. I won't be shamed into hiding who I am. My third truth is one that few people, especially few Americans ever experience. I plan to share that truth with you as soon as you arrive.

And now, just as Charles showed me the way to my first truth, I'm giving you the key to yours, dearest Vera. I suspect you might be just like me. Perhaps I'm wrong, or perhaps I'm right and you've already discovered this. Your letters never mention you're going out on dates with anyone. Of course, your parents taught you well to keep to yourself and not talk about anything as private as a young man you're attracted to. Just know that here it's safer to be who you are than it is back in Philadelphia, dear one. Following your heart's desire won't be completely free of obstacles here in Paris, but rest assured you'll find acceptance from me and from others."

Love always,
Aunt Vangie

I folded the letter and tucked it with the others. By now, I'd almost memorized its contents, maybe because my aunt's words had pierced me profoundly, in a deep place I never knew existed. I found it strange that although her words had gone right through me, they hadn't left me troubled or wounded. In fact, they'd made me feel lighter.

I peered through the train's window and realized that while I'd been reading, I'd missed seeing parts of the French countryside. I saw a landscape of fields abloom with yellow rapeseed. In the distance I could see tall poplar trees standing guard alongside narrow roads. As the train chugged its way next to a canal, I saw long narrow boats moored along the waterway. Their brightly colored roofs made it impossible to ignore them.

A little boy stood on the bank of the canal and waved at the train.

Why wasn't he at school, I wondered. And because it was impossible for me to know why he was there instead of in a classroom, I let my imagination invent the reason for his absence. Perhaps his father had died and it was left to him to get a job and care for his ailing mother. Maybe both parents had abandoned him, and he had to fend for himself. The canal would be a good source of fish. He'd be able to catch his own food and return to his humble home to cook and eat it. Maybe he was in the habit of playing hooky, and his home wasn't one of the boats lined up on this part of the canal. He just came here to look at the boats, watch for the trains, and count any fish he saw in the shallow water.

My daydreamed maybes gradually melted into real

dreams as I gave in to the exhaustion of travel and slept for the remainder of the rail journey from Le Havre.

"Paris! Gare Saint-Lazare! Paris!"

The conductor's raspy voice announced the city and station as the train slowed.

Startled, I stood and gathered my handbag and suitcase. With the train barely at a standstill, I stepped onto the platform and followed the knot of people headed toward stairs and then to the station's street-level exits.

I stepped outside into the cool air and paused to get my bearings. When I looked at the other side of the street, I noticed the long line of taxicabs. A man got into the first taxi before I could cross the street. I approached the next one and inclined my head toward the driver's open window.

"Sixteen... I mean *Rue Clauzel, numéro seize, s'il vous plait.*" The driver nodded his okay, so my suitcase, handbag and I maneuvered ourselves into the taxi's back seat.

Five minutes and a tangle of diagonal streets later, the taxi stopped in front of the address I'd uttered.

I opened my purse and removed two pieces of the colorful paper money I'd received when I traded some of my U.S. dollars for French francs at the First Pennsylvania Bank in Center City, Philadelphia.

"Merci, Monsieur," I said.

I gripped my suitcase and remembered Aunt Vangie's instructions about getting to her apartment.

When I turned away from the curb, I saw a huge wooden door with the number sixteen affixed to it. After pushing it open, I entered what looked like a short tunnel whose arched roof was made of ancient stones. Three paces later, I emerged from the structure and found myself standing on one side of a small sunlit courtyard. In the center of the courtyard there was a fountain surrounded by flowers arranged in the pattern of small *fleurs-de-lis*. A gravel path outlined the courtyard's perimeter.

I followed the stone walkway as it curved to the left and ended in front of a door painted a deep purple and wearing a tarnished, pitted metal knocker. I lifted the knocker and tapped it gently against the door.

A woman's voice answered.

"*J'arrive!*"

The door swung open and revealed a rather plump, brown woman. She wore her hair gathered in a bun and she offered her smile so willingly.

"You are Vera, right?" she asked.

"Yes, I am."

"I am Claudine, your Aunt Vangie's good friend."

"Of course," I said. "My aunt has mentioned you many times in her letters. You share this apartment with her, right?"

"Yes. Vangie asked me to be here to meet you."

Claudine's words, spoken in French-accented English, sounded like musical notes fluttering through the space between us.

"She's not here?" I asked.

"No, but come in and I will explain to you where she is."

I entered the two-level apartment's dimly lit foyer.

"Please give me your suitcase and I will take it up to your bedroom."

With Claudine and my luggage out of view, I glanced at my surroundings. To the right of the foyer, I saw a large space I figured was the living room. A lace covered rectangular table stood against one wall. I could see the table was crowded with framed photos of my aunt and other people, everyone smiling and looking happy. I noticed my graduation portrait and, as always, I wished I had smiled and not posed with such a serious expression on my face. When I compared my picture to the photos of my aunt and her friends, I was reminded of the two masks that symbolize drama and comedy.

Before I could look any further, I heard the sounds of someone descending the stairs.

Seconds before Claudine reached the landing, I noticed another photo. This one, placed atop a small, curved shelf near the stairs, was of Aunt Vangie and another woman. My aunt must have been staring directly at the camera. Her unabashedly joyful grin was so contagious that I felt my lips spread into a smile. The other woman in the photograph looked more like a silhouette than a fully realized person. Her body and face were turned away from the camera and toward my aunt.

"Did you have anything to eat before the train left Le Havre?" Claudine asked.

"No, but that's okay. I ate breakfast on the ship."

"I would offer you a cup of tea or coffee, but I know Vangie is eager to see you."

"I'm anxious to see her also. Where is she?"

Claudine opened the door and gestured for me to gather my handbag and follow her.

"Come with me. It is easy to find a taxi from here. I will explain everything to you between here and there."

Now four feet impacted the gravel walkway, making the sound of crushed stone louder than I'd made it moments ago. I followed Claudine through the courtyard, the small tunnel, and out to the street.

Claudine waved at an approaching taxi. When it slowed sufficiently, she stepped down from the curb and spoke to the driver.

"L'Hôpital Pitié Salpêtrière, s'il vous plait."

As soon as we settled into the vehicle's back seat, Claudine turned to me.

"Two weeks ago, now almost three, Vangie was leaving the *boite*, that is, the nightclub where she works. The second her feet met the street she was struck by an automobile. Gérard, a man who works at the club with her, saw it all happen. Thank God he was there." Claudine paused and with her right hand, made the sign of the cross.

"He ran back into the club and called for an ambulance and the police. When the police arrived, Vangie was unconscious. Gérard was afraid she was dead. The ambulance got there and they took Vangie to the hospital. Gérard went with her. He knew your aunt would not be able to talk, and even if she could, her French is far from perfect."

"Why didn't she write to me about the accident?"

"Because she did not want you to change your plans." Claudine patted the tops of my hands. "She thought that if you knew she would still be in the hospital, you would cancel your trip."

"No, I'd never do that. I'd want to be here all the more."

"I told her that. I reminded her how eager you would be

to see her, especially since she is in the hospital."

Claudine leaned toward the back of the taxi driver's seat.

"S'il vous plait, Monsieur. L'entrée du nord."

"Bien sûr, Madame."

"It is easier for us to use the north doors instead of the main entrance. It is not as grand, but it is not as crowded either. We will be closer to the ward where Vangie is," Claudine explained.

"There is the main entrance to the right."

Claudine pointed to a wide, light-colored walkway. At its end was an even wider building whose center section was capped by a huge dome. The dome lent the same kind of formality to this building as the one topping the U.S. capitol in Washington. I understood the importance of the latter's design. But this building was a hospital, not a symbol of the government.

Suddenly, I felt very much like a foreigner, out of place and out of any curiosity I might have had about where I was. Did the air smell different in Paris? Did the buildings seem older than the ones I was used to seeing in Philadelphia? Were there more stores and restaurants here than there were at home? I was so preoccupied with the unexpected news about Aunt Vangie's accident, I didn't hear the alternating two-tone claxon alert as an ambulance sped by and preceded our arrival at the hospital's north entrance.

It wasn't until Claudine and I entered the hospital that I remembered I had a voice.

"How was Aunt Vangie when you saw her yesterday?" I asked.

"You can thank God she was much better. Each day she has gotten better. She has received good care here. She is bandaged and strapped from her waist to her shoulder blades to help heal her ribs, and they operated on her hip the morning after the accident. She is able to walk, but not too far. And she has to use a cane."

"Will she be here in the hospital much longer?"

"I do not think so. She told me they are going to discharge her in another day or so."

"Then it's good that I'm here. I can do things for her and help her get around."

"Yes, I agree." Claudine smiled benevolently. "But you

know your Aunt Vangie. She will want to do everything for herself. They told her she might have a slight limp from now on, but that will not stop her."

Claudine lowered her voice to a whisper.

"And listen to this. Vangie told me she believes some people are attracted to a woman with a limp."

I blinked a non-verbal response.

Claudine punctuated her statement with a faint *humph.*

I looked from my left to my right. Claudine and I walked through a long corridor, both of us wrapped in the kind of silence that keeps you company as you're stepping into the unknown.

Claudine slowed in front of a wide glass-paned door.

"Her ward is near the top of this staircase," she stated.

We both took deep breaths and began climbing the marble steps, each one worn down in its center by time and circumstance. When we reached the end of our climb, Claudine turned to the right before stopping abruptly in front of a set of doors.

"Here we are, *Mademoiselle.*" With an exaggerated flourish, Claudine gestured that I should enter the room first.

Although most of the beds on both sides of the room had occupants, I had no difficulty at all finding my aunt. She was seated in a wheelchair, and she had a closed book resting on her lap.

Eager to both give and receive the hug-filled greeting I had expected to experience an hour ago, I walked quickly to her and bent down to kiss her cheek.

"Aunt Vangie, how are you feeling?"

"Oh, my dear Vera. I'm feeling so much better just seeing your smiling face. You're all grown up now. And it looks like you found your way to Paris just fine, honey," Vangie said.

"Unlike you in your present condition, Vangie. Your niece arrived in one piece," added Claudine.

Vangie looked first at Claudine, and then at me.

"Don't I have a good friend here, Vera?" she asked.

"I should say so. Claudine told me what happened and she brought me right here."

Vangie winked at Claudine.

"That's my Claudine," she said.

I looked over my shoulder at the blur of nearby patients and then lowered my voice.

"Is Claudine your special friend?" I asked, barely whispering.

"No, honey. Brickette's a great friend, but not the special friend you're asking about."

"Brickette?" I glanced at Claudine.

"That is the nickname your aunt gave me because of my red hair. She knows I do not like it, but she calls me that now and then." Claudine explained.

"Like I wrote in my letters to you, honey. There's lots of Negro Americans here in Paris," said Vangie. "One of them has the reddest hair I've ever seen on a colored woman's head. Her hair is so red, they call her Bricktop, or sometimes just Brick. Since Claudine's hair is red too, but not quite as red as Bricktop's, I call her Brickette."

Claudine rolled her eyes.

"Bricktop has opened her own jazz club and it has an after-hours room. She's been talking to me about working there for her," said Vangie.

I nodded. I knew better than to ask if working at night and coming home in the wee hours was safe in Paris. It wasn't a good idea if you lived in some parts of Philadelphia. Visualizing my aunt walking along the mostly deserted streets a few hours before dawn brought her late-night accident back into focus.

"Aunt Vangie, Claudine said you were hit by a car."

Vangie nodded.

"What happened with the driver? Did he stop? Was he drunk?"

"No. He did not stop." Claudine answered before Vangie could.

"You mean, he just hit you and then kept going?"

"That's what happened, honey," Vangie shot a warning look at Claudine.

"And someone named Gérard saw the accident? Would Gérard recognize the driver or the car?"

"I doubt it. It was too dark and it happened like that." Vangie snapped her fingers.

"Your aunt says she does not know who was behind the steering wheel, but she thinks she knows who was behind the so-called accident," said Claudine.

I looked at Claudine and then at my aunt.

"Who, Aunt Vangie?"

"Let's talk about all that later," said Vangie. "So, tell me all about yourself. Do you still want to be a writer, honey?"

"I think so. I'd really like to be a journalist. Maybe write for a newspaper," I said.

"When you wrote to me about the job rejections you'd received, I felt so bad for you."

"I felt bad for me, too."

"But you're not going to give up, right?"

"Right." I smiled at my aunt and her persistence.

"You just keep on applying, especially to the Negro newspapers. New papers keep springing up everywhere, and not just in the big cities. Your first job might be in a little town, but it will be a start for you. I'm certain somebody out there is going to hire you."

"Vangie, did you talk to the doctor today?" Claudine asked. "Did he say when you will be able to come home?"

"No, and no, Claudine. But I suspect they'll send me home in another day or so. I can get around good with crutches, and even better with a cane."

"I told your niece your theory about certain people finding cane-users intriguing, Vangie."

My aunt winked at me.

"Claudine, I didn't say *intriguing*. I said some people are *attracted* to those who use a cane."

Aunt Vangie lifted the book from her lap.

"Do you see this book, Vera?" she asked. "The person who gave it to me is my special friend. She'd be right here to meet you if she weren't traveling right now in the States." Vangie caressed the book's cover.

"She's an artist. She and her brother have gone to Chicago, Boston, and then New York to meet with art gallery owners and a couple of museum curators." Vangie paused. "What with the car accident and then the operation on my hip, I've lost track of the calendar. I thought for sure they'd be back by now."

"What's her name?" I asked.

"It's Bette. Bette Moune. And she's very special to me." Vangie reached for my hand. "Bette and I are my third truth,

Vera. She and I love each other more than you can imagine."

"Tell Vera about Hervé, Vangie," said Claudine, her voice an octave lower than it had been.

Vangie inhaled deeply. Unable to hide the pain that accompanied the deep breath, she allowed the smallest "oh" to escape her lips.

"Hervé is Bette's brother. He's not happy about Bette's relationship with me."

"Not happy? That is an understatement, Vangie." Claudine's voice regained its usual pitch.

"Claudine thinks he arranged the trip to the States to separate us for a few weeks," said Vangie. "But you know me, Vera. No man is going to stop me from doing whatever it is I want to do."

"Not even if he hires someone to run you over with a car?" Claudine asked.

"Oh, no," I said. "You think Bette's brother planned your accident?"

Vangie glared at Claudine. "I thought I asked you to keep that to yourself, Big Mouth."

"Vera deserves to hear everything, Vangie." Claudine countered.

I could tell by the tones of their voices, that my aunt and Claudine weren't really annoyed with one another.

"I do need to hear the whole story, Aunt Vangie. But maybe it can wait until tomorrow." I moved closer and kissed my aunt's forehead.

"She is right, Vangie. The poor girl had a long train ride from Le Havre to Paris. Then she learned you were hurt and in the hospital. She needs time to catch her breath."

I was beginning to value Claudine's friendship with my aunt, even though Claudine wasn't her special friend.

"We're going to let you get some rest now. I promise I'll be back to see you tomorrow." I said.

"All right, honey." Vangie smiled weakly. "You're probably tired. When you and Claudine get back to the apartment, just make yourself to home."

I smiled. I'd always been amused when my aunt said "to" home, instead of "at" home. Hearing this expression of hers delivered a familiarity I'd missed for the past five years of Aunt Vangie's absence. My ears welcomed those words the same way they'd welcome a serving of my mother's apple brown Betty or musical notes from my father's jazz records.

Aunt Vangie grasped my hands and held them in hers.

"I'm so glad you're here, Vera. It's been too long since I've seen you."

"Do not worry, Vangie," said Claudine. "I will make sure she is okay until you return home."

"*Merci, ma chère* Claudine. And Vera, when we see each other tomorrow you can tell me all that you've done during the past five years, and all that you want to do now."

Claudine and I stepped away from Aunt Vangie who blew us air kisses.

Chapter Four

We retraced our steps to the hospital's north entrance. Once we were outside, I expected Claudine to hail the first taxi she saw. Instead, she suggested we walk a few blocks to get fresh air in our lungs.

It was late afternoon and the temperature had cooled enough to revive my energy. We walked down a wide avenue crisscrossed by narrower streets whose food shops reminded me I hadn't eaten anything since breakfast. The exhaustion I'd felt before we left Aunt Vangie's bedside was now replaced by a fierce need to put food in my stomach.

After we walked a bit farther, Claudine paused.

"You must be hungry by now. Let us find a taxi and go home. It will not take me much time to fix dinner. *Par ici*," she said as she cupped my elbow with her hand and steered us toward a rank of taxi cabs.

"I got up early this morning and cooked beef with wine and vegetables. Our kitchen is not the *Café de la Paix*, but it will do for your first meal in Paris."

When we arrived at the courtyard's entrance to what would be my home for at least the next three months, I noticed a woman seated on the bench in front of the flower garden. Her thin lips were pressed together so tightly, they gave the impression they'd never be able to form a smile. Her hair might have begun the day wrapped neatly in a bun atop her head. Now, its late afternoon style was more a wispy confusion of brownish-gray shafts having their way atop her head. The renegade strands were like unruly children determined to misbehave. Despite her riot of a hairstyle and the worry her sealed-perhaps-forever lips suggested, the woman's eyes brightened when she looked up and saw us walking toward her.

"*Bonjour*, Claudine."

"*Bonjour*, Simone."

"This young woman is the niece of Vangie, right?"

"Yes." Claudine turned toward me. "Vera, this is our neighbor, Simone Blum."

"*Enchantée, Madame*," I responded. Even though I was tired and hungry, I felt a ripple of excitement as my voice resurrected a word from my high school and college French lessons.

Madame Blum smiled as she acknowledged my attempts to speak her native language.

"*Enchantée*, Vera. But now, we shall speak English, no?" she said.

Had I uttered the wrong word? Had my error convinced *Madame* Blum that continuing to speak French with me would be a waste of her time?

Apparently sensing my self-doubt, Claudine touched my arm. "Simone wants very much to learn English. Her daughter tries to teach her, but she does not visit that often."

Simone interrupted Claudine's explanations. "She does not live in Paris. And many times, she is too busy to visit. Your dear aunt helps me though. She brings me English language newspapers a couple of times each week."

I smiled and wondered which newspapers Aunt Vangie read. Was it the *Paris Herald Tribune*, or the European edition of the *New York Herald*?

"Vangie leaves it in front of my door when she arrives home from her job late at night. So, almost every morning you will see me here, sitting on this bench, reading a section of the latest newspaper delivered by Vangie. *C'est gentil à elle, n'est-ce pas*?"

"It is no problem for her," said Claudine. "She finds the newspapers at the club where she works. They belong to everyone and to no one."

Madame Blum looked up at me. "*Eh bien*, I hope to see you frequently during your visit, Vera. Perhaps my daughter will visit and meet you while you are here."

"If I do not prepare her dinner soon, no one will see her. Not me, not you or your daughter, not even Vangie. Vera will disappear due to starvation."

Claudine headed toward the entrance to her and Aunt Vangie's apartment, and I followed her as quickly as my food deprived body could.

"*Au revoir, Madame* Blum."

"I will see you soon," she replied

As we paused long enough for Claudine to place her key into the apartment door's lock, I heeded my sixth sense and turned to look for *Madame* Blum.

Still seated on the garden bench, she acknowledged my glance by nodding. Had she known I was going to look back at her? Had she expected me to do it, or was she simply being polite and waiting for us to enter the apartment?

Chapter Five

Hervé Moune paced back and forth in his home's foyer, his feet and legs propelled by annoyance. The sound of gravel flattening beneath a truck's tires compelled Hervé to go to the front door and then outside to the building's entrance.

In the twilight Hervé watched as two men climbed down from the truck and offered him half-waves.

"*Bonjour, Monsieur*," said one of the men.

"You are late." Hervé's terse greeting did absolutely nothing to hasten the men's motions.

"Come with me and I'll show you where everything must go."

Hervé followed the narrow stone path next to the side of the building. The men were only a step behind him when they arrived in front of a second structure, smaller than Hervé's residence, but no less imposing. Large windows covered much of the wall space on three sides of the building.

Hervé turned toward the men and reached into his pants pocket to retrieve a key.

"Your late arrival has delayed my leaving to keep an appointment," he said.

The men seemed unperturbed by Hervé's attitude and simply gazed at him. After a few seconds, one spoke.

"Did anyone from our company telephone you, *Monsieur*, to tell you your parcels must have been the first ones loaded on the ship, because the manifest had them listed as the last ones to be off-loaded?"

"No. No one notified me. I expected you to be here two hours ago."

"We are sorry, *Monsieur*, but there was nothing we could do until it was our turn to begin moving the crates from the ship to our truck. When we realized we would be late, we decided to offer a tip to a few of the dock workers to help us. If they had not been willing to do that, we would still be on the road, somewhere between here and Le Havre."

Hervé acknowledged the men's explanation of their late arrival with a cold stare.

"All of the crates have to be placed in here and then opened." Hervé pointed to an area at the opposite end of where they were standing.

"Put the largest crates over there, against the west wall. Put the medium-size ones against the east wall. Place the smallest crates on that table over there," Hervé said.

"After we have opened the crates, do you want us to collect all of the lumber and haul it away, *Monsieur*?"

"Yes." Hervé looked at his watch and scowled. "My sister will be here in a few minutes and she can answer any other questions, if you have them. This building is her art studio."

"That is fine, *Monsieur*. We understand what to do."

"Actually, it is not fine. My sister has other, more important things to do. Supervising you was supposed to have been my task, not hers."

"Of course, *Monsieur*."

Hervé nodded and quickly left the studio. When he returned to his and his sister's apartment, he went into the room that served as his office. He snatched a large, weathered leather portfolio from his desk, and then left the room. With one hand on the doorknob, he turned around and called out to his sister.

"Bette, I'm leaving now."

"Alright, Hervé." Bette's voice became louder as she approached the foyer.

"Are the movers still here?" Bette asked.

"Yes. They are still here because they have just arrived." Hervé shook his head.

"And you are going to be late for your meeting with *Monsieur* Brouillard."

"Yes. And my late arrival will be one additional challenge added to my task of convincing him your work should be included in his next salon."

"I am sure if you explain why you are late, he will understand, Hervé," said Bette. "And you should be able to find a taxi quickly at this hour. There is so much traffic on our avenue."

Hervé ignored his sister's remarks. "It is up to you to supervise the movers. Make certain they have done everything correctly before you pay them," he said.

Bette answered his command with an obedient but somewhat anxious air. "All right. We will talk later, after you have returned. I will be eager to hear if you have been able to reach an agreement with *Monsieur* Brouillard."

Bette's last words ricocheted off the apartment's door as Hervé slammed it shut.

In a rush to arrive at his meeting, Hervé's long strides led him past several taxis. After covering a two-block distance from his apartment, he saw the parked car that awaited him. Two people occupied the vehicle's rear seats. Hervé opened the front passenger's door and slid into the seat.

"*Messieurs*," he said as he inclined his head in a deferential bow.

The driver glanced at his newest passenger. "We feared you'd forgotten about the meeting," he said as he steered the car away from the curb.

"That would never happen," said Hervé. "Each meeting is more important that the preceding one."

****

Although Bette knew it was her responsibility to oversee the opening of all the newly arrived crates of her paintings, she continued to stare through the parlor's front window. She watched the end of the workday's usual stream of cars pass by. The pedestrians walked almost as quickly as the cars passed. They seemed annoyed when they paused at intersections in an effort to avoid colliding with each other or with the speeding cars.

As today's late afternoon became early evening, Bette wondered why her brother had walked past two available taxis instead of engaging one of them, especially since he risked being late for an important appointment. She shrugged her shoulders and with them, her curiosity. Then, she remembered several occasions in the recent past when she couldn't find a reason for some of Hervé's actions, nor for his newly acquired contentious attitude. Bette noted her brother's inexplicably rude behaviors had become more and more frequent during the past year or so.

She sighed resignedly and approached the telephone alcove in the apartment's hallway. After looking at the number she'd hurriedly scribbled on a piece of paper, she uncradled the phone and dialed.

"*Oui*. Is this the patient information center? I am calling to ask about one of your patients, *Madame* Evangeline Curtis. How is she doing? She will be discharged in the next few days? *C'est merveilleux! Merci. Bonsoir.*"

Feeling less burdened and happier than she'd been for the last month, Bette left the apartment and headed outside to the rear of the building. She needed to be sure the men who transported her artwork from the ship docked in Le Havre were uncrating each canvas carefully and placing it in the appropriate space in the studio.

Chapter Six

"Vera, I know you are tired after all that you have done today. Why don't you go upstairs while I am heating our dinner? Your bedroom is at the end of the hallway, just beyond the bathroom on the right."

"Thank you, Claudine. It'll feel good to wash my face and hands."

I climbed the stairs carefully in deference to the shallowness of each tread, and speculated that when this place was built eons ago, people probably had smaller feet than they have now.

The narrowness of the second-floor hallway, its high ceiling and walls papered with embossed blue, yellow, green and pink flowers made me feel smaller than I was. The door of the room at the end of the hallway was ajar, and I could see my suitcase atop the bed. Instead of going directly there, I turned to the right and entered the bathroom. Its grandiose size was the first thing I noticed. A small round wash basin atop a thin porcelain support, an extremely deep bathtub, and a toilet and bidet resembled four independent islands placed against three of the room's walls.

The mirror on the wall above the wash basin wore brownish-silver splotches here and there, much like a vain aged person caught in the conflict between nature's changes and the assistance of her beautician's skill with hair dye.

I used the toilet and ignored the bidet. Facing the basin, I turned on the tap and stared at my image in the old mirror. It seemed like I'd boarded the train in Le Havre two days ago instead of just hours earlier. Perhaps it was my imagination, but when I touched my face, my fingertips seemed to glide effortlessly from my forehead, over my nose, and down to my chin. I looked at the sink and wondered if I'd see the residue of an oily substance similar to the viscous deposits of coal oil that coated the train station's glass roof in Le Havre. I did see a suggestion of sheen which disappeared quickly into the folds of the washcloth Claudine, no doubt, had provided me.

Refreshed for the moment, I followed the hallway to my bedroom. Its tall ceiling gave a false impression of its size. Neither small nor large, the room was painted light-yellow. Two windows admitted daylight which would no doubt made the walls even brighter. When I recalled the sleeping quarters on the ship, instantly I appreciated the differences this one offered.

A tall walnut-hued armoire stood against one wall. I opened its doors and decided I'd unpack my suitcase and hang some of my clothes there. The armoire's two deep drawers would be a temporary home for the rest of my belongings.

I smiled at the sight of a small desk and chair placed in front of one of the bedroom's windows. What little remained of the day's sunlight lent a soft, almost blurred vision of the outdoors and illuminated the still-life portrait of what lay atop the desk. A blank notebook, one pencil, and a pen waited for me to sit down and begin using them.

"Thank you, Aunt Vangie." I uttered.

"Vera. Vera." Claudine called my name. "Our dinner is ready. *Viens, Chèrie.*"

I hurried back through the hallway, but slowed when I reached the stairs. Claudine stood at the border between the foyer and the living room.

"Come into the kitchen," she said. "Would you like a glass of wine with your meal?"

"No, thank you. A glass of wine will make me sleepy."

"Sometimes it does that to me, also." Claudine smiled as she looked over her shoulder at me.

Before we reached the kitchen, I slowed to a stop to look at the photographs spread atop a large round table.

"These people are friends of your aunt here in Paris," Claudine paused, then pointed to one picture in particular. "And this person standing next to your aunt is her *special* friend."

"But, she's white," I said.

Claudine nodded in slow motion.

"Yes, she is. You did not know that? Vangie never told you?"

"No," I said. "She never mentioned it. Not once. In all of the letters she wrote, she never used the word white to describe her friend."

Claudine motioned for me to follow her.

"Maybe she did not write about it because she did not want to worry you." Claudine watched me carefully as she tried to read the expression on my face. "Or perhaps she never mentioned Bette is white because it really does not matter."

"It would matter in Philadelphia," I said.

"Philadelphia is only a small speck on a map of the world, *ma chère*."

I considered Claudine's response. Part of me knew I'd traveled here to spend time with my aunt. Another part of me knew I'd travelled here because I suspected Philadelphia didn't represent all there was in the world. It was a parochial city entrenched in unquestioned rules, especially regarding its citizens. Old or young, affluent or poor, educated or not, white or Negro, it was taken for granted that everyone would assume the roles and behaviors prescribed for them a long time ago. This was especially true for the members of the white upper class whose generations-old lineages were connected to the city's founding fathers. It was true also for the Negro middle class, whose physical appearances often suggested ties to those same old Philadelphia lineages and most certainly guided friendships, marriages, and memberships. I didn't know if Claudine knew anything about these things. It dawned upon me that I didn't know very much about Claudine.

"How did you meet Aunt Vangie, Claudine?"

She looked up at the small chandelier above the kitchen table.

"One evening a couple of years ago, a friend of mine, an American G.I., took me to an after- hours club. Have you ever heard of the Harlem Hell fighters, Vera?"

"Yes, my father talked about them. They were U.S. soldiers who fought for France during the first world war," I said.

"Quite a few of them were musicians before they enlisted, and some of them stayed here after the war ended," she continued. "My G.I. friend knew I loved American jazz, so he took me to this club where the Negro jazz musicians gathered late in the evening after their shows ended. That is where I met Vangie. She was working behind the bar later than usual because one of the barmen was sick. She was so friendly to me, maybe because she thought I might be like her."

I felt my cheeks become warm as I listened to Claudine and pictured my aunt flirting with her.

"But you weren't…" I said and asked at the same time.

"No, I was not," Claudine paused. "My brother was gay, though. He was killed at the beginning of the war."

"Was he killed in combat?" I asked.

"No, he was killed by two of his French brothers-in-arms who hated him because he preferred men more than women."

"I'm sorry, Claudine."

"I was so very sorry for years, Vera. I did not understand why some people were gay, but I loved my brother very much, and that is all I really needed to understand." Claudine's stare shot right through me.

"I loved my brother the way you love your Aunt Vangie, *ma chère*. It is unimportant to you that she prefers the love of women instead of men, *n'est-ce pas*?"

I nodded.

"It is because I loved my brother and wanted to honor his spirit, that I offered to share this apartment, my home, with Vangie. She was forced to abandon the apartment where she was living when we met. The man who owned the place suddenly increased her rent to an amount she could not afford. You see, just like the two soldiers who killed my brother, this man hated homosexuals, men and women alike. When he learned that Vangie was a lesbian, he found a legal way to stop renting to her."

"How did he know Aunt Vangie was a lesbian?" I'd never said the word lesbian aloud and the effort to say it almost got stuck in my throat and threatened to choke me. I'd heard it spoken. I'd read it, of course. But fear of discovery had always prevented me from saying it.

Claudine peered into my eyes.

"Vangie wrote you many letters during the past five years, *n'est-ce pas*?"

"Yes."

"Did she not write about her friends, her social life, the people who befriended her at her different jobs?"

"Only in the last couple of years. She wrote to me about

her secrets," I said.

"Well, I assure you your aunt has had more than a few secrets and more than one special friend. She has never hidden that part of herself from neighbors or her bosses or her landlords. She has lived openly no matter the consequences. She told me she has always lived that way, even before she came to France."

I nodded as I recalled my mother's displeasure with some of my aunt's friends.

"And your brother, Claudine. Did he live openly also?"

"Ah, no. *Pas du tout*. My parents would have disowned him. You see, my mother emigrated from Guadeloupe to Bordeaux when she was sixteen years old. There, she met my father, whose family had lived in Bordeaux for generations. My mother was Catholic, and so was the family of my father. I believe that was the sole reason their union was accepted. Ironically, they would never have accepted my brother, their own son, if they knew he was gay. He was forced to hide that from them."

"It sounds like your brother had a difficult life."

"Yes, it was difficult. But he had his moments of joy, also." Claudine bowed her head. "I miss him. I shall always miss him."

We fell silent for a few seconds.

"I suppose I'd better go to bed now, Claudine," I said. "Thank you so much for making me feel welcome. And thanks for taking me to see Aunt Vangie."

"It is nothing, *ma chère*.

My first night in Paris I lay in bed, too tired and worried to fall asleep. I had no idea how long I'd be able to remain quiet about the woman my aunt loved so fiercely, a woman whose path I'd crossed twice in recent days. How was I going to stay mum about the evening I'd answered curiosity's summons and ventured to the *S.S. Leviathan's* first-class promenade deck, only to be questioned and insulted because of my race and social class? Why would I want to stay quiet about our second frigid encounter, the one that took place in the train station?

What will I do when this woman comes to visit Aunt Vangie? What will this woman do or say when she visits Aunt Vangie and sees me? Will she pretend we're meeting each other for the first time, or will she take partial ownership of the race-tinged wound she'd inflicted upon me when her complicit silence had been a weapon as powerful as her brother's?

"We'll see if color is less important here than it is in the States. We'll see," I murmured and gave in to sleep.

Chapter Seven

Hervé Moune exited the car two blocks away from his home. He was pleased it was late. If his sister weren't working in her studio, she'd probably gone to bed. He would talk to her tomorrow about his so-called appointment with the art dealer.

Hervé sprinted up the stairs from his building's entrance to his first-floor apartment and carefully inserted his key into the lock. He stepped soundlessly across the foyer. He was headed toward his office when he heard his sister call his name.

"Hervé ?"

"*Oui, c'est moi,* Bette. I thought you would be asleep at this hour." Hervé approached his sister's bedroom and saw its door was ajar.

"I intended to be in bed, but I knew I would not be able to sleep. I was anxious to hear about your meeting with *Monsieur* Brouillard."

Hervé bowed his head.

"It did not go as I had planned, Bette."

"What happened?" Bette pressed her hands together.

"Brouillard is an idiot. His taste for fine art resides in his mouth, not in his eyes."

"He refused to show my work?"

"Yes. And he has made the wrong decision, Bette."

"Maybe I should have met with him," said Bette. "I can explain my work, why I have painted certain colors, why I have chosen the subjects in my art."

"No. He would never understand your sensibilities. He gave me the impression that he is looking for something new, something different, something unlike the familiar."

Bette looked down.

"Perhaps I should look for a different way to paint. Perhaps I should create less realistic work with colors and shapes that suggest my ideas, instead of painting so literally."

Hervé began shaking his head. He pointed at his sister, as

if he were accusing her of doing something foul.

"Non! I will not have it. You cannot even consider producing art like that. It is degenerate and unworthy."

Bette narrowed her eyes.

"What do you mean by saying it is degenerate?" she asked. "It is simply new, not bad or forbidden."

"We will talk about this tomorrow, Bette. But I warn you. I am not going to change my mind."

"You may not change your mind, but I hope you will at least change the way you are discussing this with me."

"I cannot promise to do that. *Bonne soirée*, Bette."

"*Bonne soirée*, Hervé."

In full retreat, Bette sat on the edge of her bed and tried to decide if she should pull the covers over her and try to go to sleep. Her argument with Hervé echoed in her ears. Why had he become so officious and unpleasant? Had he insulted *Monsieur* Brouillard and made it impossible to ever display her work in his small salon?

Bette sighed. Determined to give in to sleep, she closed her eyes and thought about the moments of happiness she'd have the next day. After weeks of travel and hours of worrying about her lover's car accident, she would see Vangie. Vangie, the lover whose smiles, kisses, and caresses always took her out of herself. Vangie, the woman whose skin was so different from the others she knew she was supposed to love. Vangie, whose American English-accented French always called out her name when they made love. Vangie, whose importance to her life deeply disturbed her brother.

****

Instead of retreating to his bedroom, Hervé strode toward his office. He closed its door and sat down at his desk. He'd received a list of tasks to accomplish between tonight and next week's meeting. These meetings had nothing at all to do with an art dealer, and everything to do with the needs of France, a nation in need of many changes.

A lover of order, Hervé began writing the details involved to execute each task. His lifelong ability to prioritize things by order of their importance sped his notetaking.

One detail that preceded all the others involved *Monsieur* Brouillard. Hervé knew he had to speak to the art dealer before Bette sought a conversation with him. He had to gain Brouillard's promise to lie about their fictitious meeting and invent a reason for his turning down Bette's work. Gaining Brouillard's cooperation would not be difficult. If it were, Hervé knew he could always enlist the help of some of his friends with whom he'd met earlier that evening.

Chapter Eight

Early the third morning of my visit I stood in front of the kitchen sink and rinsed the last of the coffee from the enormous cup I'd used. After swabbing dry its bowl-like interior, I walked to the other side of the room and returned it to its rightful place on the shelf that divided the top of an oak Welsh cupboard from its lower portion. The shelf bore the stains of time and bowed here and there, no doubt from supporting heavy kitchen ware.

I touched the shelf. Its alternately smooth and rough surface surprised my fingertips. How different it was from the furniture in my parents' West Philadelphia kitchen. Their corner cabinet was half the size of this cupboard. And their maple table and chairs seemed dwarfed when I compared it to my aunt's huge oak table and heavy chairs. Yet all in all, each kitchen seemed right for its furnishings. Early American maple was fine in size and color for my parents' modest space. Likewise, the solid oak pieces that suggested an English manor house, not a kitchen in a Parisian apartment built at least a century ago, seemed right for this space. As I stepped away from the cupboard, I thought its size offered at least one advantage. Its heft would make moving it almost impossible. There would be no need to paint the wall behind it, no matter how many times you had to paint and repaint the other walls in the kitchen.

"*Bonjour, Vera.*" Claudine approached me and grasped both of my hands in hers. "Today your Aunt Vangie comes home from the hospital, *n'est-ce pas?*"

"Yes," I answered.

"I'm sorry she has had to stay there longer than we figured. She has talked about your visit for such a long time. I know she did not want to miss any of it."

"Yes, but at least I've been able to see her in the hospital. And I understand the doctors wanted her to be steadier on her feet than she was a couple of days ago."

Claudine looked at the clock atop one of the kitchen's counters.

"You have eaten your breakfast?" she asked me.

"Yes."

"Then you have time to take your morning walk. I expect Vangie will not be discharged for a few hours yet."

"Will we hire a taxi? Can the driver stay parked at the hospital's entrance while we go inside to get Aunt Vangie?"

"No, there is no need to hire a taxi. I sent a message to Gérard. He has access to a car, and I have asked him to go to the hospital to get her."

I pictured a young man jumping out of a car and sprinting to the hospital's entrance.

"Gérard is the person who saw the car hit Aunt Vangie, right?" I asked.

"Yes. He is very fond of Vangie. I thought it would be easier for her to ride in his car than try to fit the three of us and a cane inside a taxi."

Claudine was right. Clearly Aunt Vangie would be more comfortable riding in a car she didn't have to share with the two of us.

I took a step backward.

"I won't walk as far as I did yesterday, Claudine, even though Aunt Vangie always said that exploring the city on my own is a good way to learn the area."

"Mmm, yes," said Claudine. "And it is good that you can speak French, if only a little bit."

"*Oui, Madame* Claudine." I smiled as I thought about balancing my need for independence with the anticipation of not knowing what scenes awaited me.

"I'll be back soon. *Á bientôt.*"

I left the apartment and entered the courtyard. By now, I was used to seeing the familiar form of my aunt's neighbor as she sat on the bench near the middle of the courtyard.

"*Bonjour, Madame* Blum."

"*Bonjour.* And how goes your aunt? She is coming home soon?"

"*Oui,* yes today," I said.

"Oh, wonderful. We have worried about her. *Quel*

catastrophe! Did the police find the driver who hit her?"

"No, not yet."

"They will. I am certain of that."

I slowed my pace as I approached my aunt's neighbor.

"*Madame*, Claudine told me your daughter is a member of a police force."

"*Oui*. Amélie is the only woman in the police department of Les Andelys. *Imaginez*!" *Madame* Blum's raised eyebrows and wrinkled forehead were at odds with her smile. "Of course, she works in the office of the Brigade de Gendarmerie. Women aren't permitted to do the work of a policeman."

Not surprised to hear this, I nodded. There weren't any female officers in Philadelphia either.

"But she is an extremely bright and clever person. Always has been. She tells me sometimes she offers ideas about crimes that haven't been solved. She reads all the information contained in the criminals' records and then suggests the officers need to look to so-and-so. Her suspicions have been correct several times."

I was impressed with *Madame* Blum's daughter and I hadn't yet met her.

"Les Andelys is north of Paris, not too far away. I know she works many hours each week, but I wish she could come visit me more frequently."

"It's too bad she doesn't work for the Paris police," I said. "If she did, maybe she'd figure out who ran over my aunt and then drove away."

"*D'accord*. I agree."

At a loss for more words, I turned toward the courtyard's exit.

"You know, Vera? There is something about you that tells me you would enjoy meeting Amélie."

I paused. "Really?"

"*Oui*. I do not know exactly why I say this, but I suspect I am right." *Madame* Blum smiled. "Enjoy your walk. *Bonne journée*, Vera."

"*Bonne journée, Madame* Blum."

It *was* going to be a good day.

I'd decided I wouldn't tell Aunt Vangie that I'd already come face to face with the love of her life, Bette and her brother Hervé. The last thing I wanted to do was cause my aunt pain. I had to hope Bette Moune was a mind reader, that she would understand quickly what I was doing, and join me in pretending we'd never seen each other before. I had to hope I'd be able to perform this masquerade, because I didn't know how in the world I could do otherwise without hurting Aunt Vangie.

Chapter Nine

It was nine-thirty in the morning, much too early for Gérard Simonet to awaken and leave his bed. But summoned by the hand-written note atop the night table, Gérard dismissed his daily bath and shave routine and dressed quickly.

Serge must have left the note, Gérard reasoned. Other than Serge, there was only one person who knew his present whereabouts, and she was still a patient at L'Hôpital de la Pitié-Salpêtrière. And other than Serge Bonet, there were only two people in the world for whom Gérard would abandon sleep after only a few hours of rest broken by bad memories and a general feeling of hopelessness. One was the aforementioned friend in the hospital, and the other was the hospitalized friend's housemate. Both women had offered Gérard a place to stay when he could no longer live with Serge.

Gérard snatched the note from the small table and left his quarters. He descended the stairs two steps at a time and pushed open the door to the street. His pace more a jog than a brisk walk, he followed the shortest route he knew between his dwelling and Serge's apartment. His job-induced habit of not waking up until three hours later than he did today explained his being a stranger to the morning odors floating by his nostrils as he hurried past cafés and produce vendors' stalls. He inhaled coffee brewed so strong it could walk if it had legs, just-baked baguettes whose warm crusts Gérard imagined crunching between his teeth, and oranges, cherries, and over-ripe bananas whose sweet aromas were just short of dizzying.

The closer Gérard got to Serge's place, the faster he moved. He felt his pocket for the key to Serge's flat. The newness of their separation crossed his mind and warned him to knock on the door and not assume he still had the right to use the key and enter Serge's home at will.

Serge was already in the entryway and gestured for

Gérard to come in.

"Bonjour, Gérard."

Gérard nodded and remained as expressionless as he could. He barely glanced at Serge and fought off the temptation of saying *mon adorable* when he addressed him.

"You will no doubt want to borrow my car for your errand," said Serge. "It is in the usual location."

"Yes, I do need to use it. Thank you for delivering Claudine's message."

"I could see it was important, and I knew you would not receive it until you arrived home after work." Serge pointed at the note Gérard continued to clutch in his hand.

"The directions from Claudine are certainly specific, *n'est-ce pas?*" said Serge.

Gérard unfurled the paper and began reading the message aloud. "Please arrive on time… eleven o'clock and try to park the car on the Boulevard de l'Hôpital. You will find yourself very close to the North entrance. Go to Reception and explain who you are and why you are there. A hospital aide will help you take Vangie to your car. Remember to drive carefully and slowly because Vangie is still healing from her broken ribs and fractured hip. *Prends garde*, Gérard. *Merci. Ton amie*, Claudine."

"Well, at least I don't have to guess where to park the car," said Gérard.

Serge lifted a leather key fob from a hook not far from the door. "Here," he said as he handed the car key to Gérard. "Unlike Claudine, I am not giving you a precise time to return the car. You can deliver it and the key at your convenience."

"Merci, Serge."

Gérard turned toward the door and pocketed the car key. As it settled quietly against the coins in his pocket, he hesitated. "When would you like me to return your house key?"

"You will know when it is time to do that, Gérard. You will know."

Chapter Ten

This morning, I noticed three things during my walk. One was all the water either rushing down the sides of some of the streets I explored or standing inches deep next to the curbs. I had to hopscotch my way past the rivulets each time I arrived at an intersection.

Streams of water released from the Paris sanitation trucks tried their best to wash away days' worth of discards, human spit, chewing gum, and unachieved plans.

The second thing that struck me today was how many people here smoke cigarettes made with such strong-smelling tobacco. I didn't see many women dangling the foul-smelling things as they passed by. It's usually men who are busy inhaling and exhaling, whether they're seated at a café sipping coffee and reading newspapers, walking along the street, or riding the bus. Packets of *Gauloises*, *Gitanes*, or some other exotic brand peek from the tops of shirt and jacket pockets.

My father smokes Pall Malls, but only if my mother isn't at home. When she's out, he puffs away in the living room and deposits the ashes in the tray where he rests his pipes. He takes the ashtray out to the alley between our house and our neighbors where he wipes the tray just short of clean. If it were too clean, my mother would know he'd been smoking.

The third thing that caught my eye was a strange looking black symbol I saw painted on two of the buildings I passed. The designs appeared randomly and had exactly the same shape, two intertwining letter z's. I believe I saw a third one that someone tried to erase. Its shadow remained, as if it refused to disappear.

Each morning, I followed a different route, and each variation rewarded my curiosity and grew my sense of independence. Today I passed La Gare St. Lazare, the train station where I'd arrived in Paris. I walked along one side of the building and went as far as the Boulevard des Batignolles. Aware of the time, I kept glancing at my watch. I didn't want to miss Aunt Vangie's arrival from the hospital.

I remembered seeing a flower vendor at the station, and I thought it would be a good idea to buy a bouquet for Claudine and my aunt. I'd just finished paying for the flowers when I heard a man call out.

"*Ici les Nouvelles! Ici les Nouvelles! Boycottage des magasins des juifs en Allemagne!*"

The voice belonged to a man selling newspapers. He wore a black apron whose pockets bulged with coins. The frequent exchanges of money for newspapers failed to dampen his shouts.

As I traded a few coins for a newspaper, I hoped I'd be able to decipher enough of the French text to understand the headline and its story. I knew if I couldn't, Claudine would translate for me. I thought about *Madame* Blum's penchant for learning English with the help of the newspapers my aunt would bring her so I returned to the newsstand and bought the latest copy of the *Paris Herald Tribune*. Zigzagging through the crush of people hurrying toward their destinations, I spotted the train station's café and sat down at a table long enough to read the Tribune's headlines. There, near the bottom of the first page, was what I figured to be the English version of the story the vendor kept screaming.

"*German Boycott Against Jewish-Owned Stores And Businesses.*"

Just below the headline, I read *Citizens blocked entrances to stores owned by German Jews. Anti-Jewish policies are increasing under the newly appointed Chancellor, A. Hitler.*

"*Vous désirez, Mademoiselle?*" A waiter smiled down at me.

"*Non*, no, thank you," I said.

I folded the French newspaper over its English cousin, left the café, and exited the train station. The closer I got to the apartment, the more excited I became. I'd be able to spend hours with Aunt Vangie, listen to her tales, maybe go to work with her once or twice. As my pace hastened, I realized I felt something in addition to excitement. My happiness shared space with a vague emotion I couldn't name. What was interfering with my joy? Was it the newspapers' headlines about the anti-Jewish boycott? Why would that cause me any discomfort? It was taking place in Germany, not in France.

Whatever the reason for my mixed feelings, it must have been powerful enough to make me forget the flowers I'd purchased. I'd left them on the table in the café.

Chapter Eleven

Amélie Blum pushed aside the local newspaper and thumbed through the contents of the file envelope on her desk. One by one, she glanced at each page's description of a thief who'd been caught recently. The pickpocket wasn't very smart, she thought. He kept returning to the same places he'd trolled repeatedly in Les Andelys, the flower market, the small park near L' Église Saint-Sauveur, the alley next to the Post Office. Why it had taken so long to arrest him remained a mystery to Amélie. How many *gendarmes* had failed to see him during the past months?

Amélie picked up the envelope, left her desk, and walked down the Gendarmerie Nationale's first floor hallway. She entered a room dominated by wooden cabinets aligned one next to another, three sets of cabinets that stood back-to-back, separated by narrow pathways. Each cabinet bore a letter of the alphabet. When she arrived at cabinet N, Amélie stopped and pulled open the cabinet's third drawer. She let her fingers travel just past the midpoint of the envelopes until she found the right place to deposit the file, Normand.

The first object she saw when she returned to her desk was the newspaper she'd pushed away in favor of looking at the file. The paper's headline assaulted her emotions more than any of the sordid details she usually read about the thieves and criminals who'd been arrested by her male colleagues. By now, her job was so routinized she no longer looked at the criminals' photos nor read their physical descriptions. Their heights and weights, hair color, gender, and facial features were more a composite than a description of an individual. What many of the arrestees had in common were unfortunate childhood histories, bleak futures, and a tendency to be violent.

Amélie sighed and looked at the newspaper's front page. She knew immediately she had to telephone her mother's neighbor, Vangie Curtis. Vangie brought her mother an English language newspaper at least once or twice a week. Today's paper was one Amélie did not want her mother to see.

"*Allô, Madame Curtis ?*"

"Non, c'est Claudine Mistralle."

"Ah, bonjour Madame Mistralle. C'est moi, Amélie Blum."

"Ah, Amélie, I did not recognize your voice. You sound distressed."

"I do? I am sorry to bother you, but I have a favor to ask."

"Of course. How can I help you?"

"*Madame* Curtis, Vangie. She brings my mother the newspaper to help with her English. I need to ask her not to bring *Maman* the newspaper today."

"Doing that favor will be easy. Vangie has been in the hospital all of this time. She is coming home today, but I do not expect she will have a newspaper with her."

"Oh, *Madame* Mistralle. I completely forgot about the accident. She is recovered, no?"

"For the most part, yes. She will need help with a few things, and fortunately her niece Vera is here for a visit."

"Vera from *Philadelphie*, right?"

"*Oui.* She is a lovely young woman."

"My mother has mentioned her to me. She thinks we might have a lot in common."

"I agree with your mother. But tell me. Why do you not want your mother to see the newspaper?"

"One of the stories would upset her greatly. I do not want her to worry."

Claudine hesitated for a second, and then asked a question. "Are you alright? Has anything happened to you?"

"I am fine, *Madame* Mistralle. I just want to protect my mother. I will telephone her before the end of the day. She will be pleased to hear that I might be able to come to Paris in a few days. I will visit her and meet Vera."

"*Formidable.* I will not tell your mother that you called me."

"Thank you so much, *Madame* Mistralle. *Je vous aprécie.*"

Amélie turned the newspaper face down.

Our friend Serge Bonet has been right all along, she thought. He has warned us about this.

With the newspaper's headline etched in her mind, Amélie prepared to bring her workday to its close. With any luck, she'd be able to stop at home long enough to pack a weekend's worth of clothing, place the envelope protecting certain governmental forms in her bag, and hurry to the train station to buy a ticket from Les Andelys to the Gare du Nord in Paris.

Chapter Twelve

Instead of going directly to Aunt Vangie's apartment, I stopped in front of *Madame* Blum's door, knocked, and called her name.

"*Oui, j'arrive.*"

Just as Claudine's voice sounded like musical notes the first time I heard it, *Madame* Blum's voice seemed to carry a tune as well.

"Oh, it is you, Vera."

I offered the newspaper to her.

"Just in case my aunt doesn't have time to stop and get a paper for you," I said.

"How thoughtful of you. *Merci.*"

"Do you know if she's arrived yet?" I asked, realizing my walk had taken me farther from *Rue Clauzel* than I'd planned to go, and stopping to buy the newspapers had taken me longer than I'd anticipated.

Madame Blum looked beyond me. Her lips bloomed into a smile.

"She is just arriving now, *chérie.*"

I turned and saw a young man walking beside Aunt Vangie, his left forearm extended toward her in an offer of support.

Aunt Vangie walked slowly and gave her cane time to keep pace. She stared at the ground as if it were unexplored territory, not the path she'd traveled countless times before today.

"Aunt Vangie, you're here!"

My aunt stopped and looked in my direction.

"Yes, thank the Lord! I'm here."

I left *Madame* Blum's doorstep and approached my aunt.

"Vera, this is my friend, Gérard. He's the one who called for an ambulance right after the car hit me."

"*Enchanté*, Vera."

"I'm glad to meet you. Thanks for helping my aunt."

"It was nothing. She would have done the same for me had I been flattened by that car."

"You work with her at the jazz club, right?"

Gérard nodded. "Yes, for the past two years. She has been very kind to me. She treats me with respect and affection."

"Well, I do respect you," said Aunt Vangie. "As for affection, you're the nephew I've never had. That's why I knew you'd like my niece, Vera. You're two peas in the same pod."

I hardly ever form an opinion of someone the moment we meet, but in this case, I knew I liked Gérard. Maybe it was the way he treated Aunt Vangie, offering her support, but not insisting she hold on to his arm. It could also have been the kindness I saw in his eyes. I gauged him to be the gentle part of gentleman.

"Well, I've made it this far. Are you two going to see to it that I arrive at my door?"

Gérard gestured for me to lead the way.

I looked to see if *Madame* Blum were still standing outside her door. She was there, waving one hand and holding the newspaper with her other one.

"*Bonjour, Vangie! Bienvenue*! I will come to visit you later."

"Okay, Simone. I'll be here, at least for today."

"Just for today?" Gérard and I asked simultaneously.

Aunt Vangie laughed. "I wanted to be sure you two were paying attention."

I shook my head and traded smiles with Gérard.

"Was that a newspaper I saw in Simone's hand?" Aunt Vangie asked.

"Yes, she and Claudine mentioned you frequently give her a newspaper to help her practice speaking English, so earlier today I bought one for her."

Aunt Vangie looked at Gérard. "You see what I mean? Both of you like to help your elders."

"Vangie, I am so glad you have returned home."

Claudine opened the door to the apartment and then leaned into Aunt Vangie who braced herself for the discomfort their physical contact might cause. Claudine must have read my aunt's body language because instead of hugging each other, the two exchanged what I call the double-cheek-not-really-a-kiss-greeting.

"Gérard, I am so grateful you could borrow Serge's car and bring Vangie home from the hospital," said Claudine.

"It was nothing. And Serge is always generous with his automobile." Gérard's shoulders slumped. His voice was no more than a whisper.

I had a hunch his "nothing" was really "something," and the "something" was named Serge.

"Can you stay a while?" Claudine asked. "We will have a late lunch."

Gérard looked at the clock in the foyer. "I am afraid I cannot. I have to return the car and run a few errands before I go to work." He turned toward my aunt. "Can I help you to a chair, Vangie?"

"No thanks, sweetheart. I have to show off how good I can use this cane."

Gérard turned toward me. "Vera, it was a pleasure meeting you. Vangie, Claudine, let me know if there is anything I can do to further help you."

"*À bientôt,* Gérard," I said as I watched him make his way through the courtyard.

"Oh, Vera, I almost forgot." Claudine picked up an envelope from the foyer table. "This came for you earlier today."

I read the sender's name.

"It's from my mother. I didn't expect her to write to me so soon, especially since I wrote her a note to let her know I'd arrived safely."

"Maybe she wanted to remind you to avoid following in the footsteps of -a-disgrace-to-our-family," said Vangie.

I smiled, but not too broadly. I treasured my aunt and I knew before she left Philadelphia, she'd sustained many verbal wounds, all launched by my mother. I also knew I'd absorbed a lot of my mother's beliefs and standards, if not some of her behaviors. I was still more *her* than I'd had time to become *me.* That fact seemed more evident now that I was on my own in a city still foreign to me, despite my aunt's presence.

I opened the envelope and a smaller one fell to the floor. It bore my name and my home address, as well as the sender's name, Clifford R. Anderson, and his address in Chicago, Illinois. The name seemed vaguely familiar.

"My mother must have forwarded this to me. It's post-marked the day after I left Philadelphia."

"Then it must be important," said Claudine.

"I agree," said Vangie. "If my sister paid the extra post-age to mail it all the way here, it *has* to be important."

I didn't contradict Aunt Vangie. I knew she'd stock-piled an artillery of scathing words aimed at my mother, and she needed to take a potshot whenever she could. I fig-ured it was really my father who'd brought the re-addressed envelope with him to work, paid the postage, and mailed it the morning after it arrived.

I unsealed the letter and read it.

"Aunt Vangie! Claudine! You're not going to believe this. Listen."

The Chicago Recorder
4445 Constitution Avenue
Chicago, Illinois

Dear Miss Clay,

It has come to my attention that you wrote to *The Chicago Recorder's* employment office. You included your curriculum vitae which listed your experience writing for and editing your school's newspaper, *The Temple University News*. Our response to your question about a job here at the *Recorder* explained that we do not have any employ-ment opportunities at present. That situation continues to be true.

In your letter you mentioned you were planning to travel to France and stay there for at least three months. That is a fortuitous situation for you and for our newspa-per. I am offering you the same opportunity I gave to my nieces, Sarah G. Thompson and Florence Anderson, when they traveled abroad two years ago.

They wrote short, informative articles about their visits to several European countries. Their articles proved to be of great interest to our readers. Would you consider writing about your experiences in France?

If you agree to do so, we can formalize the terms of the agreement in a future correspondence. I can assure you that writing a column for *The Chicago Recorder* will give you journalistic experience as well as national exposure. Our newspaper enjoys a robust distribution.

Please do us the favor of a response as soon as you have made your decision.

Sincerely,
Robert S. Abbott, Publisher, *Chicago Recorder*

Vangie raised her cane in the air.

"I remember telling you not to give up. Sooner or later, you'd get a newspaper job," she said.

"Hold onto your cane the right way, Vangie." Claudine eyed Aunt Vangie warily and then grinned at me.

"What a day, my dears. Vangie comes home in one piece and our Vera has a job writing for a newspaper."

"It's only for three months." I wanted to keep my happiness under control, in case anything went awry.

"You don't know what might transpire, Vera," said Aunt Vangie. "This is just the beginning of your career. I'll bet you get offered a permanent position when they see how well you write."

"Well, maybe…"

Three sharp knocks on the apartment's door ended my sentence.

Claudine walked toward the noise.

"Ah, Simone. *Viens, viens.*"

Madame Blum entered quickly. She peered over Claudine's shoulder, saw Aunt Vangie and me, and rushed to us. Why she was still clutching the newspaper was a total mystery.

"Vangie, I am so happy you are here. You will be okay, right? Yes, you will be fine."

I tried to interpret the conflicting signals I saw in *Madame* Blum. Her smile was intense, but fleeting. It appeared on her lips, but not in her eyes. Her hand that held the newspaper seemed to have a life of its own as it repeatedly directed the paper to hit her upper thigh.

"Simone, are you alright?" Aunt Vangie asked.

I wasn't the only one who could see she was upset.

"*Je suis nerveuse.* There is something written in the newspaper. I think I understand the English, but I wanted to be sure."

She unfolded the paper and pointed to an article near the bottom of the first page.

"*Ici.* It says some people in Germany refuse to enter stores and businesses owned by Jews, right?"

Aunt Vangie squinted at the newsprint.

"Yes, that's what it says."

"And soon this will happen in Poland and in other countries?" *Madame* Blum's voice quavered.

"I don't think that's going to happen, Simone. I'm sure it won't happen here in France."

I wasn't sure if Aunt Vangie knew that as the gospel truth or if she just said it to lessen her neighbor's fear.

"*T'inquiètes pas,* Simone. This will pass."

Claudine approached Madame Blum and reached out to her. Just then, we heard another noise at the door.

"I'll go," I said.

Before I could cross the foyer, there was a second series of knocks, this one more rapid-fire than the first. I grabbed the knob and pulled the door toward me. In stunned silence, it seemed like forever until I could speak.

"Yes?" I said tentatively.

The woman at the door stared at me. Her eyes grew large and she began to blink quickly, as if blinking would change where and who we were.

"Who is it, Vera?"

"*C'est moi, Vangie. C'est* Bette."

"I'm in here!"

As I stood back to let the woman pass in front of me, she mouthed a few words. "You have never seen me before. We do not know each other."

I nodded quickly.

Bette Moune had just answered the question that had never left me. How would we act the first time we stood face-to-face? It appeared we would stage a charade and play let's pretend. I wasn't certain I could carry this off. I wasn't sure I *wanted* to carry it off. But certain, or not certain, the first act had begun and I had no choice other than to play the role of dishonesty personified.

By nightfall, I felt exhausted from the day's events. I'd received an offer to write a column for a Negro-American newspaper. I'd felt an unexpected tremor of concern when I'd read a disturbing headline in two newspapers, one in English and the other in French. I'd seen a look of fear cover the face of my aunt's neighbor after she'd read about the goings-on in Germany. I'd felt such joy at seeing Aunt Vangie return home. I'd begun to question if the Paris police would ever find the person who'd driven a car into Aunt Vangie. And by the power of Bette's two sentences upon seeing me at the doorway of my aunt's home, I'd been deputized to hide an ugly truth from Aunt Vangie.

My stay in Paris was becoming more complicated than I'd imagined it would be.

Chapter Thirteen

Gérard did not return Serge's car right away. After he left
Vangie's apartment, he drove the black Panhard 6DS
slowly through the narrow streets of nearby Montmartre.
His foot barely touched the accelerator any time a pedes-
trian seemed disinclined to share the road with his car.
Once or twice, he dared his vehicle to touch an arm or
brush against a shopper's bag, but he didn't want an arm or
bag to leave its mark on Serge's car. Simply imagining the
car scarred by marred metal jolted him into recalling Vangie's accident.

The car that collided with Vangie, a burgundy-colored
Citroën Traction Avant, must have suffered damage of
some sort. An anonymous employee working in an
unnamed auto repair shop must have been tasked with
restoring the automobile's wounded surface to its original
finish. How much time had the Paris Police spent looking
for this car, or asking questions of repair shop owners?

Vangie had discouraged him from doing anything
about the accident. She speculated that had this happened
in Philadelphia, the police wouldn't have put any distress
on looking for the car and its driver. They would not have
cared about a colored woman getting run over late at night.
Instead, they would have mumbled their incorrect assumptions about her and why she was out in the streets alone
after midnight.

Gérard sensed Vangie wanted to forget why she'd suffered broken bones, so he had stopped pressing her about
an investigation that seemed to be going nowhere. He
remained more than curious, though. And he welcomed
this curiosity because it became a place holder for the sadness that filled him after Serge ended their relationship.

With only two hours left before he had to report to
work, Gérard wended his way toward the garage where
Serge kept his car. He parked, turned off the ignition, and
took in deep breaths. He swore he could smell Serge's
essence in the car's leather seats. When he touched the

steering wheel, he imagined feeling the impressions of Serge's fingers as they'd gripped the wheel so often in the past, as they used to grip *his* hands, arms, and back in the past. Gérard missed the strength those fingers always telegraphed, along with the promises inherent in Serge's affectionate touches.

He exited the Panhard and walked slowly from the garage toward Serge's home. Using the key that was still in his pocket, Gérard entered the small house. Although he didn't plan to linger, he gave in to his curiosity and climbed the stairs to what had been the bedroom he shared with Serge. Surely, it would be there where he would find evidence of his former lover's unfaithfulness.

Gérard went to the armoire and looked at the trousers and jackets he'd recalled Serge wearing. He opened the chest's eight drawers and placed his hands under each stack of shirts, underwear, and night clothes he saw. Neither pleased nor saddened that his search resulted in finding nothing to suggest he'd been replaced by a new lover, Gérard sat on the bed and gave his tears permission to flow.

It would have been better if he'd seen something new in the bedroom ... some small token from a man unabashedly smitten with Serge. The absence of said gift left Gérard feeling empty and confused and returned him to the bitterness of his exile from Serge. As he'd done for months now, Gérard questioned why he'd been banished if it were not due to the existence of someone else.

Gérard stood abruptly and left the bedroom. He crossed the hallway and went into Serge's office. During a quick perusal of the room, he saw something on Serge's desk that drew his attention. As he approached the desk, he saw a short stack of envelopes held together with a ribbon. Very carefully, Gérard untied the ribbon and teased the top unsealed envelope away from the others. He extracted its contents and began reading.

Mon Chère Serge, I could barely wait to see and speak with you the other evening. The statements you made publicly were fascinating, but the words you spoke to me privately were so endearing. They gave me hope for our future. A future we'll spend together in our wonderful homeland, France.

M.

Gérard refolded the letter and put it back its envelope. Careful to place it on top of the others, he retied the ribbon, and then left Serge's office. He had found the object he'd sought, a tenderly worded note written to Serge by someone whose first initial was M.

On his way to the front door, Gérard reached into his pants pocket and withdrew the car key and the key to Serge's house. He placed them on a small table nearby, looked at them a final time, and spoke.

"You were right, Serge. You said I would know when to return your key. I know the time is now."

Chapter Fourteen

16 *Rue Clauzel*
Paris, 9ième
France

Dear Mr. Abbott,

I am honored that you have offered me the opportunity to write a series of columns about my stay in Paris. I accept. *The Chicago Recorder* is an outstanding newspaper with a fine journalistic reputation.

I've been here in Paris just short of one week, and already I've had experiences that are different from those of most American tourists. I can compose my first column today and mail it to you without delay. The Paris to New York City airmail service is in full operation, as is the air-mail service from New York City to Chicago.

Thank you for entrusting me with this project, Mr. Abbott. I will not disappoint you and your newspaper's readers.

Sincerely,
Vera Clay

"I'm off to the *Poste*, Aunt Vangie."

"Alright. It looks like rain. There are some umbrellas in the foyer closet. Why don't you take one?"

"Thank you. *Merci.* On my way back from the *Poste-Télégraphe-Téléphone* I'll stop at *Madame* Blum's apartment and get the typewriter she said I could borrow."

I walked as fast as my feet could take me. Thankfully, there were only two other customers ahead of me when I arrived. I purchased a special *par avion* envelope, addressed it, paid the postage, and handed it to the clerk.

Just as quickly as I'd sped to the *Poste*, I hurried back to begin writing my first column.

The morning's overcast sky reminded me of the day I

arrived in France. Had it really been only a week ago? Hadn't I known Claudine and *Madame* Blum far longer than seven days? So quickly my daily walks had changed once-foreign streets, stores, and signs into familiar landmarks. Strangers' smiles and greetings continued to surprise me. Didn't they notice I looked different from the average young Parisian woman? Didn't they fear or at least resent my presence in their streets and in their stores?

I knocked on *Madame* Blum's door and awaited her cheery, *J'arrive*. Instead, the door flew open and I found myself facing a person I didn't know. The stranger thrust her hand toward mine, enveloped it, and shook it briskly before I had time to register the contact.

"You are Vera, right?" she asked.

"Yes. How did you know?"

"My mother told me to expect you, that you would come by to borrow her old typewriter."

"You're *Madame* Blum's daughter?" I asked.

"Yes. I have looked at your photo several times when I have been in the living room or your aunt and Claudine."

She looked steadily at me as if she were trying to memorize my features.

"You resemble Vangie in a certain way."

"In what way?" I asked.

"The resemblance is in your eyes. They are holding onto questions, right?"

"Not really. I expected your mother to open the door. You surprised me." Although I didn't like strangers to make assumptions about me, I made the effort to frame an awkward moment within a casual smile.

"My name is Amélie Blum."

"*Enchantée*, Amélie," I said.

"Step inside. It is starting to rain."

Amélie backed herself against the door, forcing it to open wider. Her dark brown eyes stared into mine without blinking, as she seemed to be estimating my height and speculating about the cause of the half-inch scar above my left eyebrow. I figured that's a habit of police officers, or in this case, police department employees whose gender prevents them from becoming genuine police officers.

"*Maman*, Vera has arrived," Amélie ceased looking at

me and turned toward her approaching mother.

"*Bonjour*, Vera."

Madame Blum's eyes were red-rimmed and her cheeks looked pale and sunken. She spoke before I could ask if she felt okay.

"I rescued the old typewriter from its resting place in the kitchen pantry," she said. "And Amélie cleaned the keys and the carriage. I am afraid you will have to buy a new ribbon. The one that is here will shred as soon as you have typed your first sentence."

She ventured a wan smile.

"I'll be happy to buy a new ribbon. I'm so grateful to you for lending me your typewriter."

"*Ah, ce n'est rien, ma chère.*" *Madame* Blum gestured toward Amélie. "I am pleased that you are meeting my daughter. I had no idea that Amélie was coming to visit me this weekend, or I would have mentioned it to you yesterday."

"*Et voilà.* Here I am." Amélie barely smiled.

The air became dense with unspoken words. Clearly, something had upset *Madame* Blum. Perhaps she and her daughter had traded harsh words shortly before I knocked on their door.

I pointed to a box atop a chair.

"Is this the typewriter?" I asked.

"Yes," said Amélie. "I can carry it across the courtyard for you."

"That's not necessary."

I picked up the box and smelled the faint odor of aged ink.

Amélie took my umbrella from me and then opened the door.

"Thanks, but it's not raining that much," I said.

Amélie squinted at the sky." I will walk with you and hold the umbrella above the typewriter."

I nodded and took a last look at *Madame* Blum.

Amélie and I walked slowly as she did her best to protect the boxed typewriter from the rain that had become a dense mist.

"I know a place where you can buy your writing supplies, Vera," she said. "I will be happy to take you there."

I thought I saw the sharp angles of Amélie's shoulders soften.

"That's kind of you. But I can go to *La Samaritaine.* I know my way there."

"The store I am thinking of will be of interest to you," she said.

"Can we go this afternoon?" I asked. "I want to begin a writing assignment before the day ends."

"Certainly. I will stop by for you in an hour."

I watched Amélie close the umbrella and prop it near the entrance to Aunt Vangie's apartment.

"*Ça va bien?*" she asked.

For a second, I thought she was going to bow. She didn't.

"*Oui.* See you in an hour," I said. "Amélie, is your mother feeling all right?"

She narrowed her eyes, and once again, appeared to be taking a measure of me.

"She is angry with me because I have asked her to do something very difficult. I have brought her the government forms to apply for a passport and travel visas for England and for your country." Amélie paused. "I feel this is an important thing to do right now, but I hate to see her upset."

"Why is it important for her to do this now?"

Amélie's answer was hesitant. "Because now there is time. Also, I love her very much, so her tears wound me, Vera."

I was struck by the change in her voice I heard when she spoke my name. That and the deep beauty I noticed in her eyes stayed with me for a long time. The compassion-laced statement she'd made about watching her mother cry was the kind of heartfelt utterance a loving daughter would issue about a beloved mother. It was an expression of devotion to a parent, something that had never occurred to me to say.
I've revisited the tenderness of their mother-daughter bond many, many times since the morning Amélie volunteered to take me to a place where I'd be able to buy a new typewriter ribbon. I've not missed feeling that tenderness, but I have envied it.

Chapter Fifteen

Bette reached across the table and covered Vangie's hand with hers. "I am so glad to be back in Paris with you. It seemed like I was away for months instead of weeks."

"And to make matters worse, I was in the hospital for much of that time. I wasn't able to call and tell you I'd been hurt, and I couldn't hear your sweet voice say how much you loved me."

"Every time that I had a moment to telephone you, something interfered," said Bette.

"Something interfered? Or someone interfered?"

Bette blinked and then looked downward.

"I know what you are thinking, but it was not always Hervé who interfered. Sometimes it was too late to call. I knew you would be at work."

"Let's not talk about any problems, especially if they involve your brother's attitude about our relationship. Not now, anyway. Tell me about your trip. I bet you sold most of your paintings."

"No, only a few. But we met a few influential museum curators and dealers when we were in New York City, Chicago, and Boston."

"Good. Your work will have a future in the United States. If we ever travel there, you'll already be famous."

Bette smiled at her.

"Yes, but I was counting on selling more of my work now, or at least being offered opportunities to showcase some of it."

Vangie frowned.

"I thought Hervé was going to succeed in getting that done for you."

Bette released her lover's hand and stood. She drew close to Vangie and leaned down to kiss her.

"I missed doing that," she said.

"And I missed receiving it."

Needful of more than a kiss, Vangie began her own effort to stand. She placed her hands on the table's edge as she pushed herself away from it.

Not used to seeing her need assistance, Bette let a couple of seconds expire before she found her voice. "Let me help you, Vangie."

Vangie shook her head. "No. I can do this by myself."

Slowly, she eased her body up from the chair, all the while depending upon the curved edge of the table to support herself. She nodded toward one of the corners of the room.

"Hand me that cane, will you, darlin'?"

Bette obliged.

"See. I'm almost good as new. And to prove it, I'm going to the club tonight."

"*Non, non, non*!" Claudine's voice preceded her arrival as she swept into the room. "You are crazy, right?"

"No, not in the literal sense. But I am stir crazy and tired of being away from my friends at work."

"Vangie, how will you get there?" Bette asked.

"I've taken care of everything. I asked Gérard to see if the boss will let him leave the club long enough to pick me up and bring me there. When I'm ready to come home, he'll see that I get into a taxi."

Bette and Claudine stared at Vangie.

"*Ma chère*, I am sorry I cannot go with you tonight," said Bette.

"*Tant pis*, just as well." Claudine made no attempt to lower her voice.

"I won't be alone," Vangie continued. "I'm taking Vera with me. Now that she's going to write a column for that Chicago newspaper, I want her to see as many sides of Paris as she can. That includes the nightclubs as well as the museums, the musicians as well as the monuments, and the bar's clientele as well as the operagoers. I have a feeling she'll be wide-eyed at first, but after a little while, she'll feel comfortable."

"I hope you are right about that," said Claudine.

"I know I'm right. The poor girl needs a bit of entertainment. She spent just shy of a week traveling third class on a ship. Do you think she got dressed to the nines every evening and dined and danced with the first-class passengers?"

Bette blinked rapidly and held her breath.

"Since she arrived, Vera's spent her days visiting me at the hospital, helping you around the house, Claudine, and chatting with Simone Blum. Simone's a nice person, but she's older than we are. Vera needs to meet some young people."

"She made the acquaintance of Simone's daughter. Amélie is close to her age," countered Claudine.

Vangie allowed herself a few extra breaths.

"It's important for her to meet some joyful folks and hear some great jazz, the best music this side of the Atlantic Ocean. Amélie Blum might match Vera in age, but she's not always what I'd call a joyful person."

"Perhaps Vera might find Amélie's other characteristics attractive," said Claudine.

Vangie grinned. "Oh, my dear Claudine. My dear, dear Brickette. You claim you're not a lesbian, but sometimes you certainly think like one."

Claudine shook her head and walked out of the kitchen.

"*Au revoir, Bette*," she called over her shoulder.

Vangie looked at her lover. "Are you leaving, too?"

"Yes, it is getting late in the day, and I promised Hervé that I would work on some sketches for my next painting."

"And did Hervé promise you he'd sell your next painting?" Vangie straightened her posture in anticipation of Bette's answer.

"He always makes that promise."

"And he rarely keeps it."

"Please, let us not argue about my brother. He feels responsible for my well-being and he does the best he can to help support me."

"I know," said Vangie. "You two support each other."

Bette closed the space between them.

Vangie reached out with her free arm and encircled Bette's waist.

The women kissed several times before Bette pulled back.

"Be safe tonight, *ma chère*. And be sure to let Gérard get the taxi for you and Vera."

"I will. Don't worry."

Vangie walked to the door with Bette, watched her depart, and wondered how soon they'd see one another again.

"Be safe," she said.

She heard the echoes of Bette's advice to let Gérard secure a taxi when she and Vera were ready to return home from the jazz club. Vangie remembered the last time she left work and stepped from the sidewalk to the street. It seemed so long ago that the particular step she took became the last thing she recalled of that night.

Chapter Sixteen

Some people look up to the sky the second they step away from their front door, as if they need to see for themselves what the weather forecasters have said. Others instinctively glance to the left or right, cautious about their safety. In the short time I've been here, I've taken to fixing my gaze at the bench on the border of the courtyard's flower bed. Consciously or not, I'm always looking for *Madame* Blum.

An hour after I met Amélie, I saw her seated on that same bench. Somewhat taller than her mother, she sat erect. Her short dark-brown hair differed from *Madame* Blum's wispy gray-mixed-with-blond strands. In fact, it was different from the long hair styles most women were wearing now.

I watched Amélie stand up and stride toward me.

"You are ready to go?" she asked.

"Oui. Je suis prête à partir. "

"You do not need to speak French with me," she said. "My English is good I have been told."

I nodded even though Amélie's statements worked against bolstering my self-confidence as far as speaking French was concerned.

"Where did you say we're going?" I asked.

"I did not say. It is a surprise. Here, take this." Amélie handed me a bag made of fabric and embroidered with tiny flowers.

"You are going to buy writing supplies, *n'est-ce pas*? You can carry them in this," she explained.

"We're going to La Samaritaine or Au Bon Marché, aren't we?" I called the names of the only stores in Paris I was aware of.

Amélie placed her finger across her lips. "I am keeping silent about our destination," she whispered. "From here we will walk past the Opéra Garnier where we will board a city bus. When we reach the Boulevard St. Germain, we will leave the bus and walk to *Rue de l'Odéon*. There, you will see the surprise store."

As we walked, I noticed the streets and sidewalks were wider and more crowded than those in my aunt's neighborhood. We passed numerous cafés whose round tables accommodated men and women sipping coffee, beer or small cloudy-colored drinks.

And then, there was the Opera House.

"Look at all that goldleaf, marble, and quartz!" My eyes were overwhelmed. "Have you seen the inside? Is it as ornate as the exterior?"

"Only once, during a school trip."

"If it's so ornate on the outside, what can the interior look like?"

"It is excessive, I assure you." Amélie's curt description of the opera house told me volumes about her opinion of luxury.

Try as I might, I couldn't recall any building in Philadelphia endowed with similar eye-popping decoration. Not City Hall. Not the Museum of Art. Not even the Academy of Music. And if I could picture such a sight, I don't think I'd be as caustic as Amélie was in expressing her opinion to a foreigner.

Amélie pointed at the closest intersection. "The bus stop is over there," she said.

I saw three people huddled under a shop's overhang, and I figured they were waiting for the bus. At the same time, I focused on the window of a leather goods store with a display of every imaginable type of bag. I eyed huge steam-ship trunks, their halves spread apart to reveal sets of drawers, more modestly sized suitcases, men's work cases with their profusion of buckles and straps, children's school totes, and women's pocketbooks and purses. Red and black colored banners bearing the words, *Soldes Annuelles*, were suspended from the store's ceiling.

"Do you have need of a new purse?" Amélie asked.

"No. It's just that I've never seen such a big collection and in so many different colors."

Amélie tugged on my arm.

"Hurry! The bus is approaching."

We hastened our pace and were the last to climb aboard the vehicle.

As we sat next to each other, I wondered what some of the other bus passengers thought about us... two young women, one white and one colored, obviously acquainted with each other, our shoulders and arms pushed together by virtue of the seats' narrowness. With the exception of a young woman who chose to stand near our seat instead of claiming one for herself, no one paid us any attention at all.

The woman who remained standing glanced down at me and then at Amélie. Her eyes lingered on the place where Amélie's arm touched mine. She gazed once again at Amélie and offered the subtlest of smiles.

Amélie must have sensed the woman was watching us, because she traded glances with the stranger and then nodded at her.

"Someone you know?" I asked.

Amélie squinted and said, "Yes, and no."

I didn't press her for a fuller, less obtuse answer. Instead, I looked out the window as the bus navigated its way across the Pont Neuf to Paris' left bank. After a few moments passed, Amélie nudged my shoulder with hers.

"This is our terminus," she said.

We left the bus and made our way through a tangle of streets too narrow to permit automobile traffic. Young people hurried by us. University students, no doubt. The sound of their shoes quickly striking the sidewalk suggested the impatience their young age demanded. The speed with which they walked seemed at odds with the sounds of their shared laughter and implied intimacies.

"Have you seen much of the city, or been to any of our museums?" Amélie asked.

"No, not yet. I've only seen the route between Aunt Vangie's apartment and the hospital, and the areas I walk through in the mornings, but I intend to spend a few days in art and history museums. I love Renoir and Monet."

"Agh! The Impressionists. Your taste in art is very naïve and simple. How could you like their blurry, sketchy paintings? All those flowers and landscapes. I am happy their time has passed."

The truth was, I *did* like their gauzy dreamlike paintings. What I didn't like was Amélie's harsh criticism of me.

Naïve? Simple? What business was it of hers? At that moment, I would have preferred to look at Cézanne's worst crayon scribbles instead of listening to Amélie's opinions of artists whose works, by the way, were hung on the walls of reputable museums.

"You don't appreciate the beauty of flowers?" I asked.

"Not when there are more important subjects to portray, like infernal wars, poor people, and the hatred of men toward others who represent being different."

I remained silent for a few seconds.

"You are not familiar with Chagall, Jacob, Delaunay, or Laurencin?"

I shook my head.

"How about two of your countrymen, Jacob Lawrence or Archibald Motley?"

"Lawrence, yes. Motley, no."

"You must learn about them. They are more important than the Impressionists because they paint truths most people do not want to see." Amélie lowered her voice. "So far, you have lived a comfortable life, no?"

"As comfortable as possible considering I'm a colored female living in America." I paused. "Haven't you been living comfortably?"

"Not always. I am a Jewish woman in a Christian country surrounded by other Christian countries where some people are starting to speak out against us."

"Are they speaking out against Jews here in France?"

"The whispers have begun," said Amélie. "Soon, the voices will become louder."

I recalled the fear that struck Amélie's mother when she read about the German boycotts of Jewish-owned businesses.

"I may have done the wrong thing yesterday when I brought your mother the newspaper."

"*Non, non.* You were very kind to do that favor for her. You did not know how much it would upset her."

Suddenly, Amélie stopped walking. "*Le voilà.* Here we are," she announced.

We stood in front of a small bookstore, Shakespeare and Company.

"In case you are in need of any books written in English, you will find them here."

I'd heard about this bookstore owned by an American woman.

"And *Mademoiselle* Beach sells all kinds of writing papers, inks, pens, and ribbons for that ancient typewriter my mother has lent you."

Amélie touched the small of my back, urging me forward.

The low-ceilinged shop was crowded with books of all sorts. The lack of orderliness appalled and attracted me at the same time, much like Amélie's stinging critique of the artists I like versus what she values as art-worthy. Although I found the store fascinating, its disarray reflected my confusion about Amélie's non-verbal exchange with the young woman on the bus and what I felt when her hand was pressed against my back just moments ago.

I perused the books on offer and the hand-written posters hung wherever there was space. Finally, I decided to buy a small street map of Paris, two typewriter ribbons, and a box of typing paper. I placed my purchases in the bag Amélie had given me. I knew I'd return to Shakespeare and Company several times during my stay in Paris, and I made no effort to conceal the happiness I felt simply knowing that bookstore existed. If ever I felt too overwhelmed by this foreign city, estranged beyond anything Aunt Vangie could do or say, I would come here in search of the relief only a book could offer.

"I knew this place would please you, Vera." Amélie looked suddenly shy. "Do you know what you will write for your first newspaper column? I hope it will be more than a tourist's guide to Paris," she said.

"I have some ideas. I just need to decide before I sit in front of the typewriter."

Amélie slowed her pace and touched my arm. "I hope you will tell the people of Chicago that Paris continues to be a beautiful city, but it has become a city on the border of change when it comes to all its citizens being safe."

"What do you mean, Amélie?"

"We French are not that different from many others in Germany. Change is approaching. A dangerous kind of change, Vera. Not just here in France, but in other countries also. Spain has not been able to prevent a civil war from occurring. Italy is now ruled by a madman who wants to align himself with the madness going on in Germany and Spain. Our government is preoccupied with planning a technological exposition here in Paris next year. The people who are in charge here are ignoring what is happening throughout Europe." Amélie paused to catch her breath.

"I don't mean to tell you how to do your newspaper job, but if I were you, I would visit as many different sections of Paris as I could. Speak with Parisians everywhere, ask questions and listen carefully to the answers. Try to hear the unspoken words that remain sheltered under the shade of their sentences. Describe the feelings you see reflected in their eyes. Please learn and then explain to your readers why my mother has become as frightened as the pigeon who has wandered innocently into a den of ruthless, hungry foxes."

I was certain Amélie's advice was sound, but I had to admit I didn't understand her completely, and I was less than thrilled about her demanding what I should write.

What did French people have to do with Germans, or Spaniards, or Italians? What changes was she alluding to? What feelings should I expect to witness on the faces of people I might interview? Despite the burden imposed by Amélie's instructions and my unanswered questions, I was eager to begin my writing assignment, and pleased to assume the role of journalist.

"Shall we return to *Rue Clauzel*?" I asked.

"*Mais, oui*. Let's see if you can retrace our steps."

Chapter Seventeen

Dear American Readers,

It will be my privilege to bring you along with me during my three-month visit to Paris. I shall include you each time I write short pieces about the people I meet and the places I discover while staying with my aunt, Evangeline (Vangie) Curtis and her best friend, Claudine Mistralle.

Aunt Vangie left Philadelphia and came to Paris in 1931. She began writing me letters, describing some of her experiences in France. It was she who encouraged me to study French in high school and in college. She also encouraged me to pursue my desire to write and to study journalism.

So, here I am. I have accepted an invitation from the *Chicago Recorder's* owner and publisher, Mr. Robert S. Abbott, and I'm making my bid to become a professional journalist. I hope to explore as much of Paris as three months will permit and then share my experiences with you. There is a lot to be seen, heard, tasted, and felt here, especially from the perspective of an American Negro woman.

In the future my columns will be longer than this first one. I simply wanted to introduce myself to you, because at the same time, Paris is introducing herself to me.

À bientôt,
Vera Clay
Paris, France
September, 1937

I proofread my first column and addressed the mailer. Through my bedroom window I could see the sun's glow had begun to soften, so I knew it was too late for me to walk to the post office. I'd do that tomorrow morning.

I thought about Amélie and wondered if she'd like to

go to the post office with me. Then, I recalled her advice about the topics I should include in my columns, among them the tensions that simmered just below Paris' surface. I hadn't mentioned anything resembling that in my first article. I needed to remember it was I, not Amélie, who'd been hired to write a newspaper column. Perhaps I shouldn't give her opinion that much importance.

Chapter Eighteen

"Is there anything else I can do for you today, *Monsieur* Moune?"

"No, nothing more." Hervé stood and shook the banker's hand.

"I am so glad that your sister's art is beginning to sell, and to reputable buyers."

Dismissing the banker's fawning platitudes, Hervé cocked his head to one side. "What really pleases you, *Monsieur*, is my depositing most of my funds in your bank, right?"

"Well, I am certainly not displeased, especially if you are willing to keep the money here for a bit and let it grow."

Hervé stroked his chin. "I cannot make that promise. The Depression greatly affected our inheritances. We are just now beginning to recover."

"And you are recovering quite well, *Monsieur* Moune. Two years ago, you could not have sold the paintings by your sister for the sum you have just deposited. No, two of her canvases would not have earned the one thousand five hundred francs you have just put into your account."

Without uttering another word, Hervé turned and headed toward the door.

"*N'inquiétez-vous pas, Monsieur* Moune. Do not worry. We will take excellent care of your deposit."

The banker's too easily given smile faded as soon as his depositor exited the room.

Hervé left the bank and walked outside to a wide boulevard. His usually tightly closed lips relaxed and spread into a smile as he tapped his trouser pocket. He visualized how unctuous the banker would have been had he known the sum of money Hervé *could* have added to his account. He'd sold four of Bette's paintings, not just two. He could have deposited much more, but he had plans for the money that rested safely against his thigh. Plans he would discuss with two companions during their pre-arranged lunch.

Hervé's rapid pace reduced the duration of his three-block walk to mere minutes. He entered the café, nodded curtly at the host, and went directly to the bathroom. Before relieving himself, he washed his hands.

I need to get the smell of the Jew's hand off of mine, he thought. They won't always own so many banks and prosperous businesses. That will end, sooner rather than later.

Hervé spied his two luncheon companions hunched over a table at the far end of the restaurant.

"*Bonjour, mes amis.*"

"Hervé, sit down," said the younger of the two men. "Are you hungry?"

"In a manner of speaking. And now, we have the resources to feed our project."

The two men's faces reflected their satisfaction with Hervé's response.

"What should we do about Blum?"

"It is too early for us to make plans. Right now, let Blum take care of Blum."

Chapter Nineteen

True to his word, Gérard arrived on time to take us to the jazz club where he and Aunt Vangie worked. He preceded us to the street where we expected to see Serge's car. Instead, we stared at a taxi, its engine running.

"I wasn't able to borrow the car this evening. Serge told me he needed to use it," Gérard explained. "And it is his car after all."

"Don't worry about that, sweetheart. It was kind of you to get us this taxi." Aunt Vangie's voice must have landed on Gérard's ears like the soothing warmth of a coverlet offering comfort on a frigid night. His lips spread into a faint smile of thanks.

"I learned he is seeing someone, so I know there is no hope for a reconciliation." Gérard spoke the first part of his sentence with an air of certainty that disappeared completely by the time he uttered the final word.

"I'm sorry to hear that, Gérard," said my aunt.

The three of us and the driver kept silent until we arrived at the club. Gérard guided us to its unobtrusive entrance and then stood behind Aunt Vangie as we entered.

All of a sudden, he clapped his hands and shouted. "*Notre Belle Vangie est revenue*! Our beautiful Vangie has returned!"

The music ceased. The lights grew brighter, and the space filled with raised glasses all tilted in our direction.

"*Bienvenue, Vangie! Bienvenue*!"

I figured the club's regulars had missed my aunt during her absence, but I didn't realize her return would cause such exuberance. I heard her name yelled repeatedly from the mouths of strangers. I saw the musicians, two seated and three standing on a small, raised platform at the front of the room, no doubt readying themselves and their instruments for their next set.

The pianist counted down from five to one, his fingers poised above the keys. The saxophonist blew a flutter of

notes from his horn as the first strains of "Body and Soul"
filled the room.

I leaned in close to the center of attention to make sure
she could hear me.

"Aunt Vangie, you're like a queen here."

"No. Not a queen," she answered. "But maybe a duch-
ess."

Then she turned to face as many of the club's patrons as
she could, held up her hand that wasn't gripping the cane,
and waved.

"*Bonsoir, tout le monde! Je suis heureuse d'être
ici*. Good evening, everyone! I'm so happy to be here."

Gérard disappeared for less than a minute, long enough
to tuck a towel into his waistband and pick up a metal tray.
Deftly, he wove a path around and between the club's
small tables and picked up empty glasses here and there.
Pausing to speak to a young woman, he looked in our
direction. Whatever Gérard said must have pleased her
because she nodded and smiled.

A second later, I watched that same woman move
through the club's cigarette haze and approach us.

"Welcome back, *Madame* Vangie," she said.

"Well, thank you, darlin'. It feels good to be back."

"You're not ready to work behind the bar, are you?"

"No, not yet. Soon though."

The woman turned her gaze toward me.

"Have you met my niece, Vera?"

"We see each other again," she said to me.

Although she looked vaguely familiar, I had no recol-
lection of where I might have seen her before this moment.
Had our paths crossed when I visited my aunt at the hospital? Was she a regular at the train station's café where I'd
stopped to buy a newspaper more than once?

"I'm sorry. I don't..."

"We saw each other on the bus this afternoon. You were
with your friend."

"Oh, yes." Now I knew where I'd seen her. I recalled
watching her make eye contact with Amélie. "I remember
thinking that you and Amélie knew each other."

"No, we don't. Not literally, anyway," she said. "But
our world is a small one. Somehow, we lesbians know

each other without being introduced."

Instantly, I understood the curious answer Amélie uttered when I asked her if she knew the woman who'd smiled at us as we rode the bus.

"Yes, and no," she'd said.

"So, Gérard tells me you are *Madame* Vangie's niece, and your name is Vera."

I nodded. "But no one has told me your name."

The woman laughed. "You learn very quickly, Vera. My name is Isabelle." She extended her hand to me. "May I buy you a drink?"

My aunt's comforting presence of a few moments ago had vanished. In its place was an interminably long second of silence as I wrestled with what to do or say next. I spotted an ashtray atop the bar and hoped the product illustrated on its surface was an alcoholic beverage.

"Thank you. A Pernod, please."

Isabelle seemed to be amused by my request.

I was fairly amused by the familiarity of her offer. The scene and script were the same here in Paris as they were in the bars in Philly, I thought. Or at least the same as they were in the one West Philly bar I'd visited several times with Angela. One element that was different was the crowd. At home, all the patrons were Negroes, as were the bar's employees. Angela said she'd heard the owner of the bar was a white man. On this side of the pond, the club's patrons were mixed. There were white men and women, as well as colored folks whose dark complexions and accented speech suggested they were from one of France's colonial possessions in Africa. There were also a couple of people like Aunt Vangie and me, just ordinary looking Negroes whose presence comforted me.

Another big difference between this club and the one I'd been to in Philadelphia concerned the couples on the dance floor. Just as the crowd was mixed, so were the dancers. White women danced with Negro and African men, and there were a few white men who were dancing with Negro women. That was a phenomenon no one would see in a West Philly club. What you would see in both places is patrons arriving coupled or in threes or fours. Those who arrived alone didn't remain that way for very long.

I took tiny sips of my drink and pretended I liked the strong flavor of liquid licorice-mixed-with-anise. In search of my aunt, I gazed around the room until I spotted her seated at a table sharing a conversation with people she obviously knew.

"*Tu fumes?*" Isabelle asked.

"No, I don't smoke." Just then, part of me wished I were a smoker. I needed to do something to busy my hands.

Isabelle reached into her handbag and withdrew a thin, dark cigarette along with a small box of matches. As she dragged the wooden match against the box's edge, she watched me watching her.

"Do you live with your aunt?"

"No, I'm visiting her."

"Have you been to Paris before?"

"No, it's my first time. Visiting Paris, that is."

Isabelle smiled and stood even closer to me. "I could be your guide if you would like. It would cost you no more than a drink here and there and perhaps a couple romantic dinners."

"Thanks, but I enjoy being my own guide."

"That surprises me. I had the impression your friend on the bus was guiding you to a place you had never before visited."

I didn't know if Isabelle was speaking literally or metaphorically. Her comment returned me to a memory of Amélie and the smiles she couldn't suppress as she watched me explore the overfilled spaces in Shakespeare and Company. She'd seemed supremely satisfied that she'd introduced me to the bookstore and explained its American owner welcomed all writers and artists. Without my telling her, Amélie seemed to understand how important writing was to me.

"Your impression was correct, but..."

"But you do not need more than one guide, right?" Isabelle winked. "Be careful, my lovely American flower. Paris has so many pretty gardens and even prettier garden tenders."

Gérard tugged on my elbow.

I turned around and saw he'd abandoned his makeshift

apron.

"Vangie is over there, not far from the door. She just signaled she was ready to leave," he said. "I'll go out to the street and get you a taxi."

"Okay."

I turned back toward Isabelle, but she wasn't there. The only evidence of her having stood in that spot just a moment ago was the half-smoked thin, dark cigarette that continued to burn in the Pernod ashtray atop the bar.

I crossed the room and approached Aunt Vangie. The closer I was to her, the clearer I could see her exhaustion.

"Are you feeling okay?" I asked.

"Oh sure. I'm a little bit tired, that's all." She nodded toward the bar. "It looks like you made a new friend here tonight."

"*Friend* is an exaggeration," I answered.

"Good. Because she comes in here a lot. She's usually alone when she arrives, but...."

"But not when she leaves. Even I figured that out," I said. "Although I'm not really that worldly, you know?"

"I know that, sweetheart. And speaking of being grown, it's about time you started calling me Vangie, instead of Aunt Vangie. Now that *you're* all grown up, if you keep calling me aunt, my friends will be able to figure out how old *I* am." Vangie made no attempt to disguise her vanity.

"You'll never seem old to me, Vangie." I squeezed her shoulder.

"That's because you're an old soul, Vera. I swear you've been here before."

The door swung open and Gérard motioned for us come out. "The taxi is here at the curb. I've told the driver your address, Vangie."

"Thank you, Gérard. *Merci.* We'll talk to each other soon, right?"

"Yes," he said. "Very soon."

A steady rain fell as we rode to *Rue Clauzel*. The repetitive rhythm of the taxi's windshield wipers must have been a lullaby for Vangie who fell asleep soon after getting into the vehicle. Likewise, her internal compass must have alerted her about our whereabouts, because she awoke just before the driver stopped at our destination.

She paid and thanked him, and then walked a half-pace ahead of me to the courtyard.

"Would you believe she called me her lovely American flower?" I asked.

"Who called you that?"

"Isabelle, the woman at the nightclub."

"Honey, I'd believe just about anything."

"I may be a lovely American flower, but I didn't come to Paris to be picked."

Vangie laughed as she unlocked the apartment's door. "That sounds like the young woman I always knew you would be." she said.

Chapter Twenty

Writing enthralls me. Art fascinates me. When history is reduced to a chronologic list of events, it doesn't interest me. Show me the connection between history and the art and literature created at the same time, and my eyes and brain are focused on that connection.

I made the mistake of explaining this to Vangie and Claudine one evening as we ate dinner.

Vangie's eyebrows rose toward her hairline, and Claudine fought hard to suppress an extra breath from escaping her lips.

"Bette would be interested in this conversation. She's been after me to plan a get-together for the four of us," said Vangie.

"Make that the three of you." Claudine stabbed at a small potato on her plate.

I had more to say about the topic, but Claudine's response to the idea of getting together with Bette warned me away. This was a moment when I needed to introduce a different subject altogether, something that wouldn't interest Vangie's Bette in the least.

Since the afternoon Bette first saw me standing in my aunt's doorway, I'd obeyed Bette's wishes. I hadn't told anyone it was the *third* time I'd been in Bette's presence. I excused myself, make that *escaped* from their reunion, and went on one of my exploratory walks. The next time Bette came to see my aunt, I told them I'd promised to return some books *Madame* Blum had borrowed from the library.

Madame Blum complained about her daughter's failure to perform that chore during her last visit. "Amélie left in such a hurry, she forgot to do me that favor. She is always rushing here and there."

I recalled wondering why Amélie had returned so suddenly to Les Andelys, but I figured it had something to do with her job. I'd planned to show her the final draft of my first newspaper column, as a gesture of thanks for taking me to Shakespeare and Company to buy the typewriter supplies. When I arrived at her mother's apartment and learned she'd just left for the train station, I felt slightly disappointed. The feeling inexplicably deepened when I considered the possibility that her oddly timed departure might not have been connected to her job, but to a pre-arranged romantic obligation. *Tant pis,* I thought. So much the better if Amélie were already involved with someone.

Vangie's voice catapulted me back to a new challenge involving Bette Moune.

"She thought we'd enjoy going to some of the salons and studios that have opened in Montparnasse. There are some artists whose work Bette wants to see."

"I thought there were artists' salons near here, in Montmartre." I said.

"Used to be. But Bette says the more daring artists are doing their work elsewhere."

"*Elsewhere* is the word that means the rents are cheaper in the Montparnasse area than they are in Montmartre," Claudine offered.

"So, what do you say, Vera? How about spending an artsy afternoon with two older women?"

Devoid of excuses and unable to disappoint Vangie, I gave in to Bette's plan to expose me to modern art. I rationalized my surrender by acknowledging my need to visit as many different areas in Paris as possible. Experiencing a different neighborhood would give me something to write about in my next *Chicago Recorder* article. If I could cling to that rationale, perhaps I could continue pretending I knew nothing about Bette nor about her brother's overtly racist attitude.

Vangie made the plans for the art appreciation excursion, but the next morning she announced she wouldn't be able to join us.

"I'm in too much pain to walk around the streets of Montparnasse and then visit artists' studios. Too many steps to navigate," Vangie announced. "The doctors said this would happen from time to time. It takes months for ribs and hips to heal themselves."

"Let's postpone..."

"No! Don't postpone anything. I don't want to disappoint Bette." Vangie's raised voice cut me off mid-sentence.

"Is it that you don't want to disappoint Bette, or that you want Bette and me to spend time getting to know each other?" I asked.

Vangie smiled.

"Both, to tell you the truth. She's important to me, Vera, and so are you. I want you two to be friends."

Sensing the sincerity of Vangie's wishes, I gave in.

"Okay. I'll go."

Becoming Bette's friend was stretching it, but I was willing to be civil with her. I needed to learn if she shared her brother's animus toward us Negroes, and if she did harbor those same attitudes, why was she in a relationship with my aunt?

Vangie sat down at the kitchen table and reached for her frayed street map of Paris.

"Bette wants to meet us at a café named La Coupole. I'll write the address for you. It's 102 *Boulevard Montparnasse,* right here." She pointed at the map, and with a pencil drew a circle around tiny lines that represented an intersection. Barely visible letters spelled the streets' names.

"You know where to get on the bus, right?"

I nodded.

"And I can figure out where to get off the bus. I'll look at one of the large maps pasted on the panel near the front."

"You're becoming an expert at getting around, aren't you?"

"Not exactly an expert yet, but I'm learning."

I was three weeks and at least eight experimental bus rides into my stay in Paris. All of the rides had gone well, thanks to my habit of having a notebook with me, jotting the name of the street where I'd boarded the bus, the bus number, and the exact place where I'd gotten off.

In a short period of time, I'd begun to feel less like a foreigner here. I'd felt independent during the voyage from New York City to France, but this sensation went beyond independence. Empowerment bound itself to my willingness to reconnoiter from place A to place B all by myself. I'd become comfortable stopping in cafés and sipping coffee as I watched people pass by. I enjoyed entering stores and being greeted warmly instead of warily. Shopkeepers' smiles made me feel I was a square of fabric stitched into a large patchwork quilt along with all the other squares. I had my own pattern and color, but I wasn't sewn into an inconspicuous corner apart from the other squares. I had the same value as all the others, no more and no less.

"You'd better leave now or you'll be late," said Vangie. "Give my love to Bette."

Three-quarters of an hour later, I stood on the sidewalk near the edge of the Café Coupole's outdoor tables. A waiter appeared and gestured for me to choose a seat. Before I could decline, I heard my name.

"*Bonjour*, Vera."

Bette stood facing me. She seemed unsure of how we should greet each other... A quick handshake or the dual cheek-to-cheek ritual?

"*Bonjour*." I nodded and instinctively declined to offer my hand or my cheeks.

"Vangie telephoned and said she was not feeling well, but not to worry."

"She's right. There's no need to worry."

"Are you certain, Vera?"

"Yes. She sends you her love."

"*Merci*."

"Shall we begin our art salon tour?" I figured the sooner we got this over with, the sooner we could talk about her brother's hateful attitude toward me and how much longer I'd have to keep quiet about my encounters with him.

"Yes, but first I want to show you where some of the artists have lived."

We walked for several blocks before turning down a street that was more like an alley. Bette stopped and pointed at one building in particular.

"This is called La Ruche."

The three-and-a-half storied structure looked old and dilapidated. A tower built above the top floor looked as strangely out of place, as a Gothic-style church topped by a pyramid would. Laundered clothes draped from window ledges flapped in the breeze, and a statue that defied description was planted on the ground outside the building's entrance.

"*This* is where some of the modernist artists lived?"

"Yes. Chagall, Soutine, Brancusi. Brancusi made this

sculpture," Bette explained. "Do you know the work of these artists?"

"No. I mostly like the paintings of the Impressionists, although I've been told my taste in art is naïve."

"But naiveté does not exist when one talks about art. People know what delights their eyes. It is very personal, right?"

"I suppose so." A bit of faith in myself fluttered through me.

We arrived at a storefront whose window bore the artist's name, each letter painted in a different script.

"*Allons*. Let us go in," said Bette. "For a time, Chagall lived on the third floor of this building. Now, he lives in your country."

"Why did he leave Paris?"

"I don't really know. Maybe he is a person who is most comfortable not staying in one place for a long time. He was born in Russia, but he left there in search of a place where the sun would shine brighter and make the colors of his paint more brilliant."

I pointed to one canvas in particular, "This one isn't very colorful, and it's gloomy."

"I agree. But look at the figures. They are painted so gently and moving with much grace."

"Why did he paint that woman suspended in the air? And why is there a farm animal? It doesn't make sense to me."

"Many times, art appeals to our senses, even if it seems to be senseless."

In that moment, I realized Bette's last sentence explained some of the modern art I'd seen pictured in magazines or on display in Philadelphia's Museum of Art. The pieces weren't necessarily created to represent anyone or anything. If the painting's lines, curves, shapes and colors pleased my eyes, the artist had spoken to me. This was a revelation I'd no doubt mention in one of my newspaper columns.

We walked a bit farther before we paused in front of a nondescript building.

"This is the Académie de la Grande Chaumière, an art school," said Bette explained. "I take courses here, but the only person who knows that is Vangie."

"You mean only Vangie and your brother, right?"

"Ah, *non*. Hervé would never approve."

"Why? And why would you need his approval to take classes at an art school?"

"He would only approve of my learning more about classical art. But I find that I love the newer styles."

"What's wrong with that?"

"Hervé detests modern art. He thinks it should never be displayed in public, that it is an abomination."

"But don't you have the right to create the art that pleases you? He's your brother, but he doesn't own your creativity."

"Hervé thinks I have very few rights, and he controls the money we inherited from our parents. That in itself puts him in charge."

I heard both anger and resignation in Bette's voice.

"Bette, does Hervé know about your relationship with my aunt?"

"*Oui.*"

"I don't imagine he's pleased about it."

"No. He detests it. He wants me to end it."

"And if you don't?"

"He will probably arrange another foreign trip for us, in the hope that he will sell some of my paintings and Vangie will tire of my absences and find someone else."

"That second hope is not going to happen. I know how much Vangie loves you."

Bette grabbed both of my hands. "Thank you for saying that. Once or twice, I have suggested to Vangie that we might be safer if we lived in the United States."

"No, you wouldn't be safer. Trust me."

"That is exactly what Vangie has said."

I wanted to know more about Bette's brother and what threat, if any, he posed.

"The two experiences I've had with Hervé showed me he has a quick temper."

"At times."

"What bothers him the most about your relationship with Vangie? Is it her color, or is it your being with a woman?"

"There are times when he opposes my being a lesbian, but I do not think that is as objectionable as my being with Vangie. He doesn't really know her. All he sees is her color and that she is an American."

Bette's answer to my question caromed through my brain

and landed in front of my increasing suspicion that Hervé Moune had something to do with my aunt's hit-and-run incident.

"Bette, I need to ask you an important question. Do you think your brother had anything to do with Vangie's car accident?"

"*Mais, non.* We were out of the country when that happened."

"I know you were, but do you believe he could have planned the accident and paid someone to run down my aunt?"

"He would never do that."

Bette looked to one side. Her hesitation to say more belied the answer she'd offered.

We'd arrived at our earlier meeting place outside La Coupole. It was my last chance to speak to Bette about my intentions.

"I have to be honest with Vangie," I said. "I can't keep pretending that I'd never met you until the day you arrived at the apartment to welcome her home from the hospital. When she asks me if I enjoyed myself today, I'll tell her about the art I saw and the run-down monstrosity of La Ruche. I'll tell her also that I first saw you and your brother on the ship during the crossing, and then in line at the boat-train station in Le Havre. I recall every second of both of my run-ins with Hervé. They were seconds you spent in silence."

Bette looked down.

"I know you must tell her. I only hope your confession will not cause Vangie to distrust either of us. I hope you can see how much I truly love her."

"Yes, I think I can see that, at least I hope so. She's told me how deeply she loves you. How do you say it in French? *À la folie?*"

Bette smiled and said, "*Oui, moi aussi. J'aime Vangie à la folie.*"

I thanked Bette for the brief art tour, and after we agreed we'd see each other again, I turned to retrace the route I'd taken to Montparnasse. Just then I saw a strange symbol painted on the edge of the sidewalk.

"Bette, one moment, please." I pointed to the odd design. "What is this? What does it mean?" She eyed the crudely painted street tattoo. "I've seen them before when I've taken walks," I added.

"It is one of those new political symbols. Hervé told me it concerns German nationalism. He called it a swastika."

Although I knew next to nothing about European politics, I wondered why a symbol of German nationalism would be painted on Parisian buildings and sidewalks. I'd try to remember to ask Amélie what she thought about the stick-figure signs planted here and there. Had she noticed them in her small town of Les Andelys? Did these designs, these swastikas, have anything to do with the newspaper article that upset *Madame* Blum a few weeks ago? I didn't know when my path would once again cross Amélie's, but its' very possibility made me smile.

Chapter Twenty-one

"Come in, Simone. Have a cup of coffee with me." Claudine was pleased to have the company of her neighbor.

"Just one cup, Claudine. *Seulement une tasse.*" With every step she took toward Claudine's kitchen, Simone Blum tried to tamp down her anger. She walked toward the old oak table and sat down.

"I know you, Simone, and I can tell there is something wrong," said Claudine.

Simone took in a small breath and then exhaled once twice its depth.

"What is wrong with my daughter? Who puts these ideas in her head?"

"What ideas, Simone?" Claudine put milk and sugar within Simone's reach.

"She called me on the telephone and said she would visit me tomorrow. She asked if I had completed the government forms she left for me the last time she visited."

"Well, did you complete them?" asked Claudine.

"Of course not. One form was about changing my name. *Imaginez,* Claudine! Throwing away the name of my husband and child! I could never do that." Simone's shoulders lowered as her anger began to look more like resignation.

"And the other form, Simone? What is that for?"

"It is an application for a passport. I have no plans to travel outside of France. Where does she expect me to go?"

Claudine poured the two cups of coffee and then sat down. Used to her neighbor's emotional fluctuations, she spoke very gently.

"It is possible that Amélie seeks to protect you, Simone. She knows there are things happening in other countries, unfortunate events that could spread here as well."

"Are you speaking about the anti-Jewish ugliness that is occurring in Germany?"

"Precisely."

"That will not happen here. We Jews are woven into France like silk in a fine scarf. Look how France has accepted the newcomers from its colonies. You, Claudine, are an example of that."

"Not every French scarf has silk threads, Simone. And those that do are not without slubs of imperfection."

Simone stared at Claudine and slowly nodded, as if she remembered some lost piece of reality she'd known once but had forgotten.

"I know what you are saying is true, but I cannot imagine changing my name or leaving France for somewhere else."

"We can always hope for the best. I have read that the Front Populaire is increasing its membership. They are much more liberal than the Action Française Party." Claudine paused.

"And, their leader shares your last name, Blum."

Simone smiled and took a sip of her coffee.

"That is probably why my daughter wanted me to change my name," she said.

"No doubt. This Léon Blum wants to be elected to the national assembly next year. I would vote for him."

"I know very little about him," said Simone. "I have never followed politics."

Claudine hesitated before she spoke her next thoughts. "I read a newspaper article that said in Germany they wrote new rules to segregate Jewish citizens from others. That news made me angry at first, and then it frightened me. If a government is willing to separate its population based upon religion, what will be next?"

"I do not choose to think about it. It upsets me too much." Simone's hand trembled as she returned her coffee cup to its saucer.

"I think if we ignore it, we're putting ourselves in peril," said Claudine.

"*We*, Claudine? You are not Jewish."

"I might as well be Jewish. I am a Negro. I am someone born to colonized parents from an island in the Caribbean. I am a person whose color deems her less worthy of protection from France than are the native-born white citizens. If the Germans put you and me on the cups of a scale, the scale would be balanced, Simone. Whatever fate comes your way, comes to me and to those who are like me."

A moment of silence wedged its' way between the two women before Claudine spoke once again.

"What will you do with the two government forms Amélie brought you?"

"I will not change my name."

Claudine offered a nod of understanding.

"Perhaps I shall apply for a passport. But I would hate to leave France, even for a short time."

Chapter Twenty-two

Gérard leaned against the edge of the building located a block away from Serge Bonet's apartment. His nesting here had become a daily ritual. Each time a vehicle turned onto the street where Serge lived, Gérard stepped away from his roost and looked to see where the car, taxi, or truck was headed. One after the other, Gérard watched them drive past Serge's building and keep going until he could no longer decipher their taillights.

Why do I continue to do this? Gérard asked himself. He is done with me. I have to get on with my life. Follow the advice Vangie suggested the afternoon your desperation drove you to her front door to confess your obsession with Serge.

"You're spying on him? This isn't a good situation, Gérard," she'd said.

"I know this, but I still love him."

"You may always love him, honey. But your relationship with him has changed, perhaps forever."

"I do not want to go on without Serge in my life."

"That's how you're feeling now. You don't know what the future will bring, Gérard."

"You have your Bette, *n'est-ce pas*? What if she became interested in another woman?"

Vangie took a step closer to Gérard and gestured for him to come closer. "I'd be deeply hurt if Bette wanted to leave me and go to someone else," she said. "But if I were still the person I am now, I'd have the sense and the grace to let her go. And, if I still loved her as powerfully as I do now, I'd want her to take the path that would lead her to happiness."

"You speak wisely, Vangie. Maybe your wisdom will influence me."

"If I'm wise, it's because I've had a few experiences with love and with what I thought to be love when I was younger."

Gérard's shoulders slumped. He exhaled the most forlorn of breaths.

"I have to see him, to ask what happened. He owes me answers."

Answers? To what questions? Gérard thought about that every waking second, as he ate his solitary meals in his two-room apartment, as he served drinks and cleared tables at work, and whenever he stood against this building, buttressing it and himself for hours on end.

A sleek black automobile nosed its way along the avenue and turned at the corner. Its driver wore an English tweed motoring cap.

Gérard held his breath and stepped away from the building. As he watched the car's progress, he could see a male passenger in the backseat behind the driver. The car slowed and passed Serge's address before pulling over and parking on the opposite side of the street.

Gérard squinted in an effort to sharpen his view of what might happen next. Suddenly, he saw the door to Serge's house open. He watched Serge wave to the vehicle's driver, cross the street, and slide into the car's back seat just as it began moving forward.

Gérard took deep, breaths, each one punctuated by the tears falling from his eyes and landing silently on the pavement below.

Chapter Twenty-three

October, 1937

Dear Vera,

I hope this letter finds you in good health. Are you enjoying yourself in Paris? I imagine your Aunt Vangie is happy to spend a lot of time with you. How is she? Has she aged any?

I've been reading your articles in the *Chicago Recorder*. They're very interesting and well-written. Good for you for following my advice and taking a typing class in high school. If I remember correctly that skill stood you in good grace when you went to college as well as afterward, when you did secretarial work at the temporary job company. Speaking of high school and college, are you using the French you learned there? I imagine Vangie speaks it quite fluently by now. If she ever comes back home, she'll speak English with a French accent. Does she ever mention coming back here?

Are you eating a healthy diet with vegetables and fruit? I've always heard the food in France is very rich. They eat a lot of butter, cheese, and baked goods. The last photograph of herself that Vangie sent, showed she hadn't gained much weight in the last decade. As I've told you before, the women in our family tend to get fat once they reach forty. And since I've mentioned your aunt's picture, I have a question about it. Who is the white woman standing next to her? I hope it's not one of her girlfriends. If it is, I hope she's not planning to return to the States with her. Their lives will be miserable.

Is everyone treating you well? Vangie told me you'd be treated better there than you are here in Philadelphia. Tell me if that's true.

Your father sends you his greetings and a hug. For the first time in ages, he stayed home from work today. He's had a bad cold he can't seem get rid of. Now, he's coughing quite a bit. I convinced him the United States Postal Service could operate just fine without him, at least for one day. Much to my surprise, he agreed with me. So that tells you he's not feeling well.

One more question. Last night when I was listening to the radio, I heard some news about Germany. Apparently, there's something dangerous going on there. I put down the book I was reading and paid close attention. I wondered if the situation in Germany has anything to do with France. The announcer said something about a labor strike that occurred last Spring and caused a lot of people in the government to resign, but he didn't mention any problems where you are. I felt relieved.

Take care of yourself, Vera. Don't let your Aunt Vangie's late-night job and escapades influence you. And please avoid socializing with her weird friends.

Love,
Mother

Chapter Twenty-Four

Dear American Readers,

During the past week I became a different type of tourist, one who found speaking with and listening to Parisians as fulfilling as visiting their museums, strolling through their parks, or sipping coffee on the terraces of their outdoor cafés.

I've learned that a lot of Parisians speak English, and even more of them appreciate the efforts American soldiers expended during World War I. When the war ended quite a few Negro G.I.'s chose to remain here in France. No doubt their continued presence paved the way for me to have meaningful conversations with native-born French citizens.

I had questions I wanted to ask. They had questions for me as well. Was I a jazz musician or singer? Was I married to a musician? Was I related to the celebrity, Josephine Baker? Had I ever met her?

I'm not related to Miss Baker, nor have I met her. I did see her one afternoon as I was walking on the Champs Élysées. She was shorter than I'd imagined, and much more beautiful. Marcelled tendrils formed an upside-down question mark on her forehead. Her brilliant smile welcomed onlookers, a few of whom dared to match her stride, step by step. *La Bakair*, as she's called here, spoke to her admirers and seemed not to mind their presence.

After I see her show at the Folies Bergères I shall dedicate a column to her.

Recently, my aunt and I explored Le Marais, an area where many Jewish Parisians live, work, and own businesses. During lunch in a charming restaurant, we were seated close to two other diners, an older gentleman and his adult son. In no time at all, we began to share a conversation that began with questions about where we each lived, and quickly travelled to the son's desire for his father to move to Paris for the sake of the father's safety. Currently, he lives in a region of France that is close to

Germany. Germany, or rather its Chancellor, Adolph Hitler, is a cause for concern.

After we left the restaurant, my aunt and I strolled to the area's compact but memorable public square, La Place des Voges. As we sat on a bench, I noticed the first of a few scribblings defacing the sidewalk. It was a swastika, a symbol of German nationalism and superiority, and a symbolic threat to Paris' Jewish population, a threat that many Jews are taking seriously these days.

A middle-aged woman stood only yards away and watched us staring at the swastika. She approached and began to express her feelings about the painted symbol. As best as I can recall, she said the following to us.

"Three years ago, German politicians began their anti-Jewish rhetoric. They went from calling for a series of boycotts aimed at Jewish-owned businesses to railing about taking away the property rights of Jewish people."

My aunt and I listened to the woman speak without interrupting her.

"They passed laws banishing Jews from holding civil service jobs or enlisting in the German Army. They banned books written by Jewish authors, and they held public book burnings. One year ago, they enacted the Nuremberg Laws to forbid the intermarriage of Jews with non-Jewish citizens. Jewish students are not permitted to attend German universities. In fact, they are no longer citizens."

The woman's raised hands became fists and she began to cry.

"If you are from the United States, tell Americans what I am telling you."

That's when my aunt spoke. "*Ma chère, personne aux États-Unis ne veut écouter. Personne ne veut entendre.*"

I hoped my aunt was mistaken because I wanted to believe there were people in the United States who wanted to know information about the German-Jewish situation. People who cared and would want to do something.

That's when it occurred to me that I could use *my* voice to tell my American readers what was going on in Germany.

I shall never forget the woman's final words to us.

"How can it be that men like Hitler in Germany, Mussolini in Italy, and Franco in Spain have simultaneously risen to lead their governments and seize absolute power? Is there something peculiar going on at this period of time that has made it possible? Is it because every generation of men must have a war in order to prove they are strong? Is subjugating and killing those who look different or have a different God a rite of passage?"

Her questions are mine as well.

Maybe *old* men want to fight wars. But certainly not the men and women of my generation. We are the ones whose hearts, bodies, and hopes will be broken by combat; whose blood will soak the battlegrounds, whose futures will be obliterated.

Dear Readers…This is something to ponder, *n'est-ce pas*?

Vera Clay,
Paris, France,
October, 1937

Two weeks after submitting my column to the Chicago Recorder, I received an unexpected letter.

The Chicago Recorder
4445 South Constitution Avenue
Chicago, Illinois

Dear Miss Clay,

I hope you are enjoying writing your travel essays as much as we are enjoying publishing them. We have received many positive reactions from our readers. Because you are a talented writer, we have been able to edit your work quickly. That is another positive element in your favor.

We do have one recommendation, as per our readers whose goal it is to view Paris through your eyes. They want to experience, vicariously of course, the sites, restaurants, museums and places of interest that you visit. They are eager to read your descriptions of the stores, the fashions, and the restaurants you experience during your stay in the capital of France (or in any of the other towns and cities you might visit.) They <u>do not want</u> to read about the current political goings-on there, or for that matter, in Germany.

Please keep this request uppermost in your thoughts as you compose your future columns.

We trust you have had no problems accessing the payments we've sent to you thus far.

Regards,
Myra Ellison,
Editorial Board of the *Chicago Recorder*

I'll admit I wrote my last column under the influence of a lunchtime conversation I shared with Vangie and two strangers in one of the Marais' better-known restaurants as well as a startling encounter with a stranger who approached us as we visited the area's pleasant public square.

I'd gone to Le Marais at the urging of a terse message Amélie Blum asked her mother to deliver.

"Visitez le Marais," she said. No more. No less.

I did just that, and the experience resulted in my composing an article that was less a tourist's travelogue and more a commentary about the reactions I formed to that afternoon's adventure. My reactions were nerve-deep compared to those I'd carried away from my visit to artsy Montparnasse and intriguing Montmartre. The only commonality I'd seen in those three places, was the ever-startling wall and sidewalk drawings, the swastika. In the Marais, the symbols were muted, almost shadows of themselves due to repeated attempts to scrub them out of existence. Their faded remains, however, stubbornly continued to suggest an uncertain future for those who tried to erase the pattern's interconnecting lines. Who was responsible for disseminating these artless figures? And to what good?

Vangie, well into her recovery, went with me that day. She was familiar with the area and she wanted me to see a small square that held special memories for her, la Place des Voges. We took a taxi and arrived shortly after noon. I suggested we walk slowly, because the day was unusually warm by Paris' standards.

Vangie steered us to the *Rue des Rosiers*, a street devoted to restaurants. We stopped in front of several places to read the menus posted on their windows or on portable folding slate boards. Some of the menus were written in Hebrew, others in French. I couldn't decipher Hebrew, and I even had trouble understanding some of the French terms. Finally, after pausing in front of what seemed a dozen different places, we gave in to one café in particular whose aromas floating from its open door and windows drew us inside.

The tables in Chez Hanna were placed close to one another, so close that I found it impossible to ignore the diners seated next us. Two men, one older, the other younger, became our lunch companions as they sipped their cups of strong coffee.

"Bonjour, Mesdames." The younger man spoke first. *"Vous-êtes Américaines?"*

"Oui," I said, and wondered how he had guessed.

"Mais, elles parlent français." A note of surprise filled the older man's words. "Are you visiting Paris, or do you live here?"

I nodded toward Vangie. "My aunt lives here. I'm visiting."

"Ah! Where is your home in America?"

"J'habite à Philadelphie."

"Philadelphie... the Bell of Liberty, the house of *Mademoiselle* Betsy Ross and your flag."

I couldn't suppress a smile as I heard the older man's references to my home city. "Do you live nearby?" I looked at both men.

"I do, but my father lives in Alsace-Lorraine, in the east of France."

"How nice that you're visiting your son," said Vangie.

The older man frowned.

"I may be visiting here for a while. I might even decide to move here."

The son inched his hand closer to his father's. Was it a physical reaction to his parent's need for support?

"Where I live is close to the German border, too close. At night I hear the new Chancellor's speeches on my radio.

He makes sure to blaspheme the Jewish people regularly. And he preaches about restoring Germany to its rightful position as a leader of the world."

"It is possible my father worries too much about the political situation in Germany."

"Perhaps his worrying is justified," said Vangie. "Every week French newspapers carry stories about Germany's Chancellor and his hateful anti-Jewish policies. Just this past April…"

The waiter's arrival with our lunches interrupted Vangie's current events report.

What had been a neutral smile on my face became a look of mild confusion. I stared at the food on my plate and then at Vangie's meal as well. We'd ordered the same menu item and I didn't recognize a single morsel of food on either plate.

Vangie's prior experiences in Kosher restaurants left her fully prepared to enjoy the lunch before her. My only experiences with Kosher food had been one half of a matzah square smothered with peanut butter that a third-grade classmate had dared me to sample.

"What is this?" I pointed to four strips of a vaguely greenish-colored slimy vegetable perched along the circumference of my plate.

"It's eggplant, honey. Your mother has probably cooked it a million times," explained Vangie.

"Not like this, she hasn't. She always removes the skin, slices it, dips the slices in egg and milk, coats it all with breadcrumbs, and fries it," I said. "*This* eggplant resembles raw oysters."

"Perhaps you will like the lamb portions in mint sauce." The older man seated next to us offered his two *centimes*. "Put a few in the pita."

I followed his suggestion and discovered I liked it. Then, I tested the chopped tomato-onion-cucumber mixture and found it delicious.

"It's the herbs that make it so good." The older man had been watching me as I'd carefully used my fork to probe everything on my plate before eating any of it.

"What brings you to Le Marais today?" the son asked.

"My neighbor's daughter suggested Vera might find

this an interesting neighborhood to write about. Vera writes a weekly column for the *Chicago Recorder*, an American newspaper."

"I have read copies of the International *New York Herald* and the European edition of the *Chicago Tribune*, but I do not know the *Chicago Recorder*," admitted the younger man.

"It circulates widely in the United States, mostly in places where a lot of Negros live. And the railway porters have really helped it spread all over. They take stacks of papers from town to town, city to city, and coast to coast," I said.

"Vera's readers love to learn about foreign places, especially places in Europe," said Vangie.

"Are they curious about Europe because of the great war, when many Negro soldiers were shipped over here to fight?" the son asked.

"Not many of them fought," interjected Vangie. "You see, the top brass of the U.S. armed forces had second thoughts about arming our Negro boys with rifles."

"I read about that." The older man put down his fork and knife and leaned forward over the table. He began speaking in a hushed manner. "We French were wise to bring the American Negro soldiers under *our* command. They fought bravely and helped us defeat Germany. If Herr Hitler has his way, the U.S. Army might find itself fighting by our side once again."

The son rested his hand atop his father's. "And you will move to Paris to live near me, Papa."

"And that will put an end to all of my fun." His twinkling eyes punctuated his words as both men arose from their table.

"*C'était un vrai plaisir, Mesdames.*"

"For us also, *Messieurs.*"

As we watched them walk away from their table, Vangie tapped my arm.

"I see you've done okay with your meal."

"With some of it," I used the tip of my knife to point to the uneaten portions. "If you spread the rest to the north, south, east, and west on the plate, it looks like you've eaten more than you did."

"I think I remember teaching you that trick, didn't I?"

"Probably." I grinned at my aunt.

"Shall we explore more of le Marais, darlin'?"

"Are you up to it? Your hip doesn't hurt?"

"I'm feeling fine."

We walked from the restaurant toward the Place des Voges.

"Why is this a special place for you, Vangie?"

"Let's sit down on that bench over there, and I'll tell you why it's magical."

We strolled half the perimeter of the park-like square and then sat on the bench Vangie had chosen.

"This is the place where I first told Bette I was in love with her."

"Right here?"

"No. We were over there, on the opposite side of the square. I chose this spot today because it faces the place where I confessed my love for her."

"That's very romantic, Vangie. I never knew that about you."

"How would you know that about me? Until now, you were too young for me to talk about my romance with Bette, or my relationships with anyone else."

"And I never told you about my special friend from college, did I?"

"You didn't have to. You wrote her name in numerous letters. I figured she was very important to you." Vangie paused. "Did your parents know how much she meant to you?"

"I don't think so. And when Angela and I figured it out, we felt scared, so we went our separate ways. It never got to the point where my parents' opinion mattered."

"Your father might have accepted it after a while, but your mother would have thrown a shit fit."

"Did she throw shitfits with you, Vangie? Did she say your loving women was unnatural?"

"Not in so many words. But she had a way of communicating her opinions without using words."

"I'm overly familiar with that." I reflected on my mother's habit of expressing her disapproval with a loud silence and tightly clamped lips. She barely tolerated my aunt's choice of friends. How would she react if she knew Vangie's current love was not a Negro woman?

How had *I* reacted when the photos in Vangie's apartment led me to put two and two together?

"Vangie, how did you happen to fall in love with a white woman?"

"Oh my God! Is Bette white?" Vangie grabbed my arm and feigned shock.

It wasn't until her laughter reached out to encircle me that I knew she was teasing.

"Vera, these things called feelings have the power to render most differences invisible. Eons ago, I'd heard that could happen, but it sounded to me like a happily-ever-after fairy tale. I never believed it could be true until I uprooted myself and came here." Vangie looked me straight in the eye." In the short time you've been here in Paris, have you noticed people don't look at you the way you're looked at in Philadelphia?"

I nodded. "People don't seem to look at me at all. It's as if the *me* they see is just another person without any special significance."

"Exactly," Vangie agreed. "Mind you, I'm not saying I've become invisible, or I've forgotten Bette is white and I'm colored. I'm still Vangie from America, so that will never happen. What I am saying is it's possible to love someone beyond what race they are, without any of the barriers and rules society dangles above our heads. It's possible to see way past a person's skin color and know for true they love you well past yours."

I didn't doubt Vangie's words. I never questioned their veracity. Why would I? I was in the middle of my own age of possibilities. And lately, I'd found myself thinking about Amélie more than not thinking about her.

It was then when our encounter with the woman in the Place des Voges began. Her words left me without any of my own until days later, when I found myself devoting my column to her fears.

Chapter Twenty-five

I could have walked from Vangie's and Claudine's apartment to *14 Boulevard Edgar Quinet* in nearby Montmartre, but it was ten o'clock at night and I was a young woman from Philadelphia, a city where smart young women knew better than to walk unaccompanied at that time of night. I took Amélie's advice and easily found a taxi.

Amélie was waiting for me near the entrance of Le Monocle, a nightclub and bar she'd mentioned the last time we spoke on the phone.

"I read your newest article, Vera. *Formidable*."

Amélie and I exchanged our pro-forma cheek-to-cheek greeting.

"I'm glad you liked it," I said. "The newspaper's editorial board was less enthusiastic. They slapped my fingers and advised me to stick to writing a travelogue."

"That does not surprise me, Vera," said Amélie as she opened the nightclub's door for us.

"It doesn't?"

"The American government does not want its citizens to be aware of what is going on in Europe, especially in Germany."

"But we need to know. It's important." I raised my voice to compete with the loud music playing in the background.

Amélie guided us to a vacant table at the perimeter of the club's small dance area.

"I wrote about the German symbols I see everywhere I go in Paris, the swastikas. And I mentioned the fear I hear embedded in the voices of Jewish Parisians' whenever they speak about the future."

"I am glad you have heard their voices, Vera. And I am happy you have written about them."

"Where did you see a copy of the *Chicago Recorder*?" I asked.

"I found it at Shakespeare and Company. As long as you do not mind reading news that is a week old, you can always find papers from many different countries there. Will you write more columns like that one?"

"I'm not sure. If I do, I might lose the assignment."

"But if you do continue to expose your readers to the threats we are experiencing, you will win my everlasting admiration." Amélie smiled more shyly than I would have guessed she could.

"Then, I'll have to think about it."

"The subject of your next few articles, or winning my admiration?"

"Both," I said. "They seem to be inseparable."

I avoided looking directly into her eyes. I'd been avoiding them since the day I realized how beautiful they were.

Amélie stood and went to the bar to order drinks. A trio of women she obviously knew spoke to her. One of the women glanced my way. She wore a tuxedo and she'd cast aside her bow tie in favor of freeing her throat from the strictures of her dress shirt. Her hair was cut short on both sides and trimmed neatly where it met her neck. A clutch of longer strands fell over her forehead enroute to the area just above her left eyebrow. Her eyes reflected a vague ennui, and the quick movements that animated her hands telegraphed impatience.

Amélie nodded to the three women, picked up our drinks, and returned to the table.

"What do you think of Le Monocle?" she asked.

"Well, it hasn't taken me long to figure out why this club has its name. Half of the women here are wearing monocles. Is there a rule about that, or do they all have problems with their vision?"

Amélie laughed. "Neither, but I realize it must look strange to you."

"I'm used to seeing women with short hairstyles and dressed in men's suits, but a monocle?"

"It started years ago. Wearing a monocle used to signal that one was a lesbian. It was a silent way for us to recognize each other," explained Amélie.

"I don't think it would work for me. I'd keep blinking the damn thing out of my eye," I said.

A recording of a slow song began playing, more in the

foreground than in the background.

"Will you dance with me?" asked Amélie.

I was too surprised by her question to refuse her request. We stood and walked to the center of the small dance floor. Just as I'd noticed when I went with Vangie to the jazz club where she worked, no one paid any attention to Amélie and me. Failing to see nary a negative reaction to us, a white and colored couple whose bodies were pressed together as we danced, I let myself relax in Amélie's arms. Our cheeks touched and I wondered if she were aware of the heat radiating from mine. Our individual perfumes melded into one sweet fragrance. When the song ended and we returned to our table, I felt changed in the subtlest way. Now, I dared to gaze into Amélie's eyes and not mind at all if she saw me looking at her so directly.

She looked down for a second, perhaps in an effort to interrupt my gaze. Then she diverted her attention away from me and directed it to the three women still standing at the bar.

The tuxedoed one feigned a salute.

"Is she a friend?" I asked, echoing the question I'd posed weeks ago when we were on a bus.

"She is an acquaintance, nothing more." Amélie answered. "She is a well-known athlete and race car driver."

"She looks like she's angry."

"Yes. I agree with you."

I could tell Amélie didn't want to continue the conversation about this woman. I simply wanted to continue conversing with Amélie. I looked carefully at our surroundings, as if I were memorizing the scene and making a plan to write about the club. I noticed the multinational flags hung above the shelf of liquors on the wall behind the bar. I saw a woman standing alone against a pair of columns erected from the floor all the way up to who knew where.

"Who owns this club?" I asked.

"A woman named Lulu de Montparnasse. She is a shrewd business owner."

"I wonder why the club is here, and not in Montparnasse."

"It is here because this part of Paris offers a spirit of

freedom, an attitude of acceptance, you know? Everyone is permitted to live as they wish."

"That's why my aunt lives nearby, I suppose. But what about your mother? She seems rather conventional."

"She is. It was my father's idea to live in this *arrondisement*. He was an artist and a musician. He was very liberal and tolerated people who were different."

"What kinds of music did he play, what instruments?"

"He played the piano, the violin, the klezmer, and the Jewish lyre. After the war, American jazz reached his ears, both the music and its composers."

As if on cue, the first notes of "Sophisticated Lady" floated throughout the room.

"Duke Ellington was one of my father's favorite composers," added Amélie.

I extended my hand toward her. "It's my turn to ask. Would you like to dance?"

We made our way to the dance floor once again. The Duke's music, the combination of androgyny and feminism surrounding us, the delicious secrecy of all of it, the French words that filled my ears and throat, and the reality of Amélie Blum's body so close to mine made this second dance with her one I would not forget. All of these elements symbolized Paris, and for me, Paris was no longer a city. Paris had become a woman.

After we enjoyed a second drink and a third dance together, we decided to leave the club.

"Should we look for a taxi?" I asked.

"We can, but there are not as many taxis on the street as there were earlier."

"Will we be safe?"

"But not the Paris police," I said.

"That makes no difference."

The streets between the *Boulevard Edgar Quinet* and *Rue Clauzel* were mere steppingstones that disappeared beneath our feet. One moment we walked in silence, and the next minute found us chattering away. When we entered the little tunnel leading to the apartments' courtyard, Amélie linked her arm through mine. We paused in front of the bench where her mother sat so often.

"I have to return to Les Andelys very early tomorrow

morning," she said.

I felt regret course through me.

"May I kiss you?" she asked, as we stood facing one another.

No one had ever asked me that, but somehow the question seemed so natural and expected of her.

"Yes," I answered. "I was hoping you would."

Amélie leaned closer to me and kissed my lips lightly, almost tentatively. Her fingertips touched the nape of my neck and closed whatever distance there was between us.

I responded by kissing her more deeply and boldly in this public place than she'd dared to do seconds earlier.

We sought each other's gaze and smiled demurely.

"I am so happy that you came to Paris to visit your aunt," she said.

"And I'm so glad your mother is my aunt's neighbor and friend."

"Perhaps you can visit me in Les Andelys?" she asked. "If not, I assure you I'll return here soon. You have given me a sweet reason to come back."

We parted and walked our separate paths. I looked back to the place where we'd just kissed. It wasn't lost on me that my aunt and Bette shared their first kiss as they sat on a bench amid one of Paris' oldest landscaped squares. And now, the first kiss I've shared with Amélie has happened here, near a bench in a Parisian courtyard whose trees had begun their annual ritual of unburdening themselves of their leaves.

Chapter Twenty-six

"How you doing, Vangie? And who is this young lady you got with you?"

The woman's patois-flavored accent sailed past my ears, leaving them startled and curious about the place of her birth.

"I'm well, Josée. *Tout va bien.*"

Vangie put her hand on my shoulder. "This is my niece, Vera. She lives in Philadelphia and she's visiting me."

Josée smiled broadly. "A true pleasure to meet you, Vera. Welcome to our establishment."

"Thank you. *Merci.*"

"Our hair needs attention, Josée. Especially mine." Vangie covered her head with her hands. "Can we both make appointments with you?"

"Better than that. I can take care of you right now." Josée craned her neck in an effort to see her three employees.

"Berte?" she called. "Do you have enough time before your next customer to tend to this young lady?"

"*Bien sûre, Madame* Josée. Please come over here, *Mademoiselle.*"

Obediently, I crossed the length of the room. The familiar scents found in most Negro hair salons escorted me to the chair where Berte stood. Floral essences and herbal odors blended with the smell of slightly singed hair wrapped around the rods of hot curling irons.

Berte spun my chair around until it faced her. She placed her fingertips under my chin and gently turned my head to the left and to the right. Using a comb, she forged a dividing line that began at the top of my forehead and ended half the distance to the back of my head.

"This is where I'll make a part," she said. "Then, I will brush your hair to the right, comb it flat on top, and as it falls to the side of your face, I will use styling gel to give you brush curls. I will do the same on the left side also. *Ça va?*"

Berte stepped back and stared at me. It looked like she

was already visualizing her plans.

"Yes, I guess so," I answered. "But I thought you would style my hair the way it is now. I'm used to having Marcelled waves."

"They are now old-fashioned. You are a young woman. You should be stylish, right? If the brush curl does not please you, we can return to the Marcel waves of 1920."

Unexpectedly intrigued by Berte's ideas for my hair, I agreed. A shampoo and a new hairstyle made me more than pleased. I marched triumphantly to the front of the salon where Vangie and Josée were waiting for me. Vangie's hair was shorter than it was when we'd arrived. It was also freshly Marcelled.

"Oh, *très jolie*! How pretty you look." Josée gushed. "*Bravo*, Berte ! *Tu as fait bien!*"

Vangie gestured for me to turn around.

"It's very becoming, Vera."

We paid for our services, thanked the women for their time, and left the Salon des Crépus.

Vangie touched my arm. "Let's have lunch. There's a good café nearby."

During our two-block walk, we passed several clothing boutiques, a pharmacy, a bakery, and one swastika discreetly etched into the wooden doorframe of a flower business.

"Do these symbols upset you, Vangie?" I asked.

"Only if I let them bother me."

Vangie's quick answer and the decisive tone of her voice warned me to postpone the conversation until later, or perhaps cancel it totally.

We arrived at a café next to the Hôtel Mercure and sat at an outdoor table. A waiter approached, greeted us and pointed to the menu posted on a board next to the café's entrance.

I ordered first. "*L'omelette du jour, s'il vous plait.*"

"*Et la même chose pour moi.*" Vangie smiled politely at the waiter and then turned her attention to me.

"Now, back to your question about the swastikas that have popped up everywhere recently. They *do* upset me, more than I let on."

"They're anti-Jewish, aren't they?" I asked.

"They're against Jews, Negroes, gypsies, homosexuals.

The Germans want a hell of a lot of people to leave Germany… one way or another."

"But we're in France, not Germany," I said. "Why are there so many swastikas here?"

"The dictator wants to expand Germany's borders. Some people think he has a team of folks here, all ready to help him *adopt* France."

"What will happen if the Germans come here and take over, Vangie?"

"I don't know for sure, but I expect there are a lot of people who won't just lie down and let it happen. Unfortunately, many people will lose their lives."

I took a deep breath.

"Will you come back home if it looks like Germany is going to invade France, Aunt Vangie?"

Vangie shook her head. "This place is my home now," she said somberly. "I know you're worried about me, honey, because you just called me Aunt, instead of Vangie."

I nodded. "I guess old habits return and repeat themselves when a person is scared or nervous."

Vangie tapped the back of my hand. "Try not to worry. You don't want to ruin your visit thinking about the what ifs in life."

I counted to three silently. "Vangie, I have to confess something to you."

"You have a crush on Amélie Blum."

"No. Well, maybe. But that's not what I need to tell you."

"You know you can tell me anything, Vera."

"Well, the first time I met Bette at your apartment was not the first time I'd met her." I paused.

"Go on."

"I'd met her twice before. Well, not exactly *met* her. I encountered her and her brother on the S.S. Leviathan and then in the train shed in Le Havre. Her brother was very rude to me both times."

Vangie nodded as if she anticipated what I was going to say next. "Did he make you feel like you were wrong and inferior? Did he talk down to you?"

"Yes. How did you know?"

Vangie ignored my question, "And how did Bette react during these confrontations? Did she take up for you? Did she contradict whatever it was that her brother said?" Vangie's voice left its usual octave and ascended to the next higher one.

"No, she didn't know who I was. She looked down… like she felt ashamed of how her brother spoke to me, but she couldn't do anything about it."

"Vera, why didn't you tell me this sooner?"

"I couldn't tell you. Bette didn't want you to know her brother had treated me badly, so I kept it a secret all of this time."

"Why are you telling me now?"

"Because I've always been honest with you, and because you've trusted me with your biggest secret. I know how much you love Bette, but I'm afraid her brother might hurt you."

Vangie and I looked at our untouched meals. Filled with the discomfort of having made my confession, I'd lost my appetite. I suppose Vangie lost hers as well.

A moment passed before she spoke.

"I've been in Hervé Moune's company twice, and it was two times too many. He's made it clear that he disapproves of Bette's relationship with me. She has to sneak away to see me, and even then, she's afraid he's following her."

I remained silent.

"He hates the idea of his sister being romantically involved with a colored woman, especially one from the United States."

"Bette is a talented artist, and he's in charge of selling her work. Maybe he's afraid she'll go to the States with you and his income will disappear," I said.

"I think there's more to it than that, Vera. He hates colored people and Jews just for the sake of hating. Bette once told me he began expressing this hatred after the war ended and he watched a lot of Negro G.I.'s remain in France and marry French women. The two times we met face to face, every part of his being bristled with the contempt he felt for me .If I didn't know better, I'd swear he was a German Nazi. Vera, you know I'm not easily bullied, but Hervé Moune succeeded in doing just that."

"It must be his hatred for you that convinced Claudine of his involvement with your hit and run accident."

Vangie nodded. "I've tried to talk down that idea, but

between you and me, there are times when I think it's true."

Vangie picked up her knife and fork and signaled that I should do the same. She sliced her *omelette* until it was reduced to shreds, and then took the thick slice of bread from her plate and tore it into three remnants.

I copied her actions, although I preferred cutting my *omelette* in quarters and stacking two of them on top of the other two.

"Do you forgive me for holding on to my confession until today?" I asked.

"I can't forgive you if you haven't done anything wrong, darlin'. And by the way, I haven't shared *all* of my secrets with you, only the ones you've needed to know."

Chapter Twenty-seven

It was twilight when Hervé stepped across the threshold of his sister's studio. He glanced at the studio's most recent canvases before he strode quickly toward Bette.

Her back to the room's entrance and her attention focused on her brushstrokes, she wasn't aware of her brother's presence.

Hervé growled at the canvas in front of them. "What is this ugly monstrosity, Bette? It is certainly not art!"

Bette spun around.

"It is art, Hervé! It is the art I want to paint."

"This is a waste of the *francs* you have spent buying your supplies! Remember, your *francs* are mine as well!"

"That does not mean you are the one who decides what and how I paint."

Hervé turned to inspect several other newly created canvases. His arms made a sweeping gesture that included almost every new piece of work Bette had produced recently.

"And just what are these? What do they represent?"

"They do not need to represent anything. They are abstracts," Bette explained.

"Do you expect me to be able to sell any of these new paintings of yours? Salon owners want to show pastoral scenes, sunsets, the sea, gardens or portraits. Not these undecipherable shapes." Hervé spotted yet another example of his sister's new work, its reds and yellows still damp with impermanence. As the seconds ticked by, he became more enraged. His face was now crimson with anger.

"*Cette putaine noire*!" he screamed. "You have painted that black whore?"

"She is not a whore, Hervé."

"But you cannot deny she is black, can you?"

Bette remained silent.

"And you continue to see her. Even after I took you away to the United States. Even after I forbade it."

"Hervé, you cannot forbid me to do anything. I shall

always continue seeing Vangie. Why can't you understand that I love her?"

Hervé's right hand formed a fist and moved upward slightly. Struggling to still his arm and not drive his fist into his sister's mouth, he willed himself into a state of barely controlled anger. He clenched his jaw in an effort to speak calmly.

"Bette, you are determined to stain our family's reputation. You are painting worthless and degenerate pieces of something you claim is art, and you keep seeing that Negress bar worker. This is my final warning to you. You must return to creating traditional art that I can sell to dealers and to the smaller museums, and you must sever all ties to that woman."

Hervé shot one final glance at Bette and then left the studio.

****

Bette paced a path from one side of the large room to the other. In time, she left the studio, walked to the front of the building, and went to the apartment she shared with her brother.

The next day, after picking her way carefully around the puddles left by a morning rainstorm, she returned to her studio. She opened its door and gasped. Every single abstract she'd painted was scattered on the floor, slashed into unrecognizable bits of color. Hours of her labor were destroyed.

As the shock of her discovery lessened, Bette channeled her thoughts toward the immediate future. She decided it was time for her to act upon the plans she'd discussed with Vangie.

Chapter Twenty-eight

Dear Readers

My latest tourist excursion in Paris was a day-long visit to the *Exposition Internationale des Arts et Techniques dans la Vie Moderne*. The International Exposition of Art and Techniques in Modern Life is as comprehensive as its title is long. The display opened last May and it will close later this month, on November twenty-fifth. Its setting, directly across the River Seine from the Eiffel Tower, is quite picturesque.

Two of the three planned buildings are imposing structures. The third one will be built after the exposition closes. Among the displays that I most enjoyed were the Finnish Pavilion and the Pavilion of New Times. Modernity has arrived in the world of architectural design. Americans will soon be aware of the names Alvar Aalto and Le Corbusier, two architects leading the vanguard of their contemporaries.

I was especially impressed by a sculpture, Mercury Fountain, created by Alexander Calder, a well-known sculptor from my hometown, Philadelphia. His piece is displayed in the Spanish Pavilion. The most impressive painting I viewed there was Guernica, by Pablo Picasso. What made this work so impressive? It's scope and dramatic, if not frighteningly realistic, depiction of a Spanish village caught in the throes of a German bombing attack. As you know, Spain is in the midst of a civil war pitting the Republican loyalists against those who favor a more democratic form of governance.

Even the most apolitical visitor would be affected by the symbolism on view at the German and Soviet Pavilions. Located directly across from each other, the tall tower atop the German pavilion supports a huge eagle and an equally large swastika. I'm told that at night, the pavilion is illuminated by floodlights. The Soviet pavilion is topped by a huge statue of a male laborer and a female peasant, their hands fused to a hammer and a sickle.

I took it all in and as I left the exposition, I wondered where this competitive symbolism would lead Europeans, or Americans for that matter. Surely, the swastika and the word *Juden* that I see scribbled on walls and buildings, and the hammer and sickle reply I've seen also, serve to warn Europeans that troubling times are near. And as we witnessed during the first World War, the political factors impacting Europe, will impact the United States as well.

Adieu,
Vera Clay
Paris, France,
Novembre, 1937

The Chicago Defender
4445 South Constitution Avenue
Chicago, Illinois

Dear Miss Clay,

After much discussion, Mr. Anderson and the Editorial Board of the *Chicago Recorder* have decided to stop publishing your travel column. The reason for our decision is your failure to comply with our request that you omit political commentary from your articles. We expressed this policy via a letter we sent to you a month ago.

Last week's article about the International Exposition in Paris was your final column. As always, you will receive your remuneration for that work in a timely fashion.

Regards,
Myra Ellison, Editorial Board of the *Chicago Recorder*

I wasn't proud of being fired from my first newspaper journalism job, but I did find some solace in having followed my own internal compass. Why obey rules that are inherently wrong? Why keep the truth about shameful events hidden under layers of gossamer subterfuge?

Chapter Twenty-nine

"Leave this area immediately or I will arrest you for loitering," said one of the two policemen who stood in front of Gérard.

"*Allez! Allez*! Why are you here?" the second officer asked as he stood toe-to-toe with Gérard.

"I am waiting for someone." Gérard looked at one and then the other policeman. As a rule, he didn't trust *les flics*.

"You are waiting for someone? You come here a lot, do you not?" The second cop leaned in even closer to Gérard.

"I am waiting for someone to arrive." Gérard wished he could tell *les flics* the name of the person whose arrival meant so much to him, and why it was so important. He knew to make that declaration would ensure he'd spend a few very unpleasant nights in jail.

"Some of the shopkeepers have reported that you are here frequently, almost every day they say. You are intimidating their customers."

Gérard's eyes widened at the notion that he could intimidate anyone.

"*C'est vrai*?" he asked.

"But when we look at you, we know you do not scare people." The second cop took a step back from Gérard and looked at him. He began his long voyeuristic gaze at the tips of Gérard's shoes and ended his examination by directing his breath toward the tendrils of hair that fell across Gérard's forehead.

"You are very pretty. *Tu es très joli*. I'll bet you don't have to wait on this corner very long before your *someone* arrives."

"I do not know what you mean." Gérard's eyes widened with fright.

"I think you *do* know what I mean. This is where you pick up men, is it not? *Tu es prostitué*?" The policeman's voice grew louder and menacing.

"No! No! *Pas du tout*!"

"Then, leave this area and do not return!"

Grateful to be able to walk away before his interrogation became physically painful, Gérard straightened his posture.

"*Merci*," he said, and nodded submissively.

He headed toward the intersection and crossed the street. As he stepped up to the curb, he was aware of a car turning onto the street. Casually, he glanced at the automobile and watched it proceed slowly before it stopped in front of Serge's address. More than grateful to be able to glimpse Serge as he got into the car, Gérard almost failed to notice the significance of the scene. An alarm sprang to life from that place in his mind that was never at peace.

"The car!" he said aloud. "The burgundy Citroën T. A. that hit Vangie! Why was Serge getting into it?"

Chapter Thirty

I turned and saw Vangie standing in my bedroom doorway.

"May I come in, darlin'? I want to tell you something."

"Of course," I said.

"Oh, look." Vangie pointed to the window above my
desk. "That old tree out there has lost every one of its
leaves."

I had to admit I hadn't noticed the tree's state of
undress. Whenever I'd sat at this desk, I'd ignored the
window in favor of typing my thoughts upon the keys of
the borrowed typewriter. I had come to love the pock-
marked wooden desk as it supported my forearms and my
elbows during all the hours that I sat there, recording my
reactions to Paris, to my aunt's apartment, and to the sites
and people I'd seen and spoken to.

Vangie sat on the side of my bed, facing me.

"Remember how much you liked the club where I
work?"

I nodded.

"You were right when you said the owners must value
me, and that's why they'd been so generous giving me
time off to recover from the car accident. Of course, I
didn't earn any pay while I was out, but I felt lucky they
were willing to keep me employed."

"You went back to your regular salary when you
returned, right?"

"Yes. But while I was away, they hired another barman
and a new hostess, a married couple who used to work for
Joe Contini," Vangie said.

"Who is Joe Contini?"

"He's an American who owns a jazz club and he makes
more money than God. His club is about the biggest one in
Paris. It opens in the late afternoon and doesn't close until
the next day right before noon," Vangie paused. "But
that's beside the point. This barman and his hostess wife
brought some of their clientele with them from Contini's.

My boss didn't need the new guy from Contini's, the other barman who's been there forever, and me. He started losing money because he had one employee too many."

"Your boss is letting you go?" I asked.

"That's the story, Morning Glory."

I could see sadness but not defeat in Vangie's eyes.

"After all this time and all your hard work, you have to look for a new job?"

Vangie sat up straight and smiled.

"No, in fact I don't have to do that. A new job found me before I began looking for it."

"Where? Is it the same kind of work?"

"Yes, it's the same line of work. Bars and jazz clubs in Paris all belong to the same network. When a musician gets popular at one club, he knows he can easily be hired to play in another one, sometimes right down the street from the first place, and usually with no hurt feelings. The same thing goes for jazz club employees, especially the good, reliable ones."

"And everyone knows how good and reliable you are, right?"

"Vera, I've been kissed by the goddess of good fortune. This week I start a new job working for Charles Willard, the owner of L'Aigle Noir."

I must have worn a puzzled expression, because Vangie continued explaining.

"You mean you've never heard of Charles Willard?" asked Vangie. "He's a Negro from Georgia. He's also a military hero here in France. When the war ended, he didn't go back to the States. He got some odd jobs, learned how to play the drums, worked for Joe Contini in his club for a while, and earned enough money to buy his own place which he named L'Aigle Noir."

"The Black Eagle?"

"He had something like that painted on the side of his airplane."

"You'll be a barman at this Black Eagle club?" I asked.

"Yes, Ma'am. And for the first time, I'll have the honor of working for an American Negro, right here in Paris."

Vangie stood and looked like she'd grown half a foot taller than she was when she came into my bedroom.

I hugged her. "With me working for the man who owns the *Chicago Recorder* and you working for Charles Willard, we're both employed by Negro Americans." I paused. "Except... I no longer work for Mr. Abbott."

"This is just the beginning of your career, Vera. They'll be other opportunities for you. Who knows? Maybe one day you'll hire folks who'll be proud to work for a *female* Negro American."

"Maybe," I said in a hushed voice.

"Are there people from your old job that you'll miss, Vangie?"

My aunt gazed at the ceiling.

"Gérard Simonet. He's always been my sidekick. Always ready to help me behind the bar and elsewhere. He was so upset when I told him I'd lost my job. I thought he was going to cry."

I nodded and visualized Gérard.

"He's had a lot to deal with, hasn't he?"

"Yeah. If I let myself think about his trials and tribulation, I'd be worried about him."

"He needs a new boyfriend," I said decisively. "Do you know anyone who'd be interested in meeting him?"

"No. And even if I did know someone, I wouldn't suggest it. Gérard needs more time to get a hold of himself and stop obsessing about his ex, Serge."

As Vangie walked toward the door, she turned around and looked at me. "How about you? Have you heard from Amélie Blum recently?" she asked.

Chapter Thirty-one

The train from Paris to Les Andelys crept slowly over the tracks nestled between the station's platforms. A cold November mist greeted my arrival in the small town just as rain had welcomed me to France almost two months ago. I pulled the sides of my jacket close to my body as I stepped off the train and onto the platform.

Bienvenue aux Andelys!

The black lettering of the town's welcome sign seemed more a command than a greeting.

I rested my small travel bag on the station's floor and pulled a piece of paper from my pocket. Although I'd read and re-read the paper's hand-written information twice, I was sure I'd find it more practical now.

Exit the train station and turn to the right. In the distance, you will see a fortress on a hill. After a short walk, you will come upon a three-way intersection. To the left is a *pâtisserie*. Just beyond it there is a church, L'Église Saint-Sauveur. My house is in the middle of the next street. *Numéro 27, Rue de L'Église*. I will leave the door unlocked. Come in. I will be there soon. A.B.

I looked up to the top of a hill and saw the fortress, or what was left of it. I imagined the remaining turrets and crumbling walls must have belonged to a medieval age, an era of armor-wearing knights astride their similarly clad horses.

Refocused on the street, I walked past a succession of differently colored buildings, each one attached to the next. They reminded me of the Philadelphia rowhouses I'd known all of my life.

Some of the daub and stucco exteriors had tufts of what appeared to be horsehair protruding from the plaster. The buildings' second stories had half-timbered sections reminiscent of pictures I'd seen of houses in the Swiss and German Alps. I supposed the passage of time and the forces of nature had disturbed the timbers' alignments. The wooden slabs' lack of symmetry made it easy to see where a house's width began and where it ended. That, and the houses' different colors made it easy to distinguish one abode from its neighbor.

The church came into view. Smaller than the huge houses of worship I'd seen in Paris, but no less sacred for its congregants, I speculated. The church's open door gave me a view into the interior. Beyond the pews was the modestly sized altar and behind that was the wooden altarpiece which bore carvings painted in goldleaf. No doubt the carvings illustrated stories from the Old Testament. As I walked past the church, I could see a small cemetery in the rear of the property. Fallen leaves covered some of the graves. Others were blanketed in floral bouquets arranged in colorful pottery containers.

Once again, I returned to the paper with the directions to Amélie's house. Almost there, I slowed. Certainly, I was eager to see her. But the reality of opening her unlocked door and walking into her home made me nervous. What would happen if her neighbors saw me, a stranger, a *brown* stranger at that, enter the house without knocking on the door?

Les Andelys wasn't Paris. It was a small village. I figured the average Parisian was more worldly than the villagers were here. In Paris I'd seen other Negroes, but during my short walk in Les Andelys, I'd seen no one who looked like me. I supposed the worst that could happen would involve a watchful neighbor who upon seeing me enter Amélie's house, would alert the *Préfecture de Police.* If Amélie were still there, she'd be told about the call that concerned her address. She'd guess I was the unknown person who'd entered her home and assure her co-workers that all was fine.

I let that imaginary scenario persuade me to shake off my fears. I knew my caution was not unfounded, but my desire to see Amélie and where she lived convinced me to open the door.

A small, tiled vestibule led to a second door. It too, was unlocked. I opened it and saw a coat tree whose branches held an assortment of jackets, caps, and scarves.

I took off my jacket and put it atop one of Amélie's. A stairway to the house's second floor faced me, and I set down my travel bag near it. To its left was the *salle de séjour*, the living room. I ignored the room's furniture and found myself drawn to a framed photograph sitting atop a shelf on the other side of the small room. The picture was of *Madame* Blum, Amélie, and a man who was probably her father. I recognized where the photo had been taken. It was near the little tunnel that opened onto *Rue Clauzel* and ended in the courtyard where my Aunt Vangie and *Madame* Blum had their apartments. *Monsieur* Blum wore a hat, tilted slightly to the side of his head. His smile was like his daughter's, consciously rakish, broad but cautious. *Madame* Blum's unyielding lips were pressed together so tightly, I couldn't tell where her upper lip ended and her lower one began. Amélie's facial expression was one she'd worn each time we'd been in each other's company. Her dark eyes flirted with the camera's lens the same way she'd flirted with me the afternoon she guided me to Shakespeare and Company, and the evening we spent together at Le Monocle.

I heard a noise and turned around to find Amélie closing the outside door behind her. She saw me at once.

"Ah, *bonjour*, Vera! You found my little house."

"You gave me excellent directions."

As Amélie walked toward me, I realized I wasn't sure how we should greet each other. Should we shake hands, hug, exchange a casual kiss, one that would not imply I was here solely to continue what we'd begun the last time we were together?

"I am glad to see you," she said, stopping too close to reach for my hand yet too far away to offer her cheek or any other part of her body.

"And I, you," I said.

"When did you arrive?"

"A few minutes ago."

"Let me show you my house, and then we will take a short walk to the grocery store. I need to buy wine for our dinner." Amélie turned toward the staircase.

"I see your travel bag. Shall we take it upstairs?"

I followed her to the second floor where she showed me a small room furnished with a table, a chair, a lamp, and a divan. Between that room and another one was the bathroom where she'd draped a folded towel and wash cloth on the side of the deepest tub I'd ever seen.

"I could swim in this tub." I said.

"And I would like to see that, *Mademoiselle*."

Amélie bent at the waist and gestured our way forward.

"The last room is on the other side of the bath. It is my bedroom, but this evening it is where you will sleep."

"Where will you sleep?" I asked.

"In the other room, on the divan."

"It's very generous of you to give up your bed."

"I do not mind at all. It is enough that you were willing to visit me. And I believe there will be other times when I would not want to make that sacrifice." Amélie's low and serious voice held the promise of some future intimacy awaiting us.

I simply smiled my understanding.

We entered Amélie's bedroom. It too was furnished sparingly. Her bed, a night table, an armoire, and a chair were its sole contents. Interior shutters that covered the narrow expanse of a window provided her privacy.

"*Nous descendons*?" she asked. "Shall we go back to the first floor?"

I was halfway down the stairs when I heard her say she wanted to change her clothes. I turned around to look at her.

"I do not like to wear my work uniform when I am not at the *Préfecture*. The jacket suits me, but this long skirt is uncomfortable."

I smiled. I couldn't remember ever seeing Amélie dressed in a skirt. She always wore trousers when she visited her mother in Paris.

"I'll wait for you downstairs," I said.

My wait was a short one, as Amélie sped down from the second floor wearing a pair of tweed trousers and a blue shirt. She offered me my jacket and took hers from its hook on the coat tree.

"Maybe we can go and return before the mist becomes rain," she said. "But just in case, I will carry an umbrella."

Our walk to the grocery store took us in the opposite direction from my earlier hike from the train station to Amélie's house. Along the way, she narrated anecdotes about petty crimes that had occurred in one place or another, and the tale of a jealousy-fueled murder-suicide that happened outside a café we passed. She pointed to the village's narrowest street and described a jazz club located near the street's end. The club hosted special nights for lesbians and gay men, she explained, but you had to possess detective-like skills to find out which nights werc the special ones.

The tinkling bells above L'Épicerie Bonnard's entry door welcomed us just as it began to rain. We hurried inside and found two bottles of wine that Amélie said would be good with dinner. As we left the store, I took the umbrella from her and she carried her purchases. We stepped onto the sidewalk and into the path of a passer-by.

"*Chère* Amélie!"

"Luc! *Bonjour*!"

The young man gave Amélie the cheek-to-cheek greeting Amélie circled my waist with her arm.

"Luc, *je vous présente mon amie*, Vera."

"Ah *oui. La belle femme qui vous visite des États-Unis, oui ? Enchanté, Mademoiselle.*"

I felt flattered being called the pretty woman, but I wondered how he knew I was a visitor from the United States?

"Welcome to France. You have been here for some weeks, right?" He didn't wait for my reply. "And thank you for writing your newspaper articles. Americans must know the details of our present situation."

In a rush, he spoke to Amélie. "*J'ai parlé avec Robert. Tout va selon nos plans.*"

Amélie nodded and withdrew her arm from my waist. "*Bon. Á la prochaine*, Luc."

We parted ways with him and began our return to Amélie's house. Neither of us spoke right away. My questions remained unasked, perhaps because I didn't want to hear Amélie's answers. The wind became entangled with the rain and made holding the umbrella above both our heads a challenge.

"How did he know I've been in France for a few weeks?" I decided to break our silence. "And how did he know about my column? Who is Robert and what plans is he following?"

Amélie's eyes narrowed. "I will answer all your questions, Vera. But not right away. Okay?"

"All right."

We hung our wet jackets and left the umbrella in the vestibule.

Amélie tugged on my hand and smiled.

"Come with me and we'll have dinner."

With no trace of reluctance, I followed her from the living room, through a cabinet-filled pantry no larger than a closet, and into the kitchen.

Amélie went to the refrigerator, a small rectangular box that had probably been an icebox in the days when Les Andelys didn't have the benefits of electricity. She withdrew a square container made of pottery and placed it in the oven.

"I got up early this morning and prepared *coq au vin* for us," she said. "It tastes better after it has had time to sit and absorb its wine. It is my spe-cial-i-ty."

My infatuation with her made the extra syllable she gave the word specialty so charming.

"Can I help you do anything?"

"You can set the table."

She showed me where to find the plates, cutlery, and two wine glasses. Suddenly playful, she tossed a baguette my way.

We ate the meal slowly, savoring each mouthful as well as the time we had to spend together. After she cleared the table, Amélie poured what was left of the wine into our glasses.

"Thank you for a wonderful dinner," I said.

"Thank you for the gift of your company."

"Is now the right time for you to answer my questions about the young man we met when we left the grocery store?" I asked.

Amélie nodded. "Luc and I are members of a small group of people who live in or near Les Andelys. We are all very patriotic. During one of our meetings, I mentioned your name and said you write articles for an American newspaper. That is why he knew who you were."

Her explanation was logical, but it seemed incomplete.

"You must have told him I'm a Negro, as well."

"Are you?" Amélie's lips curved into a sardonic smile.

"I'll ignore that," I said. "But I won't ignore my curiosity about a person named Robert who was following the plans. What plans?"

"Vera, I am afraid I cannot answer that particular question."

Amélie sounded sincere, but her refusal to answer my question gave rise to an invisible barrier between us. A barrier that excluded me from knowing a part of her she wasn't willing to expose. I felt I'd tried too hard to enter a place where I didn't belong, and feeling out of place made me stop and think. I questioned my reasons for coming to Les Andelys and staying in her home, even if the stay was for one night only. Why had I done that, and what did I want from her?

Our awkward silence ended when she asked about her mother. "How was she the last time you saw her?"

"She seemed very well. She's still practicing English."

Amélie smiled. "Who knows? One day she may be able to visit England or your country and then she can practice what she has learned."

"Yes. If my aunt comes back for a visit, she can bring your mother with her." Even as I said this, I doubted it would happen.

"Vera, I must ask a favor of you." Amélie hesitated before continuing. "I know my mother refuses to apply for a passport or to officially resume using her unmarried name in place of my father's surname. I accept that. Vangie has several photographs of my mother along with other neighbors. Do you think you could ask her to give you one or two of the pictures?"

"I suppose so. Would they be for you?"

"Yes. I have very few pictures of my parents, and I would like to have more. Especially now that my father has died and my mother is getting older."

"I can do that for you," I said. "Vangie has photographs scattered all over the apartment."

"*Merci.*"

Amélie arose from the table and reached for my hand.

"I know I have disappointed you by keeping certain secrets to myself. I saw the sadness in your eyes when I wouldn't answer all of your questions. I felt you withdrawing from me, and that is the last thing I wanted for either of us tonight."

"Amélie, I don't know what to say."

"Then, say nothing unless it is a comment about these walls."

I smiled as she pointed to the wallpaper covering every inch of unused space in the kitchen.

"This wallcovering… *c'est horrible, non?*"

"Now that you ask, I must admit I've never seen so many tiny violets in one room."

"I know, but I cannot make any changes because I do not own this house. I rent it."

We walked through the pantry and into the living room before pausing at the bottom of the staircase. Once again, Amélie reached for my hand and we climbed the steps to the second floor. She led me to the threshold of her bedroom, where I was to sleep that night.

Facing each other, we allowed seconds to pass before we kissed. I knew I'd wanted this to happen. I blinked away the vestiges of uncertainty I'd felt moments earlier and accepted the kisses that came sweetly, then tenderly, then passionately.

Hours later I found my way back from that sweet place where gravity ceases to exist, and I looked deeply into Amélie's eyes.

"I don't want you to sleep on the divan in the other room," I said.

"And I don't want you to sleep in here without me beside you."

I had never before heard a truer call and response.

Some hours later, when it was neither night nor dawn, we were awakened by the sounds of huge rain drops splashing against the bedroom window. We answered the storm by holding each other tightly.

"Vera, I know we have known each other for a short time, but that fact does not stop me from wanting to be with you for a long time to come."

"I want that as well, Amélie."

"Soon, your travel visa will expire and you will return to the States."

I wanted to erase the reality of her words.

"As soon as I arrive in Philadelphia, I'll apply for another visa. I'll come back to France and to you as soon as I can."

Amélie smiled and touched the tip of my nose with her fingertip.

"I hope that is so," she said. "I hope it is possible."

In that very moment, I didn't doubt its possibility. I took it for granted that what we'd begun would be our future. I hadn't considered the how's, when's, and where's of our being together. Nor had it occurred to me that sacrifices would be demanded and deep losses would be suffered, before we could enter that future together.

The next morning, as we walked from Amélie's house to the train station, I could feel she was struggling with indecision. There was something she wanted to tell me, something she thought I should know.

"I will see you as soon as I can, Vera. If it were left to me, I would see you this evening, either here or in Paris. But it is not left to me. It is very complicated."

I listened solemnly, as the minutes before I had to board the train sped by, disrespectful of our need to spend more time together and plan our way forward.

"Please remember to gather some photographs of my mother. I will take them from you the next time we see each other."

We waved to each other as the train crept slowly alongside the platform. I knew I would hold close two memories of my brief visit to Les Andelys. The first memory was the village itself, whose buildings referenced the Normans and centuries old invasions. The town was different from Paris in many ways, not the least of which was the absence of swastikas defiling squares of sidewalks or walls of buildings. My second memory was that of making love with Amélie. We were different, she and I. But somehow, I'd failed to notice the most salient difference I'd learned to take note of since the days of my childhood. Being aware of that key difference had kept me safe always. Forgetting that difference when I spent time with Amélie was a surprise, especially since I hadn't felt unsafe. Being with Amélie felt natural.

My life was now divided into two parts, *before* Amélie and *during* Amélie. I dared anyone to challenge my belief that Paris, indeed France itself, was a woman. And *Amélie* was that woman.

Chapter Thirty-two

Bette sat at the far end of L'Aigle Noir's bar and watched Vangie fill drink orders as quickly as they were given to her. Two Deaths in the Afternoon? Quickly poured. A French 75? Four ingredients deftly merged. A Kir Royale? Easily mixed and pretty to boot.

Bette admired the *élan* with which Vangie performed her job and the economy of her movements in the small space where she worked. Mostly, Bette admired Vangie's constant state of optimism that convinced her to hold her head high under the weight of being let go by her former employers.

"Hey, Baby. How's it going tonight?" L'Aigle Noir's owner, Charles Willard, winked at Vangie as he passed by.

"Everything's fine, Mr. Willard," Vangie answered.

Acting on a second thought, Willard stopped and turned to face Vangie. "You know, baby, you can call me Charles."

"I'm just fine with calling you Mr. Willard, Mr. Willard. And I'm equally fine with you not calling me baby."

Willard chortled. His shoulders moved up and down in reaction to Vangie's comment.

"I know how it goes and I know your story. You're okay by me." He paused. "That's why we're both here, isn't it? You can be you and I can be me. The hell with who we had to be back in the States!"

Vangie smiled and looked toward Bette. "Exactly," she said.

Willard leaned onto the bar's polished wood counter. "Listen, Vangie. Three men dressed in suits just came through the door. Do you see them?"

Vangie glanced casually in the direction of the club's entrance. "Yup. I see them."

"When they come up to the bar, no matter what they order, make their drinks extra generous, okay?"

"Sure."

Vangie was used to following instructions like this one.

She'd received similar ones many times in the past, and she'd always complied without asking any questions. The double-shot patrons were usually guys who worked for Paris' city government. Vangie imagined them stamping unread bar and occupancy permits by day and ordering free drinks by night. She knew Charles Willard hadn't fallen into his jazz club ownership by simply showing up at a bank and the appropriate office in Paris' City Hall with a smile on his face. He had studied and learned how the system works in order to be as successful as he was.

One of the newly arrived customers sauntered to the bar and spoke his order to Vangie. While she poured the three drinks, she overheard the man speaking with her boss. Both men laughed and then ended their brief conversation.

"*Danke*," said the man.

"*Bitte, mein freund.*"

Vangie's ears hadn't deceived her. The customer spoke German, and so did Charles Willard. Once again, Vangie gave herself an imaginary pat on the back for having accepted Willard's job offer. She'd reached the conclusion that her new boss was one of the smartest Negroes she'd ever met. She wondered what other enterprises claimed his time.

Chapter Thirty-three

November, 1937

"Claudine, Bette won't be here with us permanently," said Vangie. "And after Vera returns to the States, Bette and I can sleep in the bedroom Vera's been using."

"*T'inquietes pas*. Do not worry about it, Vangie. This apartment is large enough for all of us to have our own space."

"Thank you for always being so gracious, Claudine."

"I have wondered where Bette will do her painting. She is used to the big space she has in her studio."

"We've talked about that, and decided she can use part of my bedroom. There's a lot of light in there, more than there is in Vera's room."

Claudine agreed.

"I know there are times when Bette gets on your nerves, Claudine," said Vangie. "That's why I appreciate your generosity more than I can say."

Claudine nodded.

"It is true. She does get on my nerves, especially when she talks and talks and does not give anyone else a chance to speak. When she does that, there are two things that I do. First, I think about the mean way her brother treats her, especially because of her relationship with you. How can she stand to live with him? You know I still suspect he had something to do with your accident."

Vangie nodded. "I know you do."

"The second thing I do when she is talking the color off the walls is figure out whether I should escape to a different room or to a different floor."

Vangie laughed. "Well, I want you to know how much I appreciate the sacrifices you make."

"Yes, but how much do you appreciate it when I remind you that her brother was probably involved with that car than ran into you?"

"The police haven't gotten to the bottom of it, and I

can't prove he had anything to do with it, Claudine." Vangie's frustration was evidenced by the strain in her voice.

"There was an article in the newspaper about the accident. You would think someone in addition to Gérard would have seen it happen."

"It was late at night, not the middle of the day. There was no one around."

"You'd think the police would have talked to every automobile repairman in or near Paris to ask if a damaged car had been brought in to be fixed."

"Maybe they've done that, but they haven't gotten any clues or answers."

"The next time I see Simone Blum, I'm going to ask her to remind her daughter to inquire about the accident. Even though she works with a different police district, it is possible they work hand in hand now and then, no matter their jurisdiction."

"Okay, Claudine. I can see you're not going to let this go."

"Indeed not."

"The next time *I* see Simone, I'm going to ask her if she knows what's brewing between my niece and her daughter." Vangie winked. "She might not be aware of it, but I certainly am."

"Do not interfere, Vangie. They are both adults."

"I know. I know. But one of those two adults has to return to Philadelphia in a couple of weeks while the other one stays here. We're going to be picking up the pieces of two broken hearts."

"Maybe not. You cannot predict the future."

Claudine's words became muffled under the sound of the front door knocker.

"*J'arrive*," she called.

Simone Blum tiptoed into the foyer, a folded newspaper nestled under her arm.

"*Bonjour à toutes*," she said. "As always, I am here with a question or two about an article I read in the last newspaper you gave me, Vangie."

"Fire away, Simone."

"Fire? There is a fire?" asked Simone.

"No, no, no. That is just an expression. It means go

ahead, or proceed forward with your questions, Simone."

"May I?" Simone pointed at the table in the living room.

"Sure."

Simone placed the paper on the table and unfolded it before turning its pages. "*Le voilà.*"

She showed Vangie and Claudine an article she'd outlined in pencil. "It says a United States senator spoke on the floor." She paused. "Does that mean he sat down on the floor before he began to speak?"

"No," Vangie chuckled. "It means he had permission to speak in front of the other senators, that's all."

"*Ah, oui.* I continue. *He expressed a warning to the other senators. He said there are rumors Germany's leader, Adolf Hitler, is making plans to take over other European countries. His army will be prepared to conquer his first target, Poland, within the next two years.*" Simone looked questioningly at Vangie, and then at Claudine.

Vangie eased the newspaper out of Simone's hands and quickly perused the article. "Yes, that's what it says all right."

"It says he has a particular disdain for Jews. What is the meaning of disdain?" asked Simone.

"It means he hates Jews," said Claudine, matter-of-factly.

Simone looked drawn. Deep crevasses embedded themselves across her forehead. "I feared it was bad news, and it is."

Vangie continued reading the article until she found another passage worth quoting.

"The senator urges the United States and Great Britain to pay attention to the situation and be ready to join forces to help Poland if Hitler's rumored ambitions come to pass."

"You see, Simone? There's no need to worry. Even if it happens, the U.S. and England will come to the aid of Poland."

Simone nodded.

"You are probably right, Vangie. But still, I am worried."

Although she tried to minimize her neighbor's anxiety,

Vangie understood a lot could happen in the next two years, good things as well as bad. Time never paused the way it seemed to when she was younger. Changes occurred before she had a chance to recognize them, not to mention accept them.

Since the day Vera arrived and came to the hospital to visit her, Vangie had banished all thoughts of the day when her niece would leave Paris and return to Philadelphia. Purposely, she'd stopped looking at the calendar and tracking the weeks, then the days they had left to spend together. She'd done her best to ignore how quickly time passed, compared to how slowly it crawled when she was anticipating Vera's visit. Ninety days had not given Vangie enough time to share all she'd learned about family, life, and love with Vera. So far, she'd not had the opportunity to share her final secret with Vera, the secret she counted on to survive a future that was closing in on her and so many others.

Chapter Thirty-four

Ce flic stupide, thought Gérard. Stupid cop! Did it not occur to him that I would change my look-out place? Serge lives on a two-way street. I can just as easily see his comings and goings from this end of his street as I did from the opposite end.

There were no businesses located here, only private houses and apartments. Few pedestrians strolled by as Gérard maintained his vigil. For this, he was thankful. Slowly, he walked the distance of one block past Serge's street before he crossed the intersection and reversed direction. He quickened his pace whenever a car turned onto the street where Serge lived. If a car stopped near Serge's house, Gérard scribbled its details in a small leather-clad notebook. Twice, the details included what Gérard had begun calling the killer car, *la voiture de la morte*. He was determined to learn Serge's connection to that car and its driver.

On a particularly mild day in November, a bit after noon, Gérard spied the front of the Citroën's characteristic inverted double-V as the car slowed and turned onto the street. He walked quickly and stopped at the corner. When he saw the car come to a complete stop in front of Serge's front door, Gérard noticed a man seated behind the driver. He was somewhat non-descriptive, ordinary looking. He was the same man Gérard had observed before.

As if on cue, Serge opened the door to his house, stepped out, and headed toward the car.

Gérard watched his former lover walk behind the car, open the rear door, and ease himself into the seat. Gérard whispered to the air. "I am sorry to do this, my love. But I must."

He looked through the car's rear side window, aimed a revolver at Serge's head, and quickly pulled the trigger. Then, he fired the gun twice more, aimlessly. He heard a guttural grunt spread itself into a growl as the car lurched from the curb and sped away.

Chapter Thirty-five

The Philadelphia Sentinel
1600 Mt. Vernon Street
Philadelphia, 22 Pennsylvania
November 30, 1937

Dear Miss Clay,

We hope this letter finds you well. We hope also that you are still seeking employment with a major newspaper. The columns you wrote for the Chicago Recorder attracted the attention of our editorial staff. We found your articles to be accurately researched and certainly well-written.

The Philadelphia Sentinel values accurate reporting about local, national, and international events. Our readers deserve to be informed about issues that may affect them, their families, their communities, and the entire nation.

To that end, we are offering you employment as a staff writer for our newspaper. Please do us the favor of responding at your earliest convenience. It will be our pleasure to welcome you and provide more information as it pertains to your joining our staff.

Sincerely,
Herman Scott,
Editor-in-Chief, The Philadelphia Sentinel

I pressed the letter to my chest and hurried into the kitchen where I figured I'd find Vangie eating her dinner before she had to leave for work.

"Vangie! Look! I'm employed again! I'll be writing for the Philadelphia Sentinel. I won't have to move to who-knows-where."

Vangie rested her fork on the edge of the plate and grinned at me. "That's just wonderful, sweetheart! Imagine that."

I pulled out a chair and sat down at the table, opposite her. I'd expected her reaction to my news to be gleefully boisterous, not calm and contained. I stared at Vangie long enough to give birth to suspicion.

"Did you know about this before I did? Did you know about this job offer?" I asked.

"Now, how could that be?" Vangie avoided looking into my eyes, and then continued.

"Well, I did suspect something good might come from a discussion I had with my boss a couple of weeks ago," she said. "The bar was slow that night and Mr. Willard and I got to talking. At some point, he asked me about you and what you were going to do when you returned home. I told him about your column in the Chicago paper, and how they let you go because you kept mentioning the troubles in Germany. He smacked his hand on the bar and said he might be able to help you."

"Really? How? Does he own a newspaper as well as a jazz club?"

"No, it's better than that. Remember I told you he was a war hero over here?"

I nodded.

"During the war, he joined a group of multi-national soldiers and they fought on the side of France. He and some of the other men ended up being decorated. France appreciated their bravery and honored most of those men. Mr. Willard and some of the others stayed here after the war was over. They got all kinds of jobs. One of those men was a writer. He applied for a job with an American newspaper, but he was rejected, just like you were, Vera. After a while, he decided to return to the states and try his luck again. He got hired by the colored newspaper in Pittsburgh and once he was there, he rose through the ranks. To this day, he's stayed in touch with Mr. Willard."

"From Pittsburgh?"

Her meal forgotten and now cold, Vangie leaned forward. "No. He learned all the skills he could working at that newspaper. I bet you can't guess his name."

I began to think Vangie's anecdote had relegated my good news to runner-up if this were a race to excitement.

"No, I can't guess his name."

"It's Herman Scott. He's Editor-in-Chief of *The Philadelphia Sentinel*, and it looks like he's just hired a new employee."

"Oh, my sakes and souls!" I grabbed the edge of the table.

"My sakes and souls? That's an expression your grandmother used to say. You've talked your way back to a past generation, honey."

"So, your Mr. Willard has gotten me a job? I need to thank him! Maybe I can go to work with you one evening before I leave."

"Sure, that would be grand. If I can get Bette to come also, the two of you can keep each other company while I'm working."

"I believe I'd like that."

"Do you see how things are working out, Vera? You have a job in Philadelphia. You can live with your parents and save your money instead of paying rent somewhere," said Vangie.

I was in favor of the economic part of her plan, but less than enthusiastic about living with my parents. My thoughts turned to Amélie. How could I return to Paris quickly if I accepted this job offer? But how could I afford to return here at all if I didn't take the job and earn a salary?

"I bet you're thinking about Amélie, aren't you?" asked Vangie.

"My face must be an open book," I said. "I'm afraid my feelings for her have travelled way beyond a crush."

"Maybe her feelings for you run as deeply as yours do for her. You can't predict the future."

I paid attention to the far-away expression shrouding Vangie's eyes.

"Perhaps you'll find a way to make a life together, either here or in Philadelphia."

I shook my head. "I can't see that happening at home, not the way things are in our country."

"I know, love. I don't want to frighten you, but I can't see it happening here either."

"But it's different here, Vangie. It's just like you

described it in all of your letters."

"Sweetheart, things are changing. They're changing quickly."

"What do you mean?"

"I mean some people are starting to feel afraid. The same kind of afraid you, me, and all the other colored folks in the U.S. live with all the time. We're used to it. We don't talk about it all that much, but the fear and caution are always with us. We tiptoe through life instead of planting each step firmly and leaving footprints like declarations of who we are and why we're entitled to the same freedoms others have. Fear is always in the driver's seat. Look at Simone Blum. If she reads one more newspaper article about the Germans or has one more conversation with our other Jewish neighbors, she'll snap. She's a nervous wreck."

I agreed. "What do you think is going to happen here, Vangie?"

"I don't know, honey. But I imagine it won't be good."

"If life here becomes dangerous for you, will you come back to Philadelphia?"

Vangie bowed her head and then looked up again, her eyes filled with an apology she didn't need to offer.

"Probably not. My life is here. My Bette is here." Vangie gestured toward the ceiling as if she could see Bette upstairs in their bedroom, thoughtfully applying paint to a canvas.

The joy I felt moments ago was akin to a warm coat draped upon my shoulders. Now, that coat had been snatched away, and suddenly I felt cold, inconsolably cold.

Vangie tapped the table softly. "Come on now. Let's take it one day at a time."

"I know, live for the best and plan for the worst," I said.

"Oh Lord. Now I feel like I'm talking to your mother."

I allowed myself to smile. "Amélie and I barely know each other, but..."

"But it feels like you've known each other forever,

right?"

"Yes. A friend of mine has a habit of saying there's a lid for every pot. I truly believe Amélie is my lid."

Vangie took in a deep breath and then let it escape very slowly. "I promised myself I wouldn't tell you what else I know about your new job, but…"

"Please tell me."

"Mr. Scott knows my boss has connections with all sorts of government people, and he asked him if he could get you an extension of your travel visa. I thought it was a great idea, but I told Mr. Willard the extension could be for another ninety days, no longer. After that, you need to get back to Philadelphia," explained Vangie.

"Is Mr. Willard going to do that for me?"

"He told me it will be finalized by the end of next week."

"Aunt Vangie, you and Mr. Willard have saved my life."

"I wouldn't go that far, honey. You're in charge of saving your life. And good luck telling your mother about…"

The jarring sound of a wooden object assaulting the apartment's front door stifled whatever else Vangie had to say. We heard Claudine's voice ring out a second before we left the kitchen table.

"*J'arrive! J'arrive!*"

Annoyed that someone would dare pummel her front door with something other than a fist, Vangie strode through the living room and reached the foyer just as Claudine unlatched the lock.

"*Mademoiselle* Moune?" A uniformed, mustachioed policeman spoke.

"*Non. Je suis Claudine Mistralle.*"

Claudine glanced quickly at Vangie before she spoke her next sentence.

"I will tell *Mademoiselle* Moune you are here."

As Claudine headed toward the stairs, Vangie took a step closer to the policeman whose dark-blue-nearly-black wool uniform verified his identity. She scrutinized his badge's double-edged ax at the top, shiny blue *Préfecture de Police* label in the middle, and intertwined RF at its bottom.

"And, what is your name, *Madame*?" he asked.

"I am Evangeline Curtis."

"I am Lieutenant Christophe of the Paris *Préfecture de Police*."

The police officer extracted a small leather-bound note-book from his jacket's pocket. He opened it and then pressed his already reed-thin lips even thinner.

"You were involved in a hit-and-run car accident a few months ago, *Madame*?"

"Yes." Vangie answered the question guardedly.

Hearing the sound of footsteps on the stairs, we turned and watched as Bette reached the foyer.

"*Vous-êtes Bette Moune, Madame?*"

"*Oui, Monsieur.*"

"You are the sister of Hervé Moune?"

"*Oui.*"

"Your brother has been involved in a shooting, *Madame*. He has survived and he is recovering in the American Hospital of Paris."

I looked at Bette and noticed she'd barely flinched. I was certain Lieutenant Christophe noticed that as well.

"Why was he taken to that hospital? It is located in *Neuily-Sur-Seine*. Is that where he was shot?" asked Bette.

"No, he was wounded in a quarter close to the Rothschild Hospital, but he refused to let us take him there. He said he wouldn't ever go to a hospital owned by Jews." The lieute-nant paused, perhaps to look for Bette's reaction to her bro-ther's antisemitism.

"What happened? Who shot him?" Vangie fired off her questions.

The police officer turned his attention to her. "Rest assured, *Madame*, we have the suspect in our custody as well as the weapon he used. We had also the sad task of notifying the family of the person who was killed during this attack."

"Someone was killed?" I asked, no longer willing to be silent.

"And who are you, *Mademoiselle*?"

"My name is Vera Clay." I gestured toward Vangie. "I am Miss Curtis' niece."

The lieutenant stared right through me, as if to dismiss

my presence. Quickly, he redirected his attention to Vangie and Bette.

I saw Vangie's shoulders and back stiffen, and I sensed she'd arrived at one of those moments when you know you're about to hear words knotted together like a noose tied around your throat, ready to choke a part of your life out of you. You know the words are coming, and you're powerless to stop them from changing some aspect of your everyday reality.

"The victim who was less fortunate than your brother, *Madame*, was named Serge Bonet. The person who has admitted firing three shots from his gun is named Gérard Simonet. He is the person we have arrested."

Vangie arms seemed glued to her sides. She clenched both fists.

"*Mesdames*, do either of you know Serge Bonet or Gérard Simonet?"

"I know Gérard. I used to work with him," said Vangie.

The lieutenant nodded. "And he was the person who witnessed your being run over by someone driving a car we have not been able to locate?"

"Yes. If Gérard hadn't been there that night, I might not be here talking to you."

"*Monsieur* Simonet claims he has seen the car that hit you, and in fact, his victims were in that car when he shot them. If his information proves to be true, he and his advocate have the means to spare his execution."

"Does Gérard have to prove it's the same car?" I asked.

"Not necessarily."

"Is there something we can do to help him?" asked Claudine.

"I do not know." The policeman's brief answer signaled he was ready to move on. He looked at Bette.

"*Mademoiselle* Moune, may I take you to see your brother at the hospital?"

"Thank you, but no. I shall see him soon."

Lieutenant Christophe of the Paris *Préfecture of Police* tipped his tall, flat-topped cap and in one motion he directed his words to the three of us.

"Good afternoon, *Mesdames*. We shall be in contact with you concerning the automobile mishap, and of course, the armed assault of *Monsieur* Moune."

Claudine stepped away from her perch in front of the closet door and followed the officer to the apartment's entrance.

After a moment of silence, Vangie mournfully uttered, "Oh, Gérard, you don't know what you've done.

Chapter Thirty-six

December 2, 1937

Dear Daughter,

I'm so glad you'll soon be back home. I have to admit I've missed you. When do you begin your new job? Soon, I trust. I've told all of my friends about it, and they're happy for you as well. I overheard your father talking on the telephone to one of his friends from work. He's very proud of you, as am I.

Remember to pack all of your belongings. Do you have your return tickets for the train and the ship? Perhaps you shouldn't put everything in your handbag. You don't want to cross paths with thieves.

Sorry to hear about your Aunt Vangie's friend who shot and killed someone. He *would* be one of her friends, wouldn't he? Evangeline has always had a talent for picking up odd people, women as well as men. Who is this Amélie that you've mentioned in a couple of your letters? After you've returned home, do you plan to keep in touch with her?

Travel safely, my dear. It will be good to see you.

Fondly,
Mother

December 4, 1937

Dear Mother,

I have more news about my job to tell you and Dad. The Philadelphia Sentinel's editor-in-chief, Herman Scott, wants me to remain here in Paris for a while longer. He is eager to receive reports about Europe from someone who's close to what's going on. That someone is me, apparently. An extension of my visa has been arranged, permitting me to stay here in France for another ninety days.

Vangie says she's more than happy to have me stay with her, so I won't need to look for a place to rent for the next three months. I've offered to pay her a weekly fee as soon as I receive my first paycheck, but she refuses to accept any money from me.

I've secured a refund for the steamship ticket I won't be using and for my train ticket to Le Havre. I've rescheduled both reservations for three months from now.

Mother, I know my change of plans disappoints you. While it's good news for me, it's not the best news for you. Please try to understand the enormous career advantage I will have as a result of extending my stay here. I shall learn so much about collecting information, interviewing people, and following story leads during a time of change. My newspaper journalism foundation will be all set.

I haven't forgotten the question you asked me in your last letter. Here is the answer. Amélie Blum is the daughter of one of Vangie's neighbors, Simone Blum. Amélie lives and works in a small town not far from Paris. We see each other when she comes to visit her mother (the kind woman who lent me her old typewriter). You'll have to trust my judgment when I say Amélie has become a good friend. I believe our friendship has the potential to become a very important one.

Love to you and Dad,
Vera

December 12, 1937

Dear Vera,

Yes, I am disappointed that you won't be coming home when you said you would. Your father is disappointed, also. If staying in Paris for three more months is what you want to do, so be it. I know better than to try to talk you out of your plans. Believing that you'd soon be home, I've avoided saying much about your father's health. He wouldn't want you to worry about him.

Do you recall when I wrote and told you he had such a bad cold, that he stayed home from work? He's never totally recovered. He coughs a lot and sometimes tells me that his chest hurts. I thought the pain in his chest was caused by all the coughing he does. The doctor thinks he may have had pneumonia and its effects continue to linger. Rest assured I am supervising his medicine regime. I make sure that he takes his pills and cough syrup regularly. His supervisor at the Post Office lets him come home early (without reducing his salary) whenever he doesn't feel well.

Perhaps if you'd known about this sooner, you would not have renewed your visa. You would have stuck with your original plans and come back home. Or, perhaps not. I suspect the combination of life in Paris and your aunt's influence on your thinking weigh more than my opinions.

Take care,
Mother

December 20, 1937

Dear Mother,

I'm distressed to learn about Dad's illness. I didn't know the bad cold he had never left completely. It's good that you make sure he's taking his medicines. Otherwise, he might skip some doses.

I hope your disappointment about my not coming home as soon as I'd planned will dissipate when you consider how much I'm learning every day that I'm here in France. Living in a foreign country has not only given me chances to learn about a different culture. It has afforded me the opportunity to learn about my country more deeply. I see the United States through a new set of eyes. I perceive things about America and Americans that I could not have perceived without stepping away from the U.S. for a few months. I believe my perceptions are both objective and subjective. I'd like to believe I've developed new grooves in my brain, if indeed brain grooves exist.

I'll stay in touch with you and Dad regularly.

Love to you both,
Vera

Chapter Thirty-seven

My next conversation with Amélie was brief, too brief. She phoned me from her job to say she was trying to get a two day break from work, so either she could come to Paris or I could travel to Les Andelys. When I told her about my newspaper job and my extended visa, she sounded jubilant. Excitement blended with desire as we vowed to see each other as soon as possible. Little did we know we'd see each other that very evening.

Vangie, Bette, and I left the apartment, hailed a taxi, and headed to Vangie's workplace, L'Aigle Noir. I wanted to thank Charles Willard for getting my career back on track. Bette wanted to drink a cocktail or two after visiting her brother in the hospital.

"So, how is Hervé?" Vangie asked a harried Bette.

"He is impossible. I am not going to visit him again."

"That sounds pretty final, *ma chère.*"

"Yes, it is final. I cannot bear to spend a moment more listening to his hateful rhetoric."

"Sounds like you need a couple of my French 75's."

"What's that?" I asked.

"Champagne, gin, lemon juice, and simple syrup."

"Thank you. I accept your kind offer." Bette smiled for the first time since she'd returned from the hospital visit.

The three of us walked into L'Aigle Noir just as a small group of musicians huddled near the bar and tuned their instruments.

One of them looked up and called out. "Vangie, good to see you! Charlie said he'd hired you."

"It's great seeing you too, Sidney. How have you been?"

"Better now that I'm out of jail." He flashed a smile that failed to conceal his feelings about being incarcerated.

Vangie approached him. "I was sorry when I heard about the fight and your arrest. I wished you could have ignored that knucklehead. He wasn't worth you going to jail, Sid."

"Well, it's history now," said Sidney. "Hey, who are these two beautiful women accompanying you?"

Vangie pointed my way, "This my niece, Vera. She's here to thank Mr. Willard for helping her get a job back in the States."

"A pleasure to meet you, Vera. But I'm afraid I have bad news. Charlie won't be here tonight."

"Oh, no." I said.

"Oh, yes," said Sidney. "I guess that means you'll have to make a return visit to L'Aigle Noir, maybe during another evening when I'm here playing again."

Vangie ignored the musician's attempt to flirt with me. "And this other attractive woman is Bette."

"Ah, the artist who has stolen your heart?" asked Sidney.

"You'd best believe it." Vangie inclined her head toward us. "Vera, Bette, this is Sidney Oakes, one hell of a talented musician."

"What instrument do you play?" I asked.

"Sometimes the clarinet, the drums, the piano, and my specialty… the soprano sax. Nobody plays that better than me, young lady."

"He's modest, also," added Vangie.

"Is it not time for you to set up the bar, *Madame*?"

Sidney's question amused Bette and me, and propelled Vangie to go behind the bar to check her inventory.

From our vantage point, Bette and I watched her inspect containers of lemon wedges, lime slices, olives and cocktail onions, mint leaves. She perused bottles of liqueurs and fruit juices. She finished a quick count of all the different sizes and shapes of glasses as the club's patrons began arriving. Before she fulfilled the first drink orders of the evening, Vangie set down drinks in front of Bette and me.

"Here's your French 75, sweetheart. Tell me if you like it." Vangie served the cocktail to Bette as if she were giving her a precious diamond. That is, with all possible tenderness.

"And here's a Kir Royale for you, Vera."

I picked up the tulip-shaped glass and admired its blush-colored hue.

"It's a pretty color, Vangie. What's in it?" I asked.

"Champagne, crème de cassis, and a fresh raspberry. Enjoy."

We did enjoy sitting there, sipping drinks, and listening to Sidney Oakes and his bandmates unfurl their versions of "Night and Day" and "Sophisticated Lady." I didn't know if it was the Kir Royale, my new job, knowing I'd be able to remain in Paris for the next three months, or the probability of deepening my relationship with Amélie that gave me a sensation of lightness I'd never known before. At one point, I turned to Bette and smiled what I hoped she recognized was a genuine expression of how I felt about her ties to my aunt. I liked Bette, and I'd begun to understand how two people who are so different from each other can be blind to the differences and simply give in to the most human of emotions. Because of my evolving feelings for Amélie, I finally understood the grace and rightness of Bette's union with Vangie.

Just then, the music ended, literally and figuratively. The Sidney Oakes Combo finished their first set as Amélie Blum entered the club. A rather sophisticated looking woman was by her side.

At first, I wondered if I were hallucinating. I might have wished fervently that Amélie were there, but I would *not* have wanted her to be there with someone else. I stared at them and silently forbade Amélie to not see me or worse, to ignore my presence. When she looked my way, her eyes were expressionless, and remained so for seconds at a time. How could this be happening? Had I become invisible?

Despite her mixing, pouring, and reaching across the bar to serve drinks, Vangie watched the entire scene. She became tight-lipped and telegraphed her concern by tilting her head in my direction. Almost unperceptively, she messaged me to be discreet, to control my confused feelings. Then, she listened and nodded as Amélie ordered drinks for herself and the woman. Vangie showed no sign at all that she knew Amélie, not even when she exchanged their drinks for Amélie's money. Not even as she watched them step away from the bar, sit down at a table, and act as if they were enjoying each other's company.

The lightness I'd felt moments ago vanished into the atmosphere like curls of smoke rising from a cigarette. I wanted to force my self-focused, naïve notions about falling in love into exile. I glanced at Bette and noticed the look of affection in her eyes as she watched Vangie. It was that visible affection that pushed me to hold on to the notion that love can unite two people whose differences traditionally keep them apart. The notion I needed to discard was the foolish idea I'd had of uniting with Amélie.

I stayed true to that thought days later when Vangie, witnessing the pain in my eyes, tried to comfort me. Moments before I set out to make a return visit to Shakespeare and Company, Vangie hugged me.

"I'm sorry about what happened at L'Aigle Noir the other night. I can see your feelings are still hurt."

"I'll get over it, Aunt Vangie." I opened my handbag to make sure my notebook was tucked inside it.

"Don't think badly of Amélie, and don't become so tough that you reject others in an effort to protect yourself."

"What do *you* think of Amélie? She ignored me and acted like she didn't know you. Was it because we're colored and she didn't want that woman to know she has colored friends?"

"I doubt that very seriously, Vera."

"Well, if that's not the reason for how she treated us, what is?" I couldn't stop my frustration from surging. The only good thing that came with expressing my anger was the absence of my tears. I had cried already, privately. Now, it was all I could do to staunch the tears that were constantly ready to fall. What helped was reminding myself to stay focused on writing my newspaper articles and avoiding any thoughts of a woman who wasn't worth my time or my emotions. As long as I could do that, I'd be able to focus on the people who knew my value, my aunt and Claudine for example.

"I don't know why Amélie acted like she did, Vera." Vangie sighed.

I looked at my aunt and realized I'd never before witnessed such a reflection of intense strain on her face. Her worries seemed so overwhelming they transformed her

generous mouth, round dimpled cheeks, and kind eyes into
lips drawn thin, cheeks flattened with no evidence of dimpled indentations, and eyes whose piercing gaze prohibited
my asking her any more questions.

"I do know Amélie is a good person and she cares for
you as deeply as she can right now."

"Right now?" I asked.

"Yes, right now."

"Okay," I said. "I'm on my way to interview the American owner of the bookstore I've visited. I'm sure there's a
newspaper-worthy story that woman can tell me."

Chapter Thirty-eight

Hervé Moune glared at his bloodied shirt and suit jacket as he got dressed. The bullet that tore through his shoulder opened a wound that seemed to bleed endlessly. In anticipation of being discharged from the hospital, he'd instructed his sister to bring him a change of clothes. Bette had not complied. Hervé threw his discarded hospital gown on the floor near his bed. Let the immigrants who make up most of the cleaning staff take care of this trash, he thought.

He left the room which he'd had to share with nine other male patients and spoke to no one. The man occupying the bed closest to the ward's exit called out.

"*Hé, où vas-tu? Tu nous quittes?*"

Hervé paused at the doorway.

"Where I am going is none of your business. And I don't recall giving you permission to address me in any other manner than *vous*."

Insulated by an air of superiority as well as disgust for the patient who'd just spoken to him, Hervé left the ward. He'd arranged for the car and its driver to be parked near the hospital's entrance. He wondered if the car would be the same one in which he'd been shot, but that did not bother him in the least. Instead of inventing a superstition-laden reason to avoid it, Hervé embraced the chance to ride in it again, gunman be damned. He also welcomed the inevitability of that gunman's fate. No doubt, he would be executed. Publicly, as the newly proposed law striking down public executions hadn't won passage.

Hervé neither embraced nor regretted the loss of Serge Bonet. Bonet's worth was rooted in his wealth and his political connections. Hervé knew there were other *Bonets* waiting to be called upon to contribute to the future of France.

As Hervé pushed aside the hospital's entrance door, he saw the car parked nearby.

"*Monsieur* Moune." Someone called his name. "You

cannot leave the hospital until the attending doctor has given his permission. Also, there are papers you must sign."

Hervé turned to confront the speaker.

"I am not waiting for anyone to give me permission to do anything. You may send any papers that need my signature to my home via a messenger."

Although Hervé's coldly autocratic response cowered the person who tried to delay his departure, the time it took for Hervé to speak was long enough to change the scene surrounding his car and driver. The car was still parked where it had been, but now the driver stood beside it, and faced three policemen.

Instinctively, Hervé took a few steps away from the hospital's door and made himself part of a small gathering of curious bystanders. He watched two of the police officers take the automobile's key from the driver and then manhandle him into the rear seat of one of their cars. The third policemen got into the burgundy Citroën that was to have been Hervé's transport home and drove it away.

"*Merde!*" Hervé hissed as he turned around and re-entered the hospital. He walked into the first room he came upon and spoke to a young man who was standing behind a counter.

"I need access to a telephone to order a taxi."

"I can help you, *Monsieur.*" The young man reached for the telephone and dialed. "What is your destination, *Monsieur?*"

"Home. That's all you need to know."

Having summoned the taxi, the young man said nothing more as he walked past Hervé.

Hervé stared at the man's back for as long as he could see him. Then, he exited the room and once again, headed for the hospital's front door. While he waited pensively for the taxi's arrival, it occurred to him that the young man looked a bit like Serge Bonet. Hervé was confident he'd succeed in his search for a new Serge. And, this time, he wouldn't recruit a homosexual. Hervé was certain the man who'd shot Serge was a jilted male lover whom Serge had abandoned. Gypsies, Negros, Jews, the handicapped, and homosexuals had no place in Hitler's Germany, nor in what would be Hitler's France.

Chapter Thirty-nine

Amélie reread the letter she'd just written before placing it in an envelope and sealing it. She had no idea how Vera might react to her words, but she did know that she had to reach out to her. If only she had the liberty to explain why she'd been at L'Aigle Noir and why she hadn't acknowledged Vera's presence.

15 *Rue Richard Cœur de Lion*
Le Petit Andelys, France
10 *décembre*, 1937

Ma chère Vera,

I feel so terrible about what happened two nights ago. As I passed by your table on my way out of the club, I saw the emptiness in your eyes, the hollowed-out expression of having been betrayed. I have not betrayed you, dear Vera. I wanted to speak to you, but under the circumstances, I could not. Even now, I cannot tell you why I was there, nor why I was in the company of a woman whose name I cannot offer.

I know you and I should not have secrets from each other. Yet, here I am, asking you to accept the reality that there are some circumstances about myself which I cannot tell you right now. Perhaps I can talk about these things in the future, after fate has determined what will be our history.

Please believe my sincerity when I say I love you. More than that...there is an endless depth to how much I need you to be in my life.

Je t'aime,
Your Amélie

Next, she took a clean sheet of paper from the desk drawer and began to compose a letter to her superior. She knew the absence of emotion would make this letter an easier one to write.

15 *Rue Richard Cœur de Lion*
Le Petit Andelys, France
10 *décembre,* 1937

Monsieur le Commandant Salière:

Thank you for the honor of approving my fourth application to join the Police Force of Les Andelys. I am proud to have earned a high score on the annual examination, indeed the highest score of those candidates who sat for the examination.

I have aspired to be a police officer for a long time. Despite that fact, I have decided not to enter the next class of police recruits. My reasons for this decision are two-fold. First, I am aware of the physical condition candidates must possess. My present age suggests I might have surpassed my optimum state of physical fitness. Second, my present position with the police force gives me a less than rigid schedule that allows me to travel to see my sixty-eight-year-old mother when she needs my help. If I became a police officer, I would be obliged to work the shifts assigned to me, thus making it difficult to assist my mother.

Thank you for the confidence you have expressed regarding my potential to become a very competent *flic*. I shall continue demonstrating my competence in my present position by serving the police force and the citizens of Les Andelys.

Avec le respect le plus profond,
Amélie Blum

Le 18 décembre, 1937

Dear Amélie,

I received your letter of December 10, and I read it

with some amount of interest. I respect your need for secrecy, and I hope you realize that secrets infer a lack of trust between two people. This lack of trust looms large over any possibility that you and I can have a relationship beyond a casual friendship.

Your mother told me you'd been offered the opportunity to train for and became a police officer, a goal you've long held for yourself. She said you had rejected the offer, and she cannot understand why. She hopes you will explain your reasons for turning down this opportunity. I said I imagined you would explain the rationale behind your decision. Then, a thought occurred to me. Perhaps you don't trust your mother, just as you don't trust me.

Your friend,
Vera Clay

Le 21 décembre, 1937

Ma chère Vera,

First, thank you for responding to my last letter. I welcomed it although I could feel the anger you are holding toward me. The next time I see my mother, I am planning to explain everything about the police training offer I rejected. If all goes as planned, that will be late in the evening of 24 *décembre*.

As you know, I do not celebrate Christmas. I do however, enjoy the good spirits and delicious meals of those who celebrate that holiday. I especially enjoy the music, *les cantiques de Nöel*. A few years ago, I began the custom of attending the midnight mass on Christmas Eve, simply to hear the music and the voices of the choir. If I am at home, I go to the church near my house. If I am in Paris, I go to the American Cathedral on Avenue Georges V. The music is beautiful in both churches. It offers me a sense of peace and of hope.

Until we see each other again, I remain your love.

Amélie

Chapter Forty

My new column, "From the Other Side of the Pond," took off with the speed of a summertime water bug startled by the glare of an overhead lightbulb suddenly come to life. When I said this to Vangie, she suggested I think of a different metaphor, something more pleasant to visualize.

"How about the speed of Charles Willard's airplane as it flew missions during the war?"

"Okay," I consented half-heartedly. "But not many Americans have heard of Charles Willard."

"Negro Americans have heard his name, and they're the folks who are reading your articles." Vangie paused before changing the subject. "Vera, are you sure you want to go with me to see Gérard? Visiting someone in prison isn't easy, you know."

"Yes, I'm sure. I want to see as many different places and talk to as many different people in this city as I can."

We succeeded in hailing a taxi a few moments after stepping onto the street.

"*La Prision Santé, s'il vous plaît, Monsieur.*"

The driver turned and looked at us before nodding.

"*Oui, Mesdames.*"

I thought it ironic that the day we were going to visit Gérard in prison, the weather was so lovely. Paris had shed its early-winter gray and allowed the sun to shine brightly. The cab moved slowly toward its destination, as if, like me, it didn't really want to go there.

"*Je regrette, Mesdames, que nous allons si lentement.*" The driver glanced at us via his rear-view mirror as he apologized for how slowly he was driving. Gesturing in frustration at laborers engaged in road projects. "They are wasting their time and the citizens' tax money."

"Is this another cobblestone project?" asked Vangie.

"*Oui.* But it should be a project to build tunnels."

"Tunnels ?" I asked.

"*Oui,* tunnels. So, we will have places to go and hide from our neighbors, the Germans. I have relatives living in the south of France. They tell me the Germans will come there first."

"Why there?" I asked.

"Many people who live there support the idea of a united Europe. They believe France will benefit if it belongs, even more if we are among the first to join without any struggle or resistance to the Germans. But I am not so sure of that. While some workers are laying stones in the streets, others are making guns and materials of defense for the French Army. *Merde*!"

The driver fused his hands to the vehicle's steering wheel and continued to shout profanities. "Why did that fool think he could pass me? *Salaud*!"

I swore to remember the driver's every word, at least until I had time to write his comments in my notes. I'd heard similar comments from other people I'd encountered recently. Ordinary everyday Parisians were beginning to give voice to the same thoughts.

The driver steered his taxi toward the curb and applied the brakes. Vangie opened her purse and withdrew the cost of the fare.

"*Merci, Monsieur*," we recited in unison.

"*Bonne chance, Mesdames.*"

La Santé's stone exterior reminded me of a university building or perhaps a library, but it was neither. A wide driveway split into two parts. One section continued toward the rear of the building, and the other ushered visitors to its entrance. As Vangie and I abandoned the pebble-covered path leading to the back of the prison, we heard the sound of a car's tires compacting the small stones underneath them. At the same time, we saw two women leave the entrance and descend the steps in silence.

Vangie tugged on my forearm. "We won't be here long. We're not blood relatives, so we can only stay for fifteen minutes."

That visitors' rule was fine with me. I realized I didn't know what to say to Gérard. I'd never before had a conversation with anyone who had killed another human being.

We climbed the steps, pulled open the tallest door I'd ever seen, and walked into a high-ceilinged open space. Immediately, we heard a man's voice.

"Good afternoon. You are here for what reason?" he asked.

"We are here to see Gérard Simonet, one of the prisoners. We made an appointment to see him."

"Your names, please."

"I am Evangeline Curtis."

"And my name is Vera Clay."

The uniformed greeter opened a large book and placed his index finger at the top of one of its pages. He directed his finger from the top of the page to its middle, nodded and then stopped.

"Your identification papers, please."

Vangie removed a card from her purse and I took my passport from my bag.

The man read the information printed on Vangie's card. He looked at the photo attached to my passport, glanced at my face, and returned our documents to us.

"Kindly wait here, please," he said.

The humorless man turned and entered what appeared to be an office.

"He's so curt, but we're the ones who have to act kindly," I said.

"Hush, darlin.' You don't want to stay here, do you?" Vangie faked a stern look.

Out of nowhere, a second uniformed man appeared.

"*Madame* Curtis, *Mademoiselle* Clay, please come with me."

The prison employee led us from the cavernous entrance and then through several long windowless hallways. Each one had a locked door at its terminus. The hallway floors were pitched on an incline. By the time we'd travelled along four of them, my shins' discomfort suggested we'd descended an entire level below the place where we began our hike.

After he locked the fourth door, the guard ushered us into a large room furnished with shallow wooden benches lining the room's perimeter.

"Take a seat. Prisoner Simonet will be here shortly."

I grappled with the strangeness of hearing prisoner attached to Gérard's last name. No doubt the linkage of that word to Simonet grated upon Vangie's ears as well.

An ominously loud creak accompanied by a sudden rush of air signaled the arrival of two men. A prison guard followed the first man who wore a stained ill-fitting gray shirt. His trousers were slashed in several places, and the hems cascaded over his shoes and onto the floor.

"You have two visitors and five minutes to talk." The guard barked at the three of us.

Vangie stood up slowly.

"Gérard?" she asked.

"*Oui*, Vangie. *C'est moi*."

This person couldn't be Gérard, I thought. I examined his face and tried to connect its features with those of the young man I'd met only four months ago.

Vangie moved closer to him, her arms outstretched.

"*Ne touchez-pas*! No touching permitted!" Once again, the guard's brittle voice assaulted our ears. He stood perfectly still and looked straight ahead. The only indication that he was human and not a machine was the barely perceptible motion his lips made when he shouted his directive.

Shocked into silence, I felt grateful for Vangie's presence. It was she who would speak to Gérard, not I.

"What has happened to you?" she asked.

Gérard struggled to force his eyelids open. "I seem to have enemies here," he began. "People who know me even though I don't know them."

"What do you mean, Gérard?"

"There are men here who take exception to men like me. You cannot be the least bit clever or handsome here without paying a price."

Certainly, he'd been good looking before his arrival in the prison, but handsome was the last word I'd use to describe Gérard now. Patches of his hair had been cut off or forcibly shaved, leaving bruised, once-bloodied areas of scalp. His swollen nose looked displaced and off-center. His slumped shoulders seemed caved-in, barely able to support his upper body. He kept his right hand fused to his left side. Were those ribs broken? Was he in danger of puncturing his lungs?

"And then, there is this. I am a man who loves men. I am here because I shot and killed my male lover." He paused. "It is known also that I am a Jew. That is the label shouted at me the most."

"Do you have an advocate who will defend you during your trial, Gérard?"

"I have no defense, Vangie. I am guilty."

"Your time has ended!" The guard put his hand on Gérard's shoulder and turned him toward the door.

"Vangie, *merci.* Thank you for coming to see me. Vera, write about how I've been treated here. Warn others how ugly it is to be a gay Jew imprisoned in La Santé. "

The guard stared at us. "Walk through this hallway. When you arrive at its end, you'll see a door facing you. A guard will unlock it and give you further directions."

We reversed the path we'd taken from the prison's entrance to the visitors' waiting room, but burdened by what we'd heard and seen, we walked more slowly. I linked my arm with Vangie's in an effort to support us both. When we reached the building's entrance and descended the stone steps leading to the property's driveway, I began to breathe again.

The afternoon sun spread across my face, warming it. I inhaled the air as deeply as I could, as if I were clearing my lungs of the prison's suffocatingly putrid atmosphere.

Vangie and I walked the distance of one kilometer before we paused next to a *tête de station* sign and climbed into the rear seat of a cab.

I turned toward her. "What will happen to him?"

Vangie stared straight ahead. "I don't know, and I wish I didn't care."

Gérard's present condition and the first taxi driver's prescient comments about forming a united Europe, building tunnels in Paris, and manufacturing weapons filled my next two columns.

Chapter Forty-one

I heard Claudine call my name, so I got up from my desk and walked into the hallway.

"*Oui*, Claudine."

"*Ah, tu es là. Tu as reçu une lettre de ta mère.*"

More and more frequently, Claudine spoke to me in French. She said it was the best way for me to become more fluent, and it was obvious that when Vangie and I spoke to each other, we used English.

"*Merci*, Claudine." I met her on the staircase, halfway between the foyer and the second floor. As I turned to go back upstairs, I thought I saw the tiniest stripe of light where the coat closet's door met the floorboards. More than likely, it was an optical illusion caused by the sun as it filtered its way through the thick glass sidelights that framed the front door.

Baffled by what I was going to write in my next column, I welcomed the chance to abandon it long enough to read my mother's letter.

December 21, 1937

Dear Vera,

I hope you receive this letter before Christmas Day because I'm enclosing your gift with it. Not knowing what you might need to buy for yourself for the winter, your father and I have sent you a money order. We're sure you'll know how to cash it. We had a little bit of trouble figuring out the exchange rate between dollars and *francs*, so we hope we've sent you enough money for a coat or a few warm sweaters.

It goes without saying that we miss you. We've decorated the tree and put the electric candles in the downstairs windows. Your father insists that we turn on the candles as soon as it's dark outside. I prefer to wait until later...

seven o'clock or so. The electric bill is too high as it is.

How do they celebrate Christmas in France? Do people decorate their homes? Do they go to church? Do they prepare anything traditional for Christmas dinner? What about your aunt? Does she work on Christmas Eve, or will she host a big party in her home? In the years before she left Philadelphia, she always had parties to attend with some of her questionable, if not colorful, friends. Maybe she's not that social any longer. Like me, she's getting older and perhaps slower.

Of course, I read your columns. I wish you hadn't gone with Vangie to visit her friend who's in jail. I'm sure you heard and saw things you'll always remember, even when you'll want to forget that experience. What was Vangie thinking when she took you with her? I question her judgment.

Do you remember Billy and Edna Ross and their son, James? Your father and I have invited them to come here for dinner tomorrow evening. After we have dessert, we'll play a few rounds of Pokeno. By the way, James asked for you. When I told him you were in Paris, he seemed disappointed. He seems to be enjoying his job at the bank. Edna told me he's been promoted twice since he started working there.

You haven't mentioned your friend Emilie(?) Amalia(?) in your last two letters. Are you still socializing with her?

Take good care of yourself, daughter. And Merry Christmas to you!

Fondly,
Mother

Chapter Forty-two

Vangie approached the large table in the living room where I'd spread out a map of France.

"I'm sorry I have to work tonight, Vera. Christmas and New Years Eve are two of the busiest nights of the year for restaurants and clubs. My offer still stands, though. You're free to come with me and help behind the bar, or just enjoy one of my special holiday concoctions along with the music. You might even meet someone interesting. You never know."

"Thanks. I think I'll stay right here."

I pretended I hadn't heard her remark about meeting someone interesting. According to my limited experiences, I hadn't been interested in anyone I'd met in a bar or a club. Neither in Paris nor in Philadelphia.

"Okay, then. You could go to Midnight Mass with Claudine. She goes to a nearby Catholic church every Christmas Eve, like clockwork. Mind you, she doesn't attend church any other day or night of the year."

I smiled and visualized a part-time pious Claudine bowing her head in prayer.

"I'm not particularly religious, despite my mother's influence," I said.

"Your mother's influence is probably *why* you're not particularly religious, honey."

I grinned. Vangie's unwavering ability to know the many ways in which I was not the model daughter my mother had tried unceasingly to mold always amazed me.

"Are you feeling homesick, sweetheart?"

"Not really."

Vangie's voice dropped a half-octave. "Are you missing Amélie?"

"Same answer. Not really. You can't miss a person you've barely known, especially a person who's made it clear there are things I won't get to know about her."

"I understand how you feel, but at the same time your attraction to each other seemed genuinely strong."

"Well, things aren't always what they seem."

Vangie pointed to the map I'd been examining.

"Are you looking for anyplace in particular?"

"A few towns I'd like to visit."

I used the tip of my pencil to point to Chartres, then to Rouen.

"I don't want to go too far from Paris, but I am curious about other places."

"Chartres is closer than Rouen, but after you've seen the cathedral, it's just another charming little town," explained Vangie. "There's lots more to explore in Rouen. Just like Chartres, there's a huge cathedral you can see from miles away. But unlike Chartres, it's the birthplace of Joan of Arc. There's a monument dedicated to her memory in a public square that used to be the town's marketplace. Unfortunately, it's the spot where they burned her at the stake."

I squinted.

"The idea of setting up a vegetable and fruit market in a place where a human being was burned at the stake seems horrendous. On the other hand, I'm a student of history, especially history that concerns women."

Vangie seemed thoughtful. "I have a friend who lives near Rouen. Last July we planned to get together to celebrate her birthday. I even bought her a small gift."

"Why didn't you get to see her?"

"She was ill at the time, so we postponed my visit. If you decide to go to Rouen, you could do me a favor and take the gift to her. I promise it won't take any time away from your excursion."

"Sure, I can do that. There's a train that runs from Paris to Normandy. One of its stops is Rouen. Do you think your friend can meet me at the train station?"

"I'll contact her and find out. Thanks, dear heart."

Vangie turned to get her coat from the foyer closet. "Well, I'm off to work."

"Be careful. *Prends garde.*"

"Of course, I'll be careful. I'm not planning to get run over a second time, you know."

Vangie walked toward the front door and blew me a kiss.

"*Joyeux Noël*, Vera."

"*Joyeux Noël, tante* Vangie."

I decided to visit Rouen. Now I had to decide what to do this evening. Write a letter to my parents? Begin writing my next column even though I hadn't figured out a topic?

Tonight was my first Christmas Eve away from home. Perhaps I was a bit homesick after all. Maybe I missed seeing our neighbors' over-decorated porches or smelling the slightly acrid odor of warmed chestnuts in brown paper bags, sold by street vendors who'd set up their stands at the city's busiest intersections.

When I jumped headfirst at the chance to remain in France and write my articles about life here, I must have forgotten the joy of stopping in front of Wanamaker's huge display windows and gazing at their designers' interpretations of how Christmas should appear. Surely, the thunderous sound of the department store's organ recitals had slipped my mind. The boisterous version of "Jingle Bells," that always invited shoppers to sing along, the triumphant chords of "Joy to the World" as they swirled over the heads of people whose gift purchases were encouraged by the swells and ebbs of the music. The soloist's subdued strains as she began singing "Oh, Holy Night" seemed to stop time itself. Of all the Christmas carols in existence, that song was my favorite. Its music and lyrical ascent from gentle piety to commands for subservience always reached down, grabbed my spirit, and flung it upward.

I turned on Claudine's large table-top radio, hoping I'd find a station playing Christmas music. Slowly I rotated the dial and heard a voice speaking English.

"Tune in this evening at ten o'clock to hear the Christmas Eve service broadcast from the American Cathedral here in Paris."

My thoughts turned to Amélie. That's where she planned to be. I wondered if my just diagnosed homesickness and general malaise would persuade me to go there as well. I would sit in the rear section of the cathedral and hope she wouldn't see me there. I'd make no effort to find her among all the other congregants. I would follow the Order of Service and allow its familiarity to comfort me. I'd feel grateful to be in that place. Me... an ambitious colored girl from West

Philadelphia who was fortunate to have an aunt who lived in Paris and welcomed me to stay in her home for a half-year.

I left a note for Vangie and Claudine at the bottom of the staircase because I wanted them to know I'd changed my mind about going to church. Then, I stepped out to the courtyard. The night's cold temperature had penetrated the windowpanes of each apartment I could see. Here and there electric candles shone, framed by the windows' wood mullions. It must have been the cold that gave those small flames a halo-like appearance, as if they were surrounded by an ethereal frost.

When I walked onto the street, my fear there'd be a scarcity of taxis disappeared. I hailed one a half-block away.

"*La Cathédrale Américaine, s'il vous plait*, 23 *Avénue George Cinq.*"

"*Bien sûr, Mademoiselle.*"

The ride from *Rue Clauzel* to the cathedral wasn't long, but on Christmas Eve it was a slow, glaringly bright one. Most of the big restaurants we passed had large signs advertising their respective midnight *Réveillons* celebrations. Some restaurant owners had hired artists to create posters illustrated with bottles of champagne and sumptuous platters of food. The smaller bistros and cafés had festooned menu boards near their entrances. Other businesses were closed of course, but their closure didn't prevent a few from posting signs on their doors or windows. A few signs, printed in bright red, bore the same message.

"*Tout le monde doit croire en Jésus! Soyons un pays des chrétiens!*"

Why should everyone be Christian? Why should everyone believe in Jesus? I asked myself. I'd try to remember these signs and ask Vangie, Bette, and Claudine what they thought about them.

The taxi stopped as close to the cathedral as the slowly moving traffic would allow. I followed a group of worshippers into the church and sat in a pew near the rear. Although I'd chosen a place far from the altar, I could see it clearly. I could see the choir members flanking both sides of the pathway to the altar.

An English-speaking family sat immediately in front of

me. I listened to the mother scold her three children for talking, and I thought it ironic that her voice was louder than their chatter. The smallest of the three children kept turning around to look my way. Each time she turned in her seat, she gave me the once-over. I met her gaze with a smile. The first smile took her by surprise. She turned her little head and faced front very quickly. The next two or three smiles pleased her and she responded by grinning. The two of us were enjoying each other's company immensely, so immensely that the little girl's continuous twisting from front to back undoubtedly made her dizzy. She tumbled right off her tiny share of the pew and landed on the floor. Then, because he'd become as annoyed as his wife had been with their offsprings' failure to adopt adult behavior in church, the father reached down, scooped his child from the floor, and planted her firmly on the pew's hard surface.

I wished I could have patted the child's shoulder and told her all was okay. But I couldn't, or didn't, now that the choir had begun singing "Silent Night." The worshippers nodded their approval as the soloist uttered his final note of the solemn Christmas hymn and the priest began the Mass.

"Almighty God, unto whom all hearts are open..."

I settled in under his voice, as did all three of the children now seated motionlessly in front of me.

"God spoke these words and said: I am the Lord thy God; Thou shalt have none other gods but me..."

Only one God? I thought.

"Thou shalt love the Lord thy God with all thy heart, and with all thy soul, and with all thy mind..."

Is it possible to love with all one's heart, soul, and mind?

"I believe in one God the Father Almighty, Maker of heaven and earth, And of all things visible and invisible... Who for us men and our salvation, came down from heaven... And was crucified also for us under Pontius Pilate; He suffered and was buried..."

I recited this creed from memory and realized I'd always thought of it as a short story or at best, a quickly narrated biography.

"On this most holy of nights, I shall omit a sermon and instead welcome the angelic voices of our choir." The priest traded places with the choirmaster who'd been seated on the left at the end of the choir's bench.

A flurry of trumpets sounded. The organ and then the choir took temporary control of the mass, filling every ear in the sanctuary with gratitude for being able to hear. "Oh Come, Oh Come Emmanuel" followed the last notes of "Oh Little Town of Bethlehem."

The singers' voices stilled and the instruments silenced, the priest continued the service.

"And to all thy People give thy heavenly grace; and especially to this congregation here present; that with meek heart and due reverence, they may hear, and receive thy Holy word..."

I came here to listen to the music and be reminded of the Christmases in my past. Should I receive the Holy Communion? Am I worthy of receiving the wafer and sip of wine if I prefer to love women, not men? I wondered.

"For in the night in which he was betrayed, he took bread; and when he had given thanks, he broke it, and gave it to his disciples, saying, take, eat, this is my Body, which is given for you; Do this in remembrance of me."

This is the part of the service that always reminds me of a play, with everyone invited to have a role. If we've sinned, or trespassed, or not forgiven someone who trespassed against us... If Amélie declared she loved me, and then kept seeing another woman...

An acolyte signaled the worshipers seated ten pews ahead of me to walk to the smaller altar on the left side of the cathedral. There were so many people there, it would take hours to accommodate every worshipper at the main altar. Row by row, men and women left their seats and processed to the left. I followed, knelt on the cushioned stool, and accepted the wafer and wine. Moments after returning to my pew, I heard the priest's voice.

"The Peace of God, which passeth all understanding, keep your hearts and minds in the knowledge and love of God, and of his Son Jesus Christ our Lord: and the Blessings of God Almighty, the Father, the Son, and the Holy Ghost, be amongst you, and remain with you always. Amen."

The choir began to sing once again. Their voices intoned the first lyrics of "Oh Holy Night."

I bowed my head and made no effort to stop my tears. I realized it was the expectation of this moment that had pulled me to this cathedral on this night before Christmas. It was my turn to acknowledge the gratitude I felt for all that I had and to be truthful about the disappointment I continued to feel whenever I thought about Amélie.

I left the church and decided to walk toward the lights of Les Champs-Élysées. Despite the number of churchgoers in front of and behind me, the street was quiet. A peaceful silence had descended upon us, and the air didn't seem as cold as it had been earlier in the evening.

A block short of Paris' widest avenue, I approached a *tête-de-station* and tapped on the window of the first taxi in line.

"Vera, may I please share this taxi with you? We are going to the same address."

I turned toward the sound of Amélie's voice and saw her standing inches away from me.

"Certainly," I said, without a second's hesitation.

After telling the driver our destination, I glanced once or twice at Amélie's silhouette and remained quiet. She did the same despite the driver's attempts to draw us into a conversation. Our silence may have seemed strange to him. Maybe that's why he navigated the taxi along what might have been Paris' most lit-up series of streets. He wanted us to utter our amazement in response to the holiday lights along Les Champs-Élysées, to express our wonderment at seeing the Place de Concorde and the view from there of the Arc de Triomphe behind us. He awaited our verbal swoons when he slowed the taxi's speed and drove around the always-opulent Opéra Garnier. But we rode in complete silence.

We left the taxi at the entrance to the apartments' courtyard and proceeded to walk under the stone tunnel. When we emerged, I saw there were fewer windows illuminated by candles than there had been three hours earlier.

"I suppose people have gone to bed," I said, surprised by the sound of my own voice.

"Why do you suppose that?" Amélie stopped walking, as did I.

"There aren't many candles still lit in windows," I answered.

Amélie turned partially around and faced me. "Vera, I wish I could tell you why I was at L'Aigle Noir that night when you saw me."

"With your other friend?" I asked.

"With another person."

"But not with me. You don't owe me an explanation, Amélie. You're someone I've met along with others during my stay in Paris, that's all."

Amélie shook her head. "No, that's not the complete truth of you and me."

I leveled my gaze and met her eyes. "How would you describe *our* complete truth if you can't tell me *your* complete truth?" I asked.

"I would describe it as a relationship that is struggling to bloom. A relationship that needs care and attention and above all, patience. A love that, given time, can surpass most ordinary relationships."

At that moment, I wanted to believe her. I wanted to overcome the anger I'd felt toward her because I knew the anger for what it was, my armament against my fears.

"How do I know I can trust you?"

"I am asking you to realize there are circumstances unfolding that are far larger than we are. There are perilous circumstances that must be stopped..." Amélie didn't allow herself to finish her sentence. She touched my cheek. "If you cannot risk loving me Vera, I will understand. But you can believe I shall continue to hold you in my heart for a long time and across any borders that separate us."

The writer in me adores the sounds of words, the manner in which they're linked, the images they paint. That night, 24 December, 1937, I listened to the words Amélie spoke so poetically and I quit all attempts to challenge her sincerity.

When we reached the door to my aunt's apartment, Amélie and I faced each other. We kissed and clung together until I felt a teardrop make its way over my cheek.

"Amélie, why are you crying?"

"Because I know there is a way forward for us."

We kissed once again before I turned the key to unlock the door.

"*Joyeux Noël*, Amélie."
"*Joyeux Noël et bonne nuit, ma chère* Vera."

Chapter Forty-three

One cold and damp morning in early January, I accompanied Bette to the front door of her art school. While she was engaged in starting her next piece of art, I planned to go to a café where I'd be able to strike up a conversation with other *café-habitués*. The strangers and I would drink our preferred versions of caffeine and imbibe in France's national pastime…verbally posturing about politics, jazz, books, and foreigners. There were times when these conversations paved the way to a topic for my newspaper column.

A week ago, I heard two men discussing the murder of Serge Bonet. One of the men claimed Serge had been an active member of the *Parti Populaire Français*, France's most fascist, antisemitic political sect. They debated whether Bonet's murder had been planned by the *Parti Social Français*, a rival rightist group with a larger membership. Even though I knew the true details about the crime, the space between my ears sparked with curiosity. Had Serge belonged to either of these groups? Had he been a partisan of those who despised Jews? If that were the case, how could he have entered a relationship with Gérard, a Jewish man?

I glanced at the other customers and noticed a young woman seated at a table with an older gentleman. The man's skin was dark brown. The woman was a much lighter shade of brown. Father and daughter? I thought about my aunt and Bette who represented different races while sharing their love and lives. I remembered my family's history, one that included illegal and legal miscegenation, and once again I reached the same conclusion. Neither color nor religion can extinguish an irrepressible attraction between two human beings. I knew that with certainty the first time I stared into Amélie's eyes.

After Bette's class ended, she always met me in the café and together we'd return to *Rue Clauzel*. I usually filled her ears with things I'd heard from that morning's café group, and she always described the progress she'd made with a painting, or the advice and insight she'd received from one of the instructors. Free from her brother's tyrannical influence, Bette continued to experience the heady thrill of liberation whenever she walked through the school's front door and realized there was no need for her to look around to see if he were following her.

One morning, as we arrived at the school, Bette hesitated to climb the steps and enter the building.

"Is there something wrong, Bette?" I asked.

"No. But for a moment, I thought we were being followed."

"It couldn't be Hervé," I said.

"It wasn't always my brother. I am convinced he had some of his friends lurking behind me,"

"But why would he do that? Why would he spy on you?" I still didn't understand her brother's reasons for interfering with her desire to paint.

"He wanted me to be under his control, I suppose."

"Bette? Bette Moune? Is it you?"

A voice, somewhat out of breath, called our attention to a tall, well-dressed older man walking toward us.

"*Monsieur Brouillard*!" Bette was visibly surprised to see this man.

"*Vous allez bien*?" he asked.

"*Oui! Très bien*! Vera, please meet *Monsieur* Brouillard. He is a well-known art dealer."

The man inclined his head as he looked at me. "*Enchanté, Mademoiselle*." He smiled and pointed to the building facing us.

"You are taking classes here?"

"Yes."

Monsieur Brouillard frowned. "I am surprised to learn this. Each canvas you've painted recently has been a continuation of your devotion to classic art."

Bette seemed confused. "But I have painted only abstracts for the past six months."

"Perhaps I am mistaken. Just yesterday your brother came to my gallery with three new paintings of yours. One was a pastoral scene and the other two were portraits of children. He said you were eager to sell them and you knew you could depend upon me to find the best buyers."

"I do not know the origin of those canvasses, *Monsieur* Brouillard, but I can assure you I didn't paint them."

The art dealer's eyes narrowed before they displayed a spark of recognition.

"I am so sorry if I have made a mistake, *Mademoiselle* Moune. Perhaps I have misunderstood what your brother told me."

"There is no need to apologize, *Monsieur*. I am certain you understood everything my brother said to you. Did you accept the consignments?"

"No. In fact, I became concerned that one of two situations was at play. Either your talent might be lessening because the paintings did not represent your best work, or your brother had hired someone to create imitations of your work."

Bette's shoulders sagged.

"I am glad you rejected them, *Monsieur* Brouillard. They weren't my work at all."

"If I could say one more thing." The art dealer cast a glance my way before looking again at Bette. "After your brother was wounded and the other gentleman was killed, rumors became rife that Hervé was a victim of a political feud."

"Don't miss the beginning of your class, Bette." That was the only thing I could think to say that would ease both the art dealer and Bette out of an awkward conversation.

"Your friend is right, *Mademoiselle* Moune." Brouillard began stepping away. "But I feel compelled to mention to you how important it is to maintain your good reputation with the art dealers' community. Another dealer and I had the same strange experience with Hervé. It was about a month ago. Hervé entered my gallery and he was not alone. He was accompanied by a stocky, somewhat quiet man who uttered only one question."

"What was the question?" asked Bette.

"He wanted to know if I was a Jew. He said he knew my maternal grandfather had been Jewish and my grandmother had been Catholic."

"What was your answer?"

"I told him yes, although I am not a very faithful Jew. I go to synagogue only once or twice a year…"

"What did my brother say?"

"Hervé said nothing. He just exchanged a nod with his companion."

"*Monsieur* Brouillard, I cannot explain my brother's behaviors. I am sorry if he and this other man made you feel uncomfortable."

"You are not your brother's keeper." The art dealer smiled politely.

"I am glad to have seen you, *Monsieur*."

"As am I."

Brouillard's figure faded away like a patch of fog lifting when it encounters the sunlight.

I looked at Bette and wondered about her unspoken thoughts. "You know where you can find me when your class ends, right?"

"*Oui*, Vera. I know where you will be."

Chapter Forty-four

The early morning train arrived in Rouen one-and-a-half hours after it left Paris' Gare du Nord. I felt my handbag to make sure I still had the small box Vangie had given to me for her friend, Régine Dépestre. Careful to avoid creasing the box's green gift wrap, I held my handbag close as I stepped off the train.

I peered the length of the platform and saw little else other than the backs of other travelers who were walking toward the station's enclosure. Then, I noticed a woman, the very replica of the person Vangie had described, waving her hand in my direction.

A gray-blue and burgundy tweed coat covered the woman's small frame. A black and blue silk scarf filled the space between the coat's top button and the woman's chin.

I waved as I made my way to her. The more I closed the distance between us, the more I noticed how attractive she was. Even if she'd not been stylishly dressed, her appearance would have drawn the attention of men and women alike.

"*Bonjour*! You are Vera, Vangie's niece from Philadelphia?" she asked.

"Yes."

"Your aunt described you, but she did not tell me how pretty you are."

I blushed and thought, nor did she mention how beautiful *you* are. For a second, I wondered if this woman and Vangie had been more than good friends.

"Aunt Vangie is very private. I'm surprised she told you she had a niece," I said.

"Oh yes. Vangie has mentioned you to me many times. She is very proud of you."

Grasping for a reply, I remembered the box I'd brought with me. I took it out of my handbag and offered it to *Madame* Dépestre.

"This is your birthday gift from Vangie. She asked me to say how much she regretted not seeing you in July, but she knew you'd appreciate receiving it now." I blinked and felt relieved to hand her the parcel as well as deliver Vangie's message verbatim.

"*Oh, c'est très gentil à* Vangie *et aussi à vous. Merci,* Vera."

I watched her place the little box inside her coat pocket.

"I know you are visiting Rouen for only one day, and you wish to see as much as possible, right?" she asked.

"Yes."

"If I had more time, I would be your guide. But I have an appointment I cannot miss."

"That's fine. I'm used to exploring new places on my own. Just point me in the right direction," I said.

Although that was true, however much I valued my willingness to traipse independently through new territories, I didn't want to explore by myself forever.

Régine led us past the station's ticket booths and out to the street before she turned and pointed toward an area behind us.

"The main street is in that direction, just five minutes from here. It is called the *Rue du Gros Horloge*. Soon after you are there, be sure to look up to see the huge astronomical clock. It's atop a structure that looks like an overhead bridge. And of course, you will want to see the Rouen Cathedral and perhaps our Beaux-Arts Museum."

"And the site of Jean d'Arc's execution." I added.

"You would not be the niece of Evangeline if you did not desire to visit la Place du Vieux Marché and pay your respects to our national heroine."

Régine's broad smile was one of approval. The polite silence accompanying it was her way of taking leave.

"Thank you for delivering my gift, Vera. Please hug Vangie for me and keep yourself safe and well. *Amusez-vous bien!*"

We stepped away from one another and I began my self-guided tour of Rouen, or at least a small part of the city. Right away I saw a pole with six placards affixed to it. Each placard was shaped like a broad arrow and bore the name of a street. I followed the one labeled *Rue du Gros Horloge.*

Despite the day's cold, the town's narrow streets were crowded with pedestrians. The stores I passed were filled with customers, and the outdoor cafés weren't suffering a lack of hungry or thirsty people. Many of the buildings were half-timbered, a style I'd come to learn was a gift from the Normans who inhabited much of Northen France during the ninth and tenth centuries. The buildings reminded me of those I'd seen in Les Andelys. That memory transported me to Amélie. How much I might have enjoyed walking through Rouen today with her at my side. Clearly, my hurt and angry feelings were behind me. They had dissipated like a wake fanning itself into invisibility over the surface of the sea.

Rouen's cathedral overwhelmed me with all of its Gothic splendor. I explored its interior which felt even colder than the weather outside. A moment of warmth arrived in the form of a dozen children whose high-pitched giggles were a welcome counterpoint to the gray stone walls of the church. In preparation for their first Holy Communion, each child carried a large sheet of paper that may have been a script for the big day. An adult followed them, his voice bellowing one name after another.

"Antoine!"

"Sylvie! *Silence!*"

"Marcel! *Taissez-vous*"

Unlike Antoine, Sylvie, and Marcel, I could not have been quieter. Nor hungrier. I found my way to the cathedral's exit and back to the large square in front of it. It didn't take long for me to spot a café on the other side of the square.

I walked past the vacant tables congregated in front of the restaurant and entered. A waiter smiled and pointed to a table that faced a large window. Viewing the cathedral from there, accompanied by a bowl of hot soup and several pieces of recently baked bread, was so much better than standing inside the bone-chilling structure. Once again, I scanned the building from the top of its tallest spire to the figures carved from stone and the huge doors that by now had admitted countless people to its interior.

I saw two people, a woman and a man, standing to the left of the cathedral's center door. They exchanged the cheek-to-cheek greeting and began conversing. Were it not for the inexplicable sensation of familiarity I felt, I wouldn't have continued to look at them. I dismissed the man, but not the woman.

She wore a gray-blue and burgundy tweed coat. A black and blue scarf covered her throat. In less than a second, she withdrew a green-covered box from one of her coat's pockets and placed it in the man's hand, where it ceased to be visible.

I watched the man incline his head toward the woman and then step away. After a few seconds, the woman turned to her right and left also.

I kept staring at the spot to the left of the cathedral's center door. By now my soup was tepid, but my curiosity was afire. Why had Régine Dépestre given her birthday gift from Vangie to this man? That question remained with me far longer than anything else I saw or heard that day. And that includes the conversation I shared with the U.S. Army veteran during the train ride back to Paris.

I had seen him standing on the platform and noticed him right away. He was a Negro. I don't mean to infer that I was the only person who noticed him, nor that the other passengers were color blind. It was my realization that whenever my field trips took me outside of Paris, I didn't see many people who looked like me.

"You're an American girl, aren't you?" he asked shortly after occupying the seat next to me.

I nodded.

"How can you tell?

"Oh, just something about the way you walk. And I noticed before the train arrived you kept looking around, like you were checking the signs and the track number to make sure you were in the right place."

"I was trying to memorize how the station looked and how many people were headed to Paris at this time of day. I'm a writer. Details are important," I said.

"What kinds of things do you write, if I'm not being too nosy."

"So far, just newspaper articles. I have a column I write for a Negro newspaper, *The Philadelphia Sentinel*."

"Oh yeah? What's your name?"

"It's Vera Clay. My column is titled, 'From the Other Side of the Pond.'"

"I'll be sure to look for a copy of your newspaper the next time I'm near a newsstand that sells U.S. papers." After a brief pause during which he seemed to measure my words, he continued. "So, do you write about France for the folks back home?"

"For the most part, I describe my opinions of France and French people. I also write about what's going on here."

"You mean in Europe generally or in France in particular?"

"Both, I suppose. It's hard to turn a blind eye and a deaf ear to some things," I said.

"I know what you mean." He glanced at the passengers who sat closest to us and lowered his voice. "Excuse my language, young lady. But the shit's going to hit the fan one of these days. I'd planned to stay here indefinitely because I've been treated so well. But now, I'm starting to think the best thing for me to do is go back home to Chicago while I can still remember how to deal with Charlie's foot on my neck."

Had it been physically possible, the color seemed to drain from his face.

"It's not just the Jews who need to be afraid. It's anybody who's not blond and blue-eyed," he added.

We rode along in silence until the train slowed to a stop at a station named Pinterville.

"This is where I get off, Miss. You take care of yourself and I'll look for your newspaper the next time I'm in Paris."

"Thanks. You take care of yourself, also."

I pressed my back into the seat and reflected on the conversation I'd shared with the ex-G.I.. It seemed a fitting way to conclude my one-day trip to Rouen. Of all the sites I'd seen there, including where Joan of Arc met her fiery end centuries ago, the strangest and most memorable sight I'd witnessed was that of Régine Dépestre surreptitiously handing the little box that held her birthday present to an unknown man.

Chapter Forty-five

Bette spoke to the three men she'd hired to move her canvasses from her former studio at the rear of the home she'd shared with her brother to the new space she'd rented in Montmartre.

"It is on *Rue des Trois Frères*, number 92. Look for a narrow building with a green door."

"*Oui, Madame.*"

"The owner has the key. He is in number 90 , and he will be expecting your arrival."

"That is far more than I have been expecting, dear sister." Hervé's booming voice was filled with sarcasm. He dismissed the movers with a curt nod and closed in on Bette.

"I did not expect to see you, Hervé." Bette held her ground.

"That is obvious."

Hervé turned around and gestured toward the studio's empty space.

"Were you not going to drop the smallest hint about vacating your lair? After all, I have never charged you rent. Your new landlord will expect quite a few *francs* from you."

"But I *did* pay a price to live here, Hervé. A price our parents would not have wanted me to pay."

"Do you think they would have wanted you to live so sinfully with that American Negro woman who works behind a bar in a nightclub owned by another American Negro?"

"Probably not right away. But they would have approved once they came to know Evangeline and saw her character far exceeded yours, dear brother."

Hervé's cheeks became crimson.

"And do you believe they would have approved of your hiring someone to imitate my artistic style and then trying to sell those imitations as if I had painted them? Would they have been proud of their son and his criminal acts?"

His temper out of control, Hervé swung the back of his hand forcefully into the side of Bette's face. Energized by the violent contact, he folded his fingers inward toward the palm of his hand, reared his arm backwards and charged his fist forward with a speed that surprised Bette and a fury that sent her careening onto the floor.

"*Lèves-toi*! Stand up!" he commanded.

Bette forced herself to get back on her feet and face her brother.

"Do you think our parents would have approved of your striking your sister, Hervé?"

He answered by spitting on the floor. Then, he turned his back and walked out of the empty art studio.

Bette touched her cheek and jaw before she closed the studio's door behind her. As she walked toward the street to hail a taxi, she realized she felt pain traveling from her right knee up to her hip. Her right arm felt the strain of trying to break her fall in the seconds following the closed-fist assault of her face.

For every block the taxi conquered, Bette invented a different story to tell Vangie, a series of fictions to explain the swellings and bruises that had formed already. By the time she saw her lover, she simply conceded by telling the truth and praying Vangie would not chase after vengeance.

Hervé was not worth it.

Chapter Forty-six

By the time I arrived at *Rue Clauzel* from the Gare du Nord, the apartment buildings' courtyard was swathed in darkness. I looked toward my adopted home and saw light shining through the kitchen window.

Good, I thought. My midday meal of soup was long gone and I was hungry for one of Claudine's dinners. I unlocked the door and walked in. Before I reached the foyer closet, I heard Vangie's voice. It was triple its usual volume.

"I love you, Bette. How can I ignore your bruises and pain? Your brother has crossed the line this time. He's going to answer to me."

I stood still, awaiting the next words from Vangie or from Bette. Suddenly, I felt a hand touch my shoulder.

"Vera, shush. Come with me."

Claudine tugged on my arm and guided me away from Vangie's angry ranting.

"When Bette came home after moving her art supplies to her new studio, one side of her face was red and swollen," whispered Claudine. "Vangie demanded to know what happened. She followed Bette upstairs and they went into Vangie's bedroom. They must have discovered Bette had more injuries, because I heard Vangie yelling about Bette's arm, leg and the left side of her back."

"Oh, Lord! What happened?"

"It gets worse, Vera. Bette said her brother slapped and punched her during an argument. Now Vangie wants to confront Hervé. Nothing good will result if Vangie crosses his path."

I knew Claudine was right. Vangie was always warm and charming, but if someone harmed her or someone she loved, woe unto that person.

"Is Vangie going to work tonight?" I asked.

"She called her boss and told him she would be late."

"What should we do, Claudine?"

"We should let them get through this without interfering."

Once again, I knew Claudine was right. Vangie needed time to calm down and think logically, and Bette needed a chance to tend to her wounds, the physical ones first, the emotional ones in time.

It was clear dinner would wait until the storm on *Rue Clauzel* settled. I retreated to my bedroom and decided to open the mail I saw on my desk. The first envelope's return address was a familiar one.

The Philadelphia Sentinel
1600 Mt. Vernon Street
Philadelphia, 22, Penna.

Greetings Miss Clay,

This is a short note of congratulations to you regarding your last column. I always enjoy reading your articles because they're enlightening to someone who has never travelled abroad. I especially appreciated your last piece, "The International Habit That Must End."

On a different topic, we have received requests for you to write about a few of the Negro ex-patriots who live in Paris or its environs. Perhaps you've become acquainted with them. Those of us who are stateside are curious about the everyday lives of people such as Josephine Baker (whom you once saw walking along the street,) Ada "Bricktop" Smith, and the prize fighter, Jack Johnson. The newspaper will gladly furnish you with a letter of introduction if that will pave the way for any of these interviews.

Take care. Thank you for your series of interesting articles.

Sincerely,
Barbara Green, Assistant Editor, The Philadelphia Sentinel

I smiled and considered Miss Green's suggestion. My columns about the prevailing political events were important to me, but I deserved to steer my writing in different directions now and then.

I picked up the next piece of mail and opened it slowly. I never knew what to expect when I recognized my mother's handwriting on the envelope. Whatever she'd written couldn't be any more dramatic than the scene occurring between Vangie and Bette.

February 17, 1938

Dear Vera,

I hope this letter arrives as soon as possible. I paid extra postage in order for it to get there quickly!

Your father is extremely ill. That cough he had before Christmas has returned. This time, when he coughs, he also spits a lot of phlegm and the phlegm is often tinged with blood. He's tried to hide his bloody handkerchiefs from me, but when I found them in the trash, I insisted he see Dr. Harris right away. That was last Thursday. Dr. Harris sent him to the hospital and ordered x-rays. Yesterday morning the doctor called and said he wanted to see both of us in his office. He gave us bad news, Vera.

Your father's lungs are gravely damaged. The doctor thinks the damage is the result of spending his childhood in West Virginia near the coal mines. Do you remember your grandfather? He was a hardworking miner. Your father says he can't recall ever seeing him without soot covering his clothes. From the tips of his shoes to the tops of his caps, he was always encased in coal soot. Your father swears he didn't know the real color of his father's face until the day he put on his only suit to attend your grandmother's funeral. The doctor thinks all the soot in the house probably caused your grandmother's dying of what they called consumption. And there's little doubt that it gave your father's illness a head start. That and his pipe smoking and cigarette habit.

When your father asked Dr. Harris how much time he had left, the doctor said he really didn't know. But as soon as your father turned away, the doctor looked at me and shook his head. When he walked us to his office door, he whispered in my ear, "It won't be long, Ethel." It was all I could do to keep from crying while we stood on the cold street corner and waited for the trolley to come.

I don't know what I'm going to do when he passes, Vera. You have always been his life, and he and you are my life.

Please come home as soon as you can.

Mother

I read the letter again, not because I didn't trust my eyes, but because I didn't want to believe my mother's words. I stood and went downstairs. Mercifully, all was quiet. Stopping at the telephone alcove in the foyer, I did the only thing I knew to do. I called Amélie to tell her my sad news and ask if we would be able to see each other before I left Paris.

Chapter Forty-seven

The Philadelphia Sentinel
1600 Mt. Vernon Street
Phila., 22 Pennsylvania

February 20, 1938

Greetings Charles,

I hope you are well and that everything is going gang-busters at L'Aigle Noir. Your clientele doesn't know how lucky they are to have a club like yours they can patronize. I'm certain the drinks and the jazz flow generously.

I'm thanking you yet again for interceding in an effort to renew Vera Clay's travel visa last November. I am pleased with the quality of her work and my newspaper's readers absolutely *love* reading her column. In fact, the paper's readership numbers have increased recently, no doubt due to her articles. Subscriptions are up! The Pullman Porters' organization has informed me they're receiving more and more requests for the paper when the trains pull into certain stations.

Miss Clay's current visa expires at the end of March. Would you be able once again to assist her with the proper paperwork to renew said document? Just let me know about any expenses you incur during the process. Also, please tell me how much time you spend accomplishing this task. Time is money, my friend, and I value your time and expertise greatly.

Your friend and fellow WWI veteran,
Herman Scott, Editor-in-Chief

March 1, 1938

Hello Herman,

It was good to hear from you. Things are going okay here, except for the price of liquor. It keeps going up. I need to expand my circle of *friends* in order to negotiate better prices.

Two of my regular Friday patrons might be able to help me. They're German businessmen who are working here in Paris. I still speak some German, so I usually engage them in a bit of conversation whenever they're here. For the price of a couple shots of schnapps, I hear some interesting information when we talk.

Lately, they've been discussing the French armament factories, comparing them to those in *Deutschland*. Whenever they mention how advanced their military fighter planes are compared to France's, I really sit up and pay attention. One evening, I asked for their opinions of Great Britain's Air Corps. They sneered. One of them said, "We would destroy those planes before they became airborne."

Who knows if that was the truth or the liquor talking?

Last Friday night I heard them mention Poland. Unless my German vocabulary has gone south, I believe one of them said Poland would belong to Hitler by the end of this year.

This brings me to the point of my response to your request. I could easily get another visa for Vera Clay. I could even get two more, allowing her to remain here until the end of September. But right now, I don't think extending Vera's permission to stay in France is a good idea. It's a bad one. I've suggested to her aunt, the best barman I've ever hired, that she should plan to return to the U.S. also.

Poland will not be a large enough conquest for Hitler. I think he intends to invade as much of Europe as he can. Certainly, France and probably England. It goes without saying that this is only my opinion.

Vera, her Aunt Vangie, and many others, especially Jews, Romani, and homosexuals should not be here when that happens. Hell, I shouldn't be here. We colored people are going to be victims just like the others I've mentioned.

So, tell me, my fellow trench-hugger. Should I risk staying here, or return to the U.S. where I'll always be boy? It's hard for me to decide.

Your WWI buddy,
Charlie Willard

Chapter Forty-eight

Armed with the assumption that the person knocking on his door was his sister's lover, a swaggering Hervé went to answer the summons.

On the other side of the door stood a man wearing a well-tailored suit. He was accompanied by two uniformed police officers.

"You are Hervé Moune?"

"Yes, I am Hervé Moune." *My sister probably reported me for striking her. Stupid cow!* he thought.

"I am Commandant Christophe of the Paris *Préfecture de Police.*"

"Come in," said Hervé.

As soon as the three men stepped into the foyer, Commandant Christophe began to speak. His quickly delivered recitation passed by Hervé's ears, leaving scant time for him to grasp the true meaning of the speeding words.

"On July 5, 1937, you entered an oral agreement with a person named Roland Gaspard. This agreement resulted in *Monsieur* Gaspard borrowing an automobile and using it the evening of July 16 to run over and attempt to kill, if not seriously injure one Evangeline Curtis. Your agreement involved you paying *Monsieur* Gaspard a sum of money to perform said deed. Do I have all of the facts correct, *Monsieur* Moune?"

Hervé didn't answer.

"I am arresting you for the crimes of plotting, paying a sum of money, and soliciting assistance to perform an illegal act, an attempt to murder a person named Evangeline Curtis. You must come with us, *Monsieur* Moune."

Chapter Forty-nine

Charles Willard succeeded in getting a one-way steamship ticket for me without my having to go to the steamship company's office on *Rue des Mathurins*. Mr. Willard offered to buy a two-way ticket for Vangie as well.

Vangie thanked him for his effort but turned down his offer. She'd been notified by The Paris *Préfecture de Police* about Hervé Moune's arrest and told she would have to be present in court the first day of the trial. It was scheduled the same day as my departure.

"I wish I could ride to Boulogne-sur-Mer with you, honey," she said as she perused my ticket.

"I wish that too, but being in court is more important."

"I know I shouldn't call Bette's brother a bastard…"

"But he is one, Vangie. He arranged to have you killed. He used his fist against Bette. I hope you get to see him convicted and sentenced to a long time in jail, maybe for the rest of his life."

I knew serving a life term in prison for attempted murder wasn't a realistic expectation. These days however, I wasn't thinking logically. My emotions held sway over any intellect I had.

"It's too bad Mr. Willard couldn't get you passage on the same ship you sailed on last summer. It takes less time to go from here to Le Havre than to Boulogne."

I agreed. A shorter train ride along with the familiarity of the S.S. Leviathan might have lessened my anxiety about my return trip to Philadelphia. I was not at all comfortable with the prospect of being aboard the S.S. Stuttgart, a ship owned by the North German Lloyd Company. I wanted nothing to do with Germany, but I had to return home as soon as possible. The Stuttgart's route included a stop in northern France and from there, on to New York City. It was my only option and it was scheduled to sail in less than forty-eight hours.

"I'm glad Amélie is going on the train with you to Boulogne-sur-Mer."

"I am, too." I wanted to say more about Amélie and me,

but to do so would bring me close to tears.

Vangie reached out and rested her hand on my shoulder.

"You and she are going to miss each other… a whole lot," she said.

I nodded my silent response.

"I know you'll write letters back and forth and keep the U.S. and French postal systems very busy."

Again, I nodded. I'd already spent time mentally composing my first letter to Amélie.

The morning of my departure was uncharacteristically sunny, but the day's brightness did nothing to lighten my mood. Nor did it bring any joy to Amélie who met me at Paris' Gare du Nord.

The train ride from there to the Boulogne-Maritime rail station sped by too quickly. We sat as close to each other as we dared. The swaying motion of the train kept our shoulders pressed together while we spoke in hushed tones and made promises for a future we hoped would happen, no matter what occurred. Amélie draped her jacket across her lap and right hand, giving our entwined fingers cover from the passengers seated near us, strangers who no doubt perceived our feelings for each other.

When the train reached its destination, we gathered my two suitcases and walked reluctantly to the customs and steamship terminal. Once we were inside, I stopped abruptly.

"Amélie, I forgot to return your mother's typewriter! Please apologize to her for me."

"*Ne t'inquiètes.* Don't worry, my love. You will return soon and continue to use the typewriter. It will already be where it belongs, on the desk in your bedroom."

I looked ahead at the line of passengers burdened with suitcases and steamer trunks. Amélie must have noticed the crowd also, because she hesitated to move forward. We turned toward each other.

"Vera, I need to tell you something important before you leave me."

She took me into her embrace and whispered in my ear. "I belong to a group of French loyalists. We are resisting the take-over by Hitler. My job is to gather information. That is what I was doing the night you saw me at L'Aigle Noir. The woman who was with me is a Nazi collaborator."

Amélie ended the embrace and smiled as if she'd just wished me a bon voyage. I hope I returned the smile with one of my own, but I was too stunned to remember.

"Travel safely, *ma chère*. I love you."

"And I love you, Amélie."

I watched Amélie turn and walk away. Determined to keep her in my sight until she left the building, I wanted to memorize as much about her as I could. I noted how quickly she strode toward the exit, how her jacket defined the set of her shoulders, how her boyish haircut obscured the femininity her soft mouth always suggested. I saw her turn around and look for me when she arrived at the building's exit. I watched as she wiped away tears that had escaped from her eyes and coursed a path to her lips. Clearly, Amélie had failed to hide her feelings about us, and for that I was grateful.

That night, the first of five I spent in a shared cabin aboard the S.S. Stuttgart, sleep eluded me. I took pen and paper and wrote the first of many letters I would write to Amélie. My mind remained filled with thoughts about leaving Paris, my Aunt Vangie, Claudine, Bette, *Madame* Blum, Amélie, and the spacious, old apartment on *Rue Clauzel*.

Chapter Fifty

March 10, 1938

Dear Amélie,

This will be more a note to you than a letter. As you know, my father's funeral is tomorrow. I expect the church will be crowded even though many of his friends have already come by the house to pay their respects. The service will be short and dignified, as per my mother's wishes. We'll have a repast here at home after the burial.

I'm glad I had a chance to talk with my father before he passed away. I was able to express my feelings of gratitude for everything he did for me. Even though he was weak and kept his eyes closed most of the time, he heard my voice. Whenever I touched his hand, he tried to squeeze mine. He was always my defender and I shall miss him greatly.

I miss you terribly, Amélie. I wish I knew when we'd see each other again. Right now, I must be here to help my mother.

With much love,
Vera

Le 17 mars, 1938

Ma chère Vera,

I wish I could have been by your side during your father's funeral. We are both in a state of missing, *n'est-ce pas?* I miss you and the gentle way you go about your life. I miss seeing your Aunt Vangie once a week, when I would use visiting my mother as an excuse to see you, first only in passing and then by design. I miss hearing your questions about Paris and French culture, and then feeling surprised when I would realize I had never really thought about my city and my culture.

I read a news article about the construction of underground shelters throughout Paris. The city does not have enough laborers to do this type of work, so the municipal government has requested help from the military. They have also conscripted prisoners from a couple of the jails. When I read this news, I thought about Vangie's friend, Gérard Simonet. I wondered if he was spending his days digging shelters and installing brick walls. Probably not. The prisoners who are doing this work have committed small crimes, not murder.

I have made one final appeal to my mother to consider leaving France. She insists upon remaining here, no matter what happens. I have told her all that I know about our country's southern regions and their apparent willingness to separate and exist under a different leader, Maréchal Pétain. She receives this information by clicking her tongue and waving me aside. I do not know what else I can do. This situation grieves me.

Dearest Vera, let us hope our separation will be brief. I miss the very sight of you.

Avec tout mon amour,
Amélie

March 17, 1938

Paris, *9ième* France

My Dear Niece,

I am truly sad about your father's passing. Thank the Lord you arrived home when you did, in time to see and talk to him before he died. He was a good man and he loved you and your mother very much. They had a long and loving marriage. You're the proof of their union.

You've said you're anxious to return to Paris and of course to your Amélie as well. But I imagine your mother will need your presence and help for a while yet. She'll have to make some decisions and she'll need your advice. Then, there's the matter of settling your father's final business details. Your mother has always made quick decisions before she's sorted out all their possible ramifications. She's allowed her emotions to play a big role in everything. This is where you can help her the most. You can see past the fog of your mother's present sadness and question, respectfully of course, the course she's on if it doesn't seem to be the best.

I miss you very much, but I can't be selfish. Right now, and for the next few months you should stay in Philadelphia with your mother. I assure you there will be other spring times in Paris.

You asked about Hervé Moune's trial and my part in it. The first day I went to court, (the day that you left here,) I sat there and listened to the list of crimes he was accused of. I didn't understand everything that was said, but I understood enough to know he was in a world of trouble. When he pleaded not guilty, it was hard for me to keep quiet.

The next few days of the trial were more interesting. I had to testify in front of three judges and nine jurors. My testimony was short because there wasn't much I could say about the assault itself. It happened so quickly and out of the blue. I couldn't recall what transpired after I left the club that night. Unfortunately, Gérard, the only witness, was not permitted to attend the trial because he's now a convicted felon and he's in prison. He did write a statement describing what he'd seen and the prosecuting lawyer read it aloud. The prosecutor told me he'd try to minimize his questions about my relationship with Bette, but he'd need to introduce it because it played a role in Hervé's motive for trying to kill me. I told him I wasn't ashamed of being with Bette, so his or any other court official's questions wouldn't embarrass me one bit.

On the last day of the trial, the prosecuting attorney switched his questions from how, when, and why Hervé put his criminal plans in motion to how, when, where, and why he spends a lot of time meeting with a certain political group. The prosecutor's questions laid out every detail he knew about this political group's activities. When the people in the courtroom heard all of this, they began to mumble among themselves. The mumbles grew louder and then Hervé's advocate spoke up and appealed to the judges to stop questions about Hervé's political activities. One of the three judges told the jurors they shouldn't pay any attention to the past few questions they'd heard. I paid attention though. And so did Bette.

The jurors deliberated until late in the afternoon when they returned to the courtroom and announced their verdict. Guilty! The judges wanted to confer and said they'd announce Hervé's sentence the next day. They've done just that. Hervé was sentenced to a prison term of twenty years.

Bette and I wondered where her brother will serve his time. Will it be in La Santé, the prison that houses Gérard?

One more thing, sweetheart… You wrote that Amélie shared something of importance with you before the two of you parted in Boulogne-sur-Mer. I suspect I know what she told you. Moreover, I would expect nothing less of her than what she's doing. She is a good person. She is *your* good person, Vera.

With affection,
Vangie

June 5, 1938

Dear Bette,

I feel I owe you a letter, as I'm always writing to Aunt Vangie. I hope she shares my letters with you. I stay busy here writing my column and helping my mother with the details of my father's will. Anytime she has to fill out papers related to his passing away, she has to send a copy of his death certificate. I go with her to Philadelphia's City Hall where his certificate is on file. The task isn't difficult, but it is time consuming.

Over the years Vangie has probably talked to you about my mother. Of course, Vangie is my mother's sister. Their sibling relationship differs greatly from my daughter-mother relationship. Vangie's relationship with me is far different than my mother's relationship with me. For as long as I can remember, Vangie has been my source of affection and approval. My mother has been my source of rules and standards. Perhaps I am lucky to have had both.

How are you doing with your painting? Is contemporary art still your focus? How do you like your new studio space in Montmartre? When I return to Paris, from time to time I'd like to accompany you to your weekly painting class in Montparnasse. I miss the talks we used to have going to and returning from your art school and at the café also.

The larger U.S. newspapers, like the *New York Times* and the *Washington Post*, are finally running stories about political events in Europe and *the demon in Berlin*. Assuming their sources are genuine, things seem to be worsening.

This brings me to an important question.

Is Vangie still opposed to coming back to the U.S.? I hope she'll have a change of heart, and if she does, I know she'll bring you with her.

Bisous,
Vera

19 *juin*, 1938
Paris, *9ième* France

Chère Vera,

Merci pour ta lettre.
You are correct in saying the situation with Germany is becoming worse. Violent acts against Jewish people are becoming more frequent, even here in France. We suspect some of the violence has been committed by members of the political group to which my brother belonged. I should say belongs because the group exists in the prisons, also. Quite frequently, inmates are found in their cells badly beaten, or worse. Not only Jewish prisoners, but Negro inmates as well. The hateful swastika appears painted on walls in more and more places.

Vangie is determined to remain here in Paris. I shall stay with her.

Your Amélie has failed to convince her mother to leave. I have witnessed her offering to take *Madame* Blum to England, but to no avail.

While Vangie and I understand Amélie's frustration, we sympathize with her mother's desire to stay here. We have sworn to Amélie that we will make sure her mother is safe no matter what happens.

Take the best care of yourself, Vera, and we will do the same.

Bisous,
Bette

Chapter Fifty-two

September 12, 1938

My dear niece,

The next-to-the-worst event has happened and I'm sure you've read about it. Hitler's Nazis have invaded Poland. They've taken it over...the entire country. They did it piece by piece, assault by assault. Then, two nights ago they began what's been called Kristallnacht. They smashed store windows and set fire to Jewish-owned businesses and homes. This, along with their book burning bonfires and random arrests and threats of deportation aimed at those who do not have Polish citizenship, is horrible! It must cease! But how do you stop a depraved tyrant like Hitler? And how do you stop ordinary people from following him?

Amélie's mother asks me these questions each time we see each other, and that's very often. Two months ago, she taught me how to play Mah Jong and then I taught her how to play Pinochle. Now, she loves both games. Every Tuesday evening (my night off from work,) Simone comes over here and we have a game night. A couple of times she's fallen asleep in the midst of a run or during a bit of confusion about her Mah Jong tiles. Bette and I have convinced her to go up to your bedroom and sleep. She leaves early the next morning and then returns with something she's baked for our breakfast. Amélie knows all about this. I believe she's glad about it because she knows her mother is safe with us.

Because you and I were Gérard's only visitors, the commandant of La Santé Prison sent me a letter asking if I wished to witness Gérard's execution. Even though he led the police to Hervé who plotted the attempt to injure or kill me in a hit and run car accident, Gérard received the death sentence for murdering Serge Bonet. I hoped that by now public executions in France would be outlawed. The government plans to make them illegal, but not until 1939. I responded no. I won't be able to watch my young friend meet his maker. The best I can do for him is claim his body and arrange for his burial. According to the present law, the burial must be done without any ceremony, and certainly without any pomp. I have arranged for my young friend to be laid to rest in the Montmartre Cemetery. His grave marker will be small and simple.

Take good care of yourself and your mother, sweetheart.

Love,
Vangie

Chapter Fifty-two

Les Andelys, France
le 12 novembre, 1938

Ma chère Vera,

By now you have read the details of the crimes that occurred in Poland two months ago. The atrocities did not end that night. The German Gestapo chief ordered actions against the Jewish population. More than one thousand synagogues were burned to the ground. Ninety-one Jewish people were killed and thirty-thousand Jewish males were arrested. Probably, they will be taken to concentration camps.

One by one, the Nazis are invading their neighboring countries. It is only a matter of time before they come for France. That is why I have begged my mother to leave here and go to England. That is why I have suggested to your aunt that she and Claudine should leave as well. It is why you cannot return to Paris any time in the near future, my love.

As for me, I plan to continue doing all that I can to help my country. My role is small, but I am told it is significant.

Dearest Vera, when I said *au revoir* to you at the embarkation terminal in Boulogne-sur-Mer, it was my greatest hope that I would go to whatever port your return ship would dock. The hopeful part of me still clings to that dream. My growing pessimism acknowledges the probability of our reunion is becoming hazy.

Je t'aime,
Amélie

November 21, 1938

Ma chère Amélie,

Yes, I know about Kristallnacht. I've just submitted my second article about it to my editor. Kristallnacht. I can't understand how such a poetic sounding word can be used to name such a barbaric series of events. Do you know what became of the Polish student who shot the German diplomat in Paris? If he is still alive and has learned about the horrible consequences of his deed, what is his present state of mind?

I worry constantly about you, your mother, Claudine, Bette, and Vangie. If I could have my way, the five of you would be sailing to the U.S. right now. I know Vangie will not leave France, even in the face of a Nazi invasion. Your mother shows no sign of changing her mind, and I know better than to beg you to leave. I only hope I have the wisdom to truly understand your allegiance to your country and the strength to accept our fates, whatever they may be.

Life goes on as usual for us colored folks in Philadelphia. In an effort to earn more money than I receive from the newspaper, I applied for a teaching position in the city's school district. I have enough credits to earn a state teaching certificate as a high school English instructor. I overlooked one stumbling block. Negroes are not permitted to teach in the city's high schools... only in the elementary schools. It looks like you and I are facing similar situations. Your life is threatened by the approach of Nazis. Mine is restricted by racism's refusal to abate.

I think about you every day and night, and I'll never give up hoping to see you again.

I love you,
Vera

December 10, 1938

Dear Vera,

This will be a short letter because I don't want to be late for work.

Here's what's happening on this side of the pond. Mr. Willard is thinking about starting a new business. L'Aigle Noir is still doing okay, but some nights the club is only half full. A lot of the regulars have dropped off, maybe because some of the musicians have left town. Some have left France altogether. Bricktop's is now closed three nights a week, and the place where I was working before the car *accident*, is closed completely. I feel lucky to be employed.

I see your Amélie at least once a week. She's concerned about her mother, so she tries to visit her more often than she used to. We've had some serious conversations lately. The only time she smiles is when I mention your name, so I try to tell her what you were like when you were a little girl. Actually, those memories make me smile as well.

Amélie's mother spends two or three nights here with us. Simone is afraid, worried, and lonely. Being with Bette, Claudine, and me seems to make her feel better. We have plenty of room here and we never mind her company.

My love paints almost every day, mostly in her studio but some days here. Before the weather turned cold, she set up her easel in different quarters of the courtyard. She was successful in selling a few of her pieces for good prices. But all of a sudden, the buyers disappeared. Her favorite dealer, *Monsieur* Brouillard, advised her to return to classical themes, because few of his patrons were willing to shell out their *francs* for Bette's abstract canvasses.

I have to go now. Try not to worry much about us. We don't hear the storm-troopers' boots on our streets yet. We'll be okay. Say hello to your mother and have sweet dreams of your father.

Your loving aunt,
Vangie

Chapter Fifty-Three

Amélie peered through the sheer curtains covering her bedroom window and saw the headlights of a car parked across the street from her house. The headlights went dark and then bright again, the signal that her transport from Les Andelys to Paris awaited her. She grabbed her suitcase and descended the stairs to the first floor where she paused for only seconds and glanced at the living room. She'd decided some time ago that when this day arrived, she wouldn't feel sorry to leave her home. After all, it was only a building.

She passed the narrow table in the house's entryway and picked up an envelope addressed to Les Andelys' *Commissariat de Police*. She planned to deposit it in post box at the edge of the next town. Within three days her *commandant* would learn that she'd resigned from her job.

"*Salût*, Luc." Amélie put her suitcase in the car's back seat and then slid into the front passenger's seat.

The two rode mostly in silence, passing through small villages as they made their way toward Paris. The darkness kept the countryside between the towns they skirted invisible. And for that, Amélie was grateful. She didn't want to be reminded of the vistas she would miss. The very act of *missing* played too large a role in her life, and it promised to continue for a long time to come.

An hour and a half later, Luc steered his car onto *Rue Clauzel* and stopped at the curb near the familiar apartment buildings.

"*Merci pour tout*, Luc." Amélie got out of the car and opened its back door to gather her suitcase.

Luc slid across the front seat in order to speak to his passenger. "It was my pleasure more than my duty to help you, Amélie." he said. "Take care of yourself, Amélie. *Vive la France!*"

Amélie smiled. "You've been like a brother to me. I appreciate you."

When she walked the familiar path that bifurcated

toward her mother's apartment or led to Vangie's and Claudine's, Amélie noticed dim lights shining through Vangie's windows. She was aware of the women's plans to make alterations to their apartment, and it made sense to construct those changes at night when fewer eyes would be watching.

Amélie turned toward her mother's building. She placed her key in the lock and opened the door quietly. Tiptoeing past her mother's bedroom, she entered the smaller one, kept her clothing on, and stretched out on the single bed. She knew she didn't have the wherewithal to awaken her mother and explain why she'd arrived so late in the night and where she was headed the next day. It would have to wait until morning, perhaps in Vangie's presence. Vangie always knew the right words to calm her mother's worrying.

The next day, there were no right words. Nor was there anyplace for Simone Blum to deposit her panic after Amélie told her she was going to England and she had no idea when she would return to France.

"But what about your job in Les Andelys?"

"I have resigned."

"What about me? How can you leave your mother?"

"I did not want to leave you. But all of these months you have refused to consider going elsewhere. You would not apply for a passport. You worried about the news you heard involving violence against Jews. You decried what occurred in Poland. And now there are few choices left for you."

Simone seemed to ignore her daughter's words of reproach.

"Will you write to me so I know you are safe?"

"Yes, I will write, but I will not be able to say where I am, and I will post my letters far from my location."

"Send the letters to Vangie's address. I stay there more and more frequently."

"I shall do that, *Maman*."

Amélie gently hugged her mother and then took a step back to look at her.

"*Maman*, you have done your best to raise a proud, intelligent daughter. I am doing my best to accomplish what I must. Always remember how much I love you."

Simone's shoulders began to heave. Her lips trembled in their attempt to say good-bye to Amélie.

"You are just like your father. Stubborn. No matter who the stubbornness hurts."

"Some circumstances demand a stubborn response, *Maman*." Amélie knew her conversation with her mother had met its point of diminishing returns. She turned to pick up her suitcase and leave.

"*Au revoir, Maman.*"

As she walked away, Amélie could hear her mother sobbing. The sorrowful sounds filled her ears until she arrived at Vangie's door.

"I am sorry to come here so early," she said. "But I am leaving and I do not have much time."

"Will you be safe? Is anyone helping you?" asked Vangie.

Amélie nodded. "I am not allowed to tell anyone my details, but I feel I must tell you. You have shown my mother so much kindness and you have promised to help her when the time arrives. When I leave here, I am on my way to *Dunkerque*. There, I will board the night train ferry on the return crossing to Dover. An English farmer will meet me at the dock and drive me to a town in Surrey where I will stay with a doctor and his family."

Vangie squinted as if narrowing her eyes would imprint Amélie's route onto her memory.

"Don't worry about your mother. Claudine and I have almost convinced her to sell her apartment and move in here with us."

"I am grateful to you for that." She reached into the breast pocket of her jacket. "I have a letter I have written to Vera, the last one for a while, I fear. Would you post it for me, please?"

"Of course, honey."

"I have written only the address on the envelope, no return information."

"That's understood."

"Your project is going well?" Amélie glanced at the pile of lumber and tools laying on the floor. "The workers are doing a good job?"

"Under the circumstances, fairly well. We'll be glad when they finish and leave. It's hard living with all this mess underfoot, not to mention taking turns staying awake until all hours of the night."

Amélie stepped closer to Vangie and hugged her.

"Thank you, Vangie, for all that you have done for my mother and will do if the worst comes to pass."

Vangie grabbed one of Amélie's hands.

"You and I are engaged in the same grand tasks, ma chère. One of those efforts involves this country's right to remain free, and the other effort is about you, my niece, and your right to have a life together. So, go forward. Go with God and stay safe."

Chapter Fifty-Four

It was January 30th and I hadn't received a letter from Amélie in more than a month. Had something happened to her? Had either France's Poste-Téléphone-Télégraphe system, or the United States Postal Service lost her letters? When I wrote to Aunt Vangie and expressed my worries about the absence of news, she wrote and reassured me everything was fine. She suggested Amélie's job might be keeping her busier than usual because it seemed like crimes against people and property had become more commonplace in the smaller cities and villages as they had in Paris.

"*N'inquietes pas,*" she wrote. "Simone tells me even she hasn't seen much of her daughter for the past few weeks or so."

But I did worry. I worried each time I thought about Amélie, and I thought about her constantly. This evening, when I spotted an envelope bearing the familiar postmark atop the rest of today's mail, I tore it open quickly. But not so quickly that I failed to notice the absence of a return address. Leaving the envelope's upper right hand corner blank was not Amélie's habit. Nor was omitting the date at the top of the letter.

I went into the living room and sat on what had been my father's favorite chair.

To Vera who owns my heart,

I shall not be able to write to you for a while. In fact, I cannot tell you where I am right now. Know that I am safe and well, and in the company of others who are supportive. I have learned bad news about my friend, Luc. You met him the first time you visited me. He was found dead, shot in the head. I have not yet accepted this terrible news about such a good person.

Please be assured that I shall do whatever I must to be

with you, and I shall always be faithful to our love.

A.

February 15, 1939

Dear Aunt Vangie,

The very short letter I've received from Amélie has upset me. She writes that she's safe and not alone, but she cannot tell me <u>where</u> she is. She also writes she won't be able to send me letters for a while. When I add that news to your account of Parisian workers digging trenches that will be used as bomb shelters in some of the city squares, I feel afraid for you, Bette, Claudine, Simone Blum, and everyone who showed me kindness during my stay in Paris. I suppose it's naïve of me to wish the Germans would be satisfied with the destruction they've already wrought. And it's foolish of me to wish people wouldn't hate each other simply because they practice a different religion or have a different skin color.

Although my wishes are childish, my heart loves like an adult. I am fearful for your life and I live in fear of losing Amélie.

With love,
Vera

16 Rue Clauzel
Paris, 9ième France
March 25, 1939

My dearest niece,

I'm sorry you're so worried and I won't deny how sobering it is to know one day we might have to go to a bomb shelter for protection. A week ago, they distributed gas masks to all of us here in our apartments. They showed us how to put them on. It's easy. Of course, Simone was a nervous wreck. Claudine helped her with the mask and told her she should practice with it.

I have to cut this short because I have an interview for a new job. Mr. Willard plans to close his club in July or August, so I thought it would be wise for me to line up something else in plenty of time.

Stay well and say hello to your mother. Is she still annoyed with me because I didn't travel to Philadelphia when your father passed away?

With all my love and a big hug,
Aunt Vangie

P.S. I know you call me Vangie, without the Aunt. That's fine. But sometimes when I remember what a loving, affectionate child you were, always hugging me and asking me questions I couldn't always answer, I feel the need to sign my letters Aunt Vangie.

December 2, 1939

Dear Vera,
It's been 6 months since the Nazis bombed Paris. Fortunately, there wasn't too much damage. Most of the destruction occurred in our minds and spirits. There's a lot of tension in the air. What's missing is the sound of children's voices. Their absence has nothing to do with the cold, damp weather that's upon us. In late August, many parents in Paris joined the effort to evacuate their children from the city to the countryside. How sad it must be to see your kids go away from you while you stay here.

My friend Régine Dépestre came to visit us in mid-August. You remember her from your visit to Rouen, right? She's familiar with the social group that Amélie belongs to, and she'd heard about A.'s leaving France. She'd heard also that A. is well. So, that's good news.

I told Régine that you'd seen her give the box that held her birthday gift to a man near the Rouen Cathedral. She laughed and said, "I never doubted she was your niece, Vangie. But now, I know for sure." She assured me the gift was put to good use, intelligence-wise. Of course, I believe and trust her.

My new job at the lawyer's office doesn't pay as well as my former one at L'Aigle Noir. No tips. But that's okay. I can manage. I'm not on my feet for hours at a time, and I don't have to work on the weekends. Thank the Lord for that. *Monsieur* Arthritis has made himself at home in my injured hip. Damn Hervé Moune and his henchman!

Bette decided not to renew her lease for the art studio in Montmartre. Did I mention someone threw rocks through the windows of several art dealers' establishments? Each place that was vandalized had modern paintings on display. Two of Bette's canvasses were ruined. She has reacted to all of this without much emotion. She'll keep painting, but she's not looking to make money, only to engage in a pastime.

Speaking of art, we've heard a lot of famous paintings and statues have been removed from the Louvre and from private homes and galleries. They've been taken to parts unknown in an effort to protect them from the Nazis. We figure some of the rich Germans with high posts in the Nazi government knew which works were the most valuable and they've already arranged to take possession of them.

Claudine has decided to move back to Bordeaux. She still has family there. I can't tell you how much I'm going to miss her. She's been my best friend and confidante for years. I offered to pay for her share of the apartment, but she said she wouldn't hear of it. We plan to stay in touch with each other no matter what.

Simone has moved in. She sold her apartment and most of her furniture to a family that sold their much larger house and bought another one somewhere on the outskirts of Paris. They plan to use the apartment whenever they're in the city. Can you imagine that? What's it like to have so much money that you can own two homes?

I realize this is a long letter. But, as you're fond of saying, I didn't have time to write a short one. Also, this might be my last one for a while. I've heard rumors that mail headed to the U.S. is sometimes opened and read by clerks who are sympathetic to the Nazis. Some of those letters never arrive at their destinations. I don't want to compromise your or your mother's safety.

I continue to love you and your mother as well, even if she cannot say the same about me. Please remind her that she and I are the only people on earth who know what it was like to grow up in our family.

Keep us in your prayers, my dearest sweet niece. I shall think about you and your Amélie every day that God blesses me with life.

Your Aunt Vangie

Chapter Fifty-Five

The news of June fourteenth, 1940 arrived on my desk at the *Philadelphia Sentinel* before I left work for the day. It was startling, but not a surprise. The precious few one paragraph letters I'd received from my Aunt Vangie prepared me for the announcement.

Hitler's Army had arrived in Paris. France was now under German occupation. What would that mean for the people I loved and left there? What would become of the Jewish people, the colored citizens, the people who like me, loved those of their own gender? What would happen to my aunt, to Bette, to Claudine, to Simone Blum, to their friends and neighbors who were Jewish? What had happened to Amélie?

I thought of her each day and tried to recall every detail of every moment we'd spent together. As the days and months passed, I found it more difficult to remember things I thought I'd never forget. When we stood toe-to-toe, which one of us was shorter than the other? What was it about her voice that I'd found so mesmerizing? Why had her eyes been so disarming any time I'd gazed directly at them? How did her skin look and feel against mine the few times we'd made love to each other? What about her very being had compelled me to be convinced we were destined to be together forever, whatever forever meant?

As I rode the subway and then the el to my West Philadelphia home, I wondered why the other passengers didn't appear to be upset by the latest news from Europe. Was I the only one who had family living in Paris? Even without family living abroad, didn't anyone else realize the consequences for the United States of the invasion of France? What was Hitler's next target, England?

I wanted to scream, *Wake up!* as I stepped off the el, but I knew my cries would do nothing except convince those who heard me to be aware of the crazy woman in their presence. So, I stilled my voice and let my tears of despair speak for me during the two-block walk from the el station to home.

I opened the front door, walked through the vestibule and looked instinctively at the table where today's mail would be. During all of these months of wanting to see a letter from my aunt, Bette, Claudine, or Amélie and not receiving one, I never failed to look for an envelope bearing my address written by one of them. Today's mail included no letters from abroad.

I rested my handbag and workbag on my father's favorite chair and walked to the kitchen. The combination of the day's warmth and the spirit-draining news left me without hunger but with a tremendous urge to drink something, anything, the first liquid I'd see in the icebox. My eyes downcast and my senses blunted, I didn't notice I wasn't alone.

"Vera?"

I looked in the direction of the voice I heard.

"Amélie?"

Amélie stepped away from the kitchen table and walked toward me.

As we embraced, I felt my knees begin to give way. At the same time, I felt Amélie's arms pulling me closer and closer, giving me permission to either fall or stand with her, our bodies pressed together. Seconds later, we stood facing one another. Amélie's words sketched a portrait of where she'd been and briefly, what she had done since we'd last been together. I listened as she said the word resist countless times, but I knew she couldn't tell me everything. I knew also that she'd done what she could for her country before she left it, that she had never left me or her mother. Her exile from France was her bid to stay alive, if not in the country where she was born, then in different place.

As days, months, and years passed, Amélie shared some of her memories. She'd fan them over my ears as if she were spreading Pinocle cards atop a table. She told me about a woman named Violette Morris whom she'd met at Le Boeuf Sur le Toit, a pre-war spot frequented by gay people in Paris.

Recruited by the Gestapo and then invited by Adolph Hitler to the 1936 Olympics in Berlin, Violette gave the

Germans the plans for the Maginot Line, the plans and design of the French Army's most powerful tank, and the places within Paris that were integral to the German's ability to invade the city. Morris also kept a list of people who formed the resistance teams determined to defeat the Nazis.

Amélie knew her name was on that list. Two years before it occurred, she whispered her prediction of Morris' demise. She said it would happen shortly before or soon after the war ended.

"*La Résistance va réussir*," she said.

Fate caught up with Morris in 1944. While driving her car along a road on the outskirts of Paris, she was ambushed, shot to death, and unceremoniously buried with other collaborators in a communal grave.

It was Violette whom I saw with Amélie at L'Aigle Noir that unhappy night I was there. Amélie feigned not seeing me and not knowing Vangie in order to keep us safe. She knew Violette's reputation for memorizing faces and names and putting her memorizations to good use.

Bette sent us a cryptic letter about Amélie's mother. In the first section of her letter Bette claimed that Simone Blum was still living with them. Near the end of the letter Bette wrote that Simone had been arrested along with a group of Jewish worshipers outside her synagogue in Paris, and then deported to a concentration camp during the winter of 1943. This was among the cruelest information we received. It took us months to find out which part of Bette's letter held the truth. It took us more than a year to learn to which camp Simone been sent, and then another few months to learn the date when she had died.

Just as crushingly cruel was the absence of information about my Aunt Vangie's disappearance. One of the neighbors who survived the occupation by accepting shelter in my aunt's reconfigured basement wrote to tell me Vangie had agreed to meet a friend in Rouen. After she boarded the train, no one saw her again.

Shortly after France was liberated, Amélie and I tried to contact Régine Dépestre. We were told that no one of that name had ever lived in Rouen.

I was disconsolate, as was my mother, much to my surprise. I'd like to believe that despite her critical attitude regarding Vangie, my mother loved her sister deeply.

The same neighbor who took shelter in my aunt's basement wrote to us about Bette. She told us Bette left the apartment a few weeks after Vangie's disappearance. She simply walked out to the courtyard and kept going. Before she left, she'd begun acting strangely. Late at night she would pace from the kitchen to the foyer repeatedly. She would shout her brother's name and wail Vangie's. She painted odd images on some of the walls in the apartment. Little by little she stopped eating. When the neighbor spoke to her, Bette stared at her but remained silent. It was as if part of her left the safety of the apartment shortly after Aunt Vangie disappeared.

Epilogue

August, 1977

It took me months to reread all the letters I'd saved from Aunt Vangie, Bette, my mother, and Amélie. The memories those letters awakened were so overwhelming that I couldn't read more than one or two of them in a sitting. Sometimes their words made me smile, even laugh out loud. Other times they filled me with such wonder about the courage they'd possessed. Aunt Vangie was the bravest person I'd ever known, a warrior decades before people dared to name and claim their sexuality and live as they wished. Even though her bravery became the path that led to her death, it never dissuaded her from bringing her truth to light. To the contrary, her life and death gave me the strength to keep writing my stories about other brave characters who dared the world to stop them from accepting who they were. If I believed Vangie's spirit were still alive and living in that charming, old apartment on *Rue Clauzel*, I would write her one final letter, similar to this one...

Dear Aunt Vangie,
You were correct the day you said you hadn't told me all of your secrets. There remained one final secret you didn't disclose. You held it inside your heart. It was your plan to save as many of your Jewish neighbors from the Nazis as you could. You used much of your savings to pay for the construction of livable space in your apartment's basement. Your agreement with the workers stipulated the project had to be done at night when most of your neighbors were asleep. You must have been planning this long before it took place.

I remember a time when I descended the stairs, stood in the foyer, and thought I saw a ribbon of light between the edge of the closet door and its casing. I convinced myself it was the sun's reflection, even though I knew sunshine never reached that side of the foyer. What I never knew about the closet was how well it disguised an entry door to steps leading down to the basement. That tiny bit of light I saw once was real. Someone, perhaps you, forgot to extinguish a light shining up from below.

I treasure the memories of moments I spent with you and Bette, and I wonder how famous Bette would have become had she continued painting. While reading a recent issue of *Smithsonian Magazine*, I saw an article about some of the art that was stolen by the Nazis, especially the work taken from galleries and private collections. There, in the list of artists whose canvasses were plundered, was the name Bette Moune. Imagine the satisfaction she would feel (and you, as well,) knowing her paintings were valued alongside those of Chagall, Klimt, Matisse, and so many others.

I miss you, Vangie. I haven't returned to Paris for a long time now. Some of my memories are sweet, but others ravage their way through my mind and exit my eyes in the form of tears.

Amélie has no desire to return to the place of her birth even though she risked her life to keep it free from the Nazis. When she reminisces about France, her sadness looks more like rage and less like melancholia despite all of the years that have passed since she left there.

You would be happy to know she helped me petition the French government to create a plaque that's been affixed to the wall outside your old apartment. You wouldn't believe all the red tape that was involved in that project. On second thought, yes, you would believe it. You always understood why Webster's Dictionary identified the word, *bureaucracy,* as being *of French origin, used to express the long and unnecessary process of dealing with government's outdated rules in order to get something done.*

Your plaque is inscribed with this message:

Ici vécut Evangeline Curtis, une Américaine noire qui aida ses voisins juifs pendant l'Occupation Allemande de la France. Le seul couleur compris par Madame Curtis fut le couleur de la liberté.

Here is where Evangeline Curtis, a Black American woman, lived. She helped her Jewish neighbors during the German Occupation of France. The only color Ms. Curtis understood was the color of freedom.

I think of Gérard Simonet from time to time, and I regret not understanding the depth of his feelings for his former lover, Serge Bonet. I now know he needed help to restore his self-confidence, to believe he could survive without Serge. Amélie has described to what extent the resistance movement mourned Serge. His penetration of the pro-Hitler political faction played a critically important role in France's ability to collect intelligence. Who knows what would have happened as a result of Serge's work if Gérard hadn't fired that bullet?

As for Amélie, she continues to be the greatest gift I've ever known, apart from you, of course. She's had her American citizenship for quite a few years now. Although she curses those French people who collaborated with Hitler's government, she's never renounced France itself. She's kept the door open to returning there one day. She believes no one who belongs to a minority group can feel safe and protected anywhere, not even here in the United States. We're both lesbians, and I'm Black. We can't be any more minority if we tried.

Amélie has lived through France's entry into the Second World War and the pure evil of the Holocaust. She recalls the signals she heard and saw as the war approached. Despite her (and my) advanced age, she still has radar-like instincts always on alert should the unthinkable occur again. I trust her instincts completely.

But back to you, Aunt Vangie. Please know if France ever gives your contemporary, Josephine Baker, its highest honor, and moves her remains from her resting place near Monte Carlo to the Panthéon in Paris, I shall be there to witness the event. I'll stand with others who recall her brave actions as a member of the French Resistance Movement. Instead of chanting her name however, I'll chant yours, because in sheltering your Jewish neighbors, you were as much a member of the Resistance as was La Bakair. You resisted homophobia, the ugliness of racism, and the Nazi regime's pathological, murderous antisemitism.

I love you, Aunt Vangie, and I shall miss you always.

Your adoring niece,
Vera

Books by Renée Bess

Breaking Jaie
Re: Building Sasha
The Butterfly Moments
Leave of Absence
The Rules
Between A Rock and A Soft Place

With Lee Lynch:

Happy Hours: Our Lives in the Gay Bars

Bringing rainbow stories to life.

Flashpoint Publications welcomes submissions from writers of every color and books featuring characters of every color. In addition, Flashpoint Publications encourages job applicants of every color whenever a staff position becomes available. We believe that EVERYONE is entitled to a seat at our table.

www.flashpointpublications.com